THE WITCHING TREE

THE AUTHOR

Alison Prince, who lives on the Isle of Arran with two dogs and two cats, is known for her many children's books, including *The Sherwood Hero*, joint winner of the 1996 Guardian Children's Fiction Award, as well as her television programmes, particularly *Trumpton* with its popular catch-phrase, 'Pugh, Pugh, Barney McGrew . . .' In 1994 she turned to biography and *Kenneth Grahame: An Innocent in the Wild Wood* was published by Allison & Busby to huge critical acclaim. She is now working on a new biography and a second adult novel.

THE WITCHING TREE

Alison Prince

a&b

First published in Great Britain in 1996 by
Allison & Busby Ltd
179 King's Cross Road
London WC1X 9BZ

Copyright © 1996 by Alison Prince

The moral right of the author is asserted

This book is sold subject to the condition that it shall not, by way of trade or otherwise, be lent, resold, hired out or otherwise circulated without the publisher's prior written consent in any form of binding or cover other than that in which it is published and without a similar condition including this condition being imposed upon the subsequent purchaser.

A catalogue record for this book is available from the British Library

ISBN 0 74900 238 7

Typeset by N-J Design Associates
Romsey, Hampshire

Printed and bound in Great Britain by
The Ipswich Book Company Ltd
Ipswich, Suffolk

To my children and grand-children,
and to Sandy, with love and thanks.

We must face the fact that our world, with its time, space and causality, relates to another order of things lying behind it or beneath it, in which neither "here and there" nor "earlier and later" are of importance.

C.G. Jung
Memories, Dreams, Reflections

PART ONE

I, Mary McGuire, am a witch.

These words worry me. I've just typed them on my old Imperial, but they cause an uneasy catch of the breath, like the quick heart-thump that wakes you at night to the memory of something awful that you said at a party. How very odd. I mean, my granddaughter and one or two friends have long called me an old witch in an affectionate sort of way, but there was never anything shocking about it. The people who come up the weedy path to tell me their concerns or describe their malaises don't expect to find mandragora or powdered batwing beside the instant coffee – why, then, should this confession cause a flicker of fear?

When I say I am a witch, I am not, of course, talking about white cockerels or chalk circles or any of that nonsense. There can be few less attractive ways of spending a Saturday night than capering about in wet woods with naked Town Clerks. No, my witchcraft is concerned with the useful working of coincidence. One can achieve a state in which events fall into an effortless, convenient pattern, and this is not accidental – it's a skill. Some readers will know what I mean, because in these practical terms, a lot of us are witches. We have this bat-sense of what lies in our path, and can avoid unpleasant collisions. Our instinct is to look for the way through rather than to heave the obstructions aside.

That's what people have never understood about magic – it's an allowing, not an imposing of will. But nowadays, children are taught that the important thing is to overcome opposition, and that's a much cruder technique, a pushing ahead through one collision after another.

We are all by instinct either witches or non-witches. One day, this will be the only political divide which counts. Already, witching people within the existing parties are wondering why the old arguments seem so irrelevant, and why there is no policy which expresses how they feel – but it will come. Meanwhile, we who are witches know each other instantly, even though we meet as strangers. People of our kind will read what I have to say with immediate recognition, whereas the others will dismiss it as rubbish. There is no neutrality. But my main concern remains centred on the question of responsibility. If I accept, as I must, that I have had a hand in shaping the course of events, then I am open to the old charge of maleficium, the sin of witches, an interfering with fate for malign reasons. I've tried hard not to be malign, at least since I grew up and learned a bit of sense, but I'm still not sure that I didn't cause damage. That's why I want to look back over the things that happened, so that I can work out where I stand. It would be so humiliating to die in a muddle. Nobody can help with this task – except perhaps Mari.

I don't know who Mari is. Sometimes, I've hardly been sure whether she is myself or somebody else. Only once, when my searching for her led to the dusty records of old brutalities, did I feel the prickle of certain connection, and that was when I found the name of Alison Balfour, executed for witchcraft on December 16th, 1596. She was forced into a false confession because she could not bear the screams of her little daughter, seven-year-old Agnes, whose small thumbs were being crushed in the "pillie-winks" in her mother's presence. Alison recanted her confession on the scaffold, explaining why it had been necessary. She was garrotted and burned just the same; but there was no record of the child's death. Unusually among those accused of supernatural practices, Alison Balfour was no poverty-stricken old crone, but a woman of some influence, well able to have a hand in the future. Somebody took Agnes from Edinburgh Castle after the execution, and gave her into the care of her grandmother, to be brought up in the small cottage that lay like a wintering sheep in the shelter of the hill, with a wild cherry tree outside its door.

Such certainties are not intellectual ones. They belong to their own truth, just as the primroses that grow today belong by seed and root connection to primroses seen by Agnes Balfour, the child with the mutilated thumbs. When she grew older, Agnes in her turn gave birth to a daughter, and sat with her under the cherry tree. And that child was Mari.

*

There is a dazzling brightness. I reach up to grasp it, but my hands are empty and I cry with disappointment. I am held close and a firmness is in my mouth. No crying. My tongue is too busy sucking.

The brilliance is still there.
I am seeing.
I am.
I am.

*

Agnes Balfour looked down at her baby and smiled. Sunlight filtered through the white blossoms of the cherry tree and laid moving shadows across the child's downy cheek. Such moments of pure happiness, she thought, dispelled all fear. And then, lest she should tempt providence, she looked up, narrowing her eyes against the sun in acknowledgement of the way things were. The fast-changing skies of Scotland could never be taken for granted. And neither could anything else.

*

We still have our witch-hunters, the fox-hound people who will persecute to order, and they still come in sharply-cut dark clothes as they always did, but their purpose is less physical now, in this more abstract age. Their underlying righteousness is the same, but they carry narrow black briefcases rather than the soiled twist of cloth in which their long needles used to be wrapped. They no longer probe for the nerveless spot in the body which proves the protection of Satan, but they scrutinise the mind for tell-tale signs of unorthodoxy.

"Mrs McGuire," my bank manager said as he impounded my cheque book, not for the first time, "you really must try to take your financial affairs more seriously." Silly man. With finances like mine, all you can do is laugh and pray. It's as good a system as any, and better than most. I wonder if he knows that they used to make you pay for your own execution – I'm sure he'd approve of that. But his kind don't believe in witches. Not any more.

*

Billy McGuire followed his brother up the hillside. Fear churned in his stomach, and the sun frowned upon him from the sky. His disobedience was public, known to the gorse and the heather and to the jackdaws whose dark wings chopped up the brightness above the hill's edge. "Clack!" they called, as if tut-tutting. "Clack, clack!" They knew he was going to the witch's house.

Hugh, four years older, was well ahead, climbing steadily towards the thicket of hawthorn trees that hid the turf roof of the cottage from any casual glance. He paused and looked back, arms akimbo as he waited impatiently. Billy knew his brother would have liked to shout to him to hurry up, but he was too close to the house for that. If they were to spy on Agnes Balfour, they must not warn her of their approach.

Billy saw a chicken hop over the wall where a black cat slept on the warm stones, and felt glad he had not hurried. Had the boys been any closer, the silly bird might have given the alarm, setting all the others a-cackling and flapping, and alerting the witch. As it was, everything remained still. The trees were motionless in the sun, heavy with creamy blossom. If he disturbed a single leaf, Billy thought, the witch would know it. And what then? Would he wake in the night, unable to cry out because his tongue was swollen and black, as they said Callum McNair's had been when they found him dead? And it was Callum's cousin, Robert Stewart, who, at the witch-trial, had forced Agnes Balfour's thumbs into the pilliewinks that her screams might bring her mother to confess. For Alison Balfour, as everyone knew, had made a wax image of the Earl of Orkney. They had found the thing, dressed roughly in a bit of cloth. The child said it was her dolly, but who knew what pins had been thrust through its heart and brain?

Trying to still the fast beating of his own heart, Billy reminded himself that Hugh still had the stone, and such a rare thing must surely be a protection. They were found so seldom, the spherical white pebbles milled to smoothness by centuries of tumbling water, but yesterday, swimming in the deep pool below the waterfall, Hugh had given a shout of triumph and his arm had come up, white as peeled willow from the dark water, with the stone held in his fist. Billy had felt afraid of it, for the paleness and perfection seemed too magical for human possession. He knew he was not brave. Hugh could swim like a trout, but Billy liked to feel the contact of his feet with the stony slippery bottom, and would soon come out of the water to lie on a warm rock, safe in the sunshine. Had he found the stone, he thought now, he would probably have dropped it back into the water. But Hugh was ten. Almost a man. Billy ran to catch up.

Hugh put his finger to his lips as his younger brother

joined him. Inch by inch, they edged their way between the trees to the wall, overgrown by its tangle of ivy. Reaching it, they crouched and stared at each other. Hugh's dark hair clung damply to his forehead, and he brushed his arm across his face to ward off a circling horse-fly. He was pale with excitement. Raising a finger to tell Billy to keep still, he stood up very slowly and gently parted the ivy leaves above the wall to peer through. He made no sound. After a few moments, he beckoned.

Billy's knees seemed reluctant to straighten, but Hugh's hand was under his elbow, pulling him up. Through the screen of dark leaves, he saw Agnes Balfour sitting with her back to them on a three-legged stool under the cherry tree, her shawl slung loose about her shoulders and her head bent as she looked down at the baby she held to her breast. Billy stared, and found himself shaken by a feeling he did not understand. She looked so young. Seventeen, they said she was, but he had still expected that a witch would be crabbit and ugly. Her neck was so slender. He thought of the rope they used for hangings, and his stomach heaved.

The girl turned her head very slightly and said, "Go away."

The words shattered the limpid silence of the day. Terror flooded through Billy. Careless of the crashing leaves, he tore his way between the branches and ran full-pelt down the track. The chickens flew in all directions with a clatter of wings and squawks of alarm, and the black cat stood like a furry demon on the wall, twice its size with anger.

Billy heard Hugh panting behind him, and imagined that Agnes followed, with her dark hair streaming out above her white neck and her shawl billowing in the air like a cloud of vengeance. Hugh turned and hurled something in the air, and Billy knew with a pang of renewed horror that it was the white stone. He had no breath for protest. The blood hammered in his head as he ran, but he thought that he could hear the strangely slow patter of the stone as it dropped through the leaves of the cherry tree. He dared not look back.

They were well out of sight of the house before they slowed down. Far below them, the sea sparkled, blue and tranquil. Billy looked fearfully over his shoulder, but nothing moved on the hill except the slow white dots which were sheep.

"She saw us!" panted Hugh. "Even wi' her back to us, she knew we were there!" He seemed triumphant.

Billy stared at him. He felt paralyzed with dread.

Hugh ran on down the track, then vaulted through the gap in the wall to the rabbit-nibbled turf on the far side. "We'll go back across the Fairy Glen," he said exultantly. "It's quicker."

The sky seemed to tighten in disapproval, like pursed lips.

"No," begged Billy, "it's near to Midsummer's Day. Please, Hugh."

But Hugh was revelling in recklessness, ready to take on all the Wee Folk who ever turned a cow's milk sour in her udder or switched a human baby for an evil-tempered imp. "I'm no' feared," he boasted. "Come on, Billy – or I'll tell mother it was you that thought of going to the witch's house."

Billy gasped at the injustice of it – but his brother was already away across the strangely brilliant green grass. As he scrambled through the gap in the wall after him, Billy found himself wondering whether the Wee Folk had already been up to their mischief with Hugh. Why else should he, of all the boys who had ever swum in the pool below the waterfall, have found the white stone? Maybe he was a changeling, a heartless elfin creature, devoid of human feeling.

Billy ran down the grassy slope after his brother to where the beech trees grew, tall and shady, by the burn. The sky jigged in time with his running, and a thousand eyes watched, mocking, from behind each foxglove and each damp-loving fern that grew in the shelter of a rock. The fairies knew the truth. They could see the guilt that lay like a cold stone in Billy's stomach because of going to the witch's house. And they knew his bad thoughts about Hugh as well. The day seemed doomed to wickedness.

A group of shaggy black cattle stood drinking at the burn's edge, and raised dripping muzzles as the boys approached. Billy hesitated. Last year a man had been killed by a bull, not far from this place. But Hugh hardly paused in his stride as he grabbed up a pebble and pitched it high, so that it splashed into the water just short of the cattle. The cows nearest to it jerked away in alarm and set off across the grass, followed by their half-grown calves. The others followed more slowly, the bull with them, heavy-shouldered and long-horned, but peaceable. Hugh's stone had been well placed.

Billy heard again the patter of that other stone dropping through the cherry tree into Agnes Balfour's garden. The sound was weirdly sinister. Secretly, he crossed the fingers of both hands, to ward off evil.

As if aware of his brother's misgivings, Hugh turned and laughed, hopping backwards on his way up the gentle bank. Then he turned and ran out of the trees' shade towards the open hill, making for the path on the further side which led to the village. Billy followed. Up here, the turf gave way to bracken and heather, studded with outcrops of stone and cut with deep fissures where runnels of water ran, half-hidden under the thin, wiry grass and the scrubby bushes that would bear blueberries in August.

Suddenly Hugh stopped and bent down to look at something. Catching up, Billy saw a very small calf, lying curled up like a dog, its head turned to rest across its hindquarters.

"Red!" said Hugh, astonished.

Billy nodded, staring at the calf's velvety, rowan-bright

coat. Nobody had red cattle. Where had this strange small creature come from?

"New-born," said Hugh, "or not much more." He offered his hand towards it, and the calf extended a curving tongue towards his fingers.

Something came crashing through the bracken above them.

"*Mind!*" screamed Billy, flinging himself away.

The cow was on them with the speed of a falling tree. For an instant, Billy saw a curved horn slice across the sun, then he tripped and fell, rolling down the slope, helpless to avoid the stones between the bushes. He crashed into a large rock that stopped his fall, and lay there with the breath knocked out of him and his face pressed into the grass, waiting for the great horns to kill him.

Nothing happened.

Billy dragged a long, sobbing breath into his lungs and, infinitely slowly, turned his head and opened one eye. The cow had not followed him. She stood further up the hill, her blackness silhouetted against the sky. Her horned head was lowered to lick at the red calf, which had staggered to its feet and was now butting at her swollen udder with its nose.

Very carefully, Billy wriggled backwards until the rock hid him from the cow's view. Then he got to his feet and ran.

He expected to see Hugh ahead of him as usual, probably waiting impatiently, but when he rounded the brow of the hill and saw the path winding down to the village and the sea, his brother was not there. Billy paused irresolutely, his ribs aching with his fall and his breathlessness. He could not go home without Hugh. Flies buzzed about his sweaty face. He was very afraid of the cow with the red calf, but he knew he would have to go back. He turned and retraced his way up the hill. It seemed deserted.

Above him, the heather gave way to bare rock. It would

be a steep climb, but from up there, Billy thought, he would have a much better view. He pushed away the terrible belief that Hugh was lying dead, hidden from sight until the circling of crows and buzzards marked the place. His bruises throbbed as he laboured upwards, and blood trickled down his right leg from a cut knee. At last he reached the slabs of rock and sat down on their hot surface, panting. He could see across the moor to the green sweep of the Fairy Glen, but he could not see Hugh. And there was no sign of the black cow.

Renewed terror swept over Billy. For a red calf to be born was surely witchcraft. It had been a punishment for disobeying his parents' warning to keep away from Agnes Balfour's house, and for coming across the forbidden Fairy Glen, and for thinking that Hugh might be a changeling. At any moment, the cow might materialise again, as vast and angry as a thunderstorm, with horns like sickle blades, reaching across the sky from sunrise to sunset.

If Hugh really was a changeling, perhaps the Wee Folk had taken him to their secret place under the green grass. Billy put his hands over his face and prayed in the sweaty darkness where red sunlight flowed like lines of fire between the bones of his fingers. "Oh, God, let him not be a changeling," he whispered. "Let him not be dead. Please, God. Lord, have mercy upon us. Christ, have mercy upon us, and give us Thy peace."

He let his hands fall, clasping them instead round his bent legs and laying his head on his knees. A sense of utter weariness overcame him. He would have liked to curl up like the red calf in the sunshine, and go to sleep. His limbs began to slacken.

Then he heard a distant whistle. He jerked his head up, scanning the hillside with renewed urgency. Something moved in the bracken, far below him. An arm, waving. Billy scrambled to his feet and waved back. He could see Hugh's face now, a lighter patch in the thick growth. "Stay there!" he yelled, and realised in the same breath that Hugh must be hurt, or he would already have moved. He started down the hill towards him.

Hugh was sitting very still. There was a lumpy bruise on his forehead, and when he looked up, his face was white and frightened. "She sent it for a punishment."

Billy nodded, glancing fearfully at the blue sky. "Let's away home," he said. Then he saw Hugh's ankle, swollen and already discoloured. "It's awful sore," Hugh whined. "I think it's broken." Then he is no changeling, Billy thought. The prayer had been answered.

"That Agnes Balfour!" his brother burst out. "There was no need. I only threw a wee pebble!" His face contorted with resentment, and he rubbed his sleeve across his eyes. Billy found himself thinking about the calf's sweet breath as it had raised its head, and the velvety ripples of its red coat. Could it have been a witch-sending? It seemed so real.

Hugh struggled to his feet, clutching at Billy for support. Together, they began to lurch and stagger down the difficult slope, Hugh leaning heavily on the younger boy, hopping and gasping with pain.

It was slow going. When they reached the path, they rested for a few minutes. "We'd best say we were birds-nesting and I fell out of a tree," Hugh said.

Billy made no reply. He dared not promise to lie, not in this place where they were watched and heard by a thousand invisible beings. There were more things to be afraid of than the witch. The Wee Folk knew everything, and so did God. Sins had to be confessed and repented. "I thought something bad about you," he blurted out for the unseen listeners to hear. "It was stupid, but I thought you were a changeling. I'm sorry."

Hugh's face was tight and bitter. "You thought that because Agnes Balfour has taken you to herself," he said. "She has laid a curse on me, and you are part of it."

"No!" Billy protested, horrified. "No, Hugh!"

Through clenched teeth, Hugh said, "I wish I had never seen her."

Billy could not answer. He stared at the silver line of the sea as they resumed their painful way along the path, but he saw in his mind's eye the white nape of the witch's neck, slender between the strands of hair which were, he saw now, as red as the coat of the calf. It must be part of the day's helpless enchantment, he thought, that he found it so beautiful.

*

"I would burn the bloody bitches, and I have said that on several occasions . . ." Thus the Reverend Anthony Kennedy, on the proposed ordination of women priests in the Church of England. His words were reported in the Guardian newspaper, March 11th 1994.

In the spring of the previous year, I had been to Salem, Massachusetts, where the white-painted clapboard houses and the washed maritime sky still quiver with rectitude, though of a correctly humorous kind. Each of the yellow cabs run by Witch Taxis has on its side the silhouette of a flying figure on a broomstick, and the place is full of tee-shirts printed with such slogans as 'DROP BY FOR A SPELL.' I walked boldly about with camera and guidebook, and was secretly afraid.

*

Agnes tucked the sleeping baby into the shawl she wore across her shoulders, knotting its ends firmly to bind the child closely to her. She dared not leave Mari to sleep in the sunshine in her rush basket, not after the stone had come down through the blossom of the cherry tree. There was something more to happen. The familiar prickle of caution narrowed her eyes and made the skin creep a li[ttle at the] back of her neck, above the comfortable wei[ght of the] baby. Her thumbs throbbed as they always did i[n times of] stress, and she clenched them gently in her cl[othes,] trying to soothe their aching. They were ugly things, nailless and shiny-skinned, a constant reminder that people were not to be trusted. She turned away uneasily, as restless as an animal which has scented danger, and picked up the white stone from where it lay in the grass. Then she stopped, frowning at the sky. Why had a vision of dark horns, curved like sickle blades, flashed across her mind? There was a blackness in the sun. She went into the house and barred the door.

Later that day, a man climbed the track towards the turf-roofed cottage. The kettles and pans dangling from his pack made a merry clatter, and when Agnes heard it she jumped up from where she crouched with the baby by the fire. She pulled the heavy bar from the door and ran out into the sunshine as Liam Tarbert came across the grass towards her.

For a moment, it seemed to Agnes that there was safety as Liam's arms came round her and she buried her face in his neck. Wordlessly, he led her into the house and dumped his heavy pack on the floor. Then he turned to look at her.

"What is it?" he asked. "What's wrong?"

Agnes told him about the boys and about the stone. She did not mention her vision of the scything horns. Liam was her true love and the father of her baby, but she dared not burden him with the things of which she herself was only half-aware. Although he scoffed at the gossip of the housedwellers, it was dangerous to try and rely on him. He was as handsome and as transient as a dragonfly, with the same ability to side-slip and hover a little further away, out of reach.

Liam laughed at her story. "There's no harm in a pebble thrown by a wean," he said, and bent his shaggy head to at Mari, still cradled in her mother's arms. "And now's my bairn?" he asked, touching the baby's face with a gentle finger.

"She's grand," said Agnes, and moved away to the window, to run her fingers through the pile of herb leaves which lay drying in the sun.

Liam watched her. "Tell me what it is," he insisted. "You are the one with the Sight. What is going to happen?"

"I think the men will come," Agnes said reluctantly. Liam sounded bold enough, but she knew his question had been put in order to elicit a reassuring answer. There was a trace of fear mixed with his love for her, and she tried not to touch on it. He would not want to share her feeling that this was something more than a child's prank. Something lasting, which would go on when she herself had been washed away by time like a yellow leaf down the burn in the autumn.

"Agnes, come with me," Liam urged. "You've been on your own long enough. You could hawk my tinware and baskets, and in the winter we'd stay with my family, in the big camp by Furnace."

Agnes shook her head. "The travellers have no truck wi' witches," she said. "Everyone knows that. I'd not be welcome among them."

"You're no more a witch than I am!" Liam said angrily. "Why do you accept what they call you? Why be what they want?"

"Liam, how can I hawk for you?" Agnes held out her hands with the ugly deformed thumbs. "How can I stand on a doorstep and offer some henwife a pot or a basket? She will see my hands and know who I am and what I am. It is only a witch's child who is put in the thumb-screws."

Liam's face darkened as he turned away. "Some folk are barbarians," he said.

Agnes felt a moment's amused envy for the innocence which enabled him to be so outraged. "There's very few who are not," she observed. "But I am lucky."

"Lucky!" He gave a bark of derisive laughter. "When you are afraid of your own shadow?"

Agnes smiled, letting him think she had conceded the point. She could not start to explain the sense of illumination which gave every moment such magical significance. In the long sleep before she was born, there had been dreams. They were forgotten now, but they made all present things familiar. She could see how the same spirit moved in the uncurling of the ferns and the leaping of the water over the stones in the burn and in the air that filled the spaces between all things. The same intelligence laid down the pattern for a new-born animal to replicate, and provided the capacity of all things to learn, so that a dandelion could flower close to the ground on a well-trodden path but long-stalked among summer grasses. For a time, she would be anxious and fearful for Mari's survival, but her own death held no fear for her, provided it could be accomplished without much pain. She had died before, it seemed. And if she had not, the seeming was good enough.

Liam took her face between his hands and kissed her. "Come with me tonight, at least," he begged. "If they are angry in the village, it is best for you to be away from here. For the child's sake, if nothing else."

Agnes thought about Billy's face, huge-eyed with terror among the ivy leaves. A vibration had existed for a moment between the boy and herself. Some kind of connection had been made through the vision of the dark horns. He knew it as well as she did. There had been a retribution, perhaps, for which she would be blamed. Maybe she had caused it, in that moment of fear and dislike when she had sensed the boys' presence. "The younger one will tell his father," she said aloud, "although he means no harm." She hoped devoutly that the boy would not die. "I will come with you," she told Liam, "but only for this night." The travelling man would not want it to be longer.

The mist lay heavy over the hills in the grey light of the next morning. Agnes and Liam came quietly through the heather from the cave behind the leaning rock where they had slept, and their breath steamed in the sunless air.

It was Agnes who heard the men first, a roughness of heavy feet on the track ahead of them, a murmur of voices. They were coming down the hill from her house. She crouched in the shelter of a gorse bush, catching at Liam's sleeve. He listened, narrow-eyed. "Stay here," he said. And he was away like a shadow, circling round to intercept the men from the track below.

Agnes pulled her shawl tight round the baby, willing her not to choose this moment to cry. Even from this distance, she could feel the harshness of the men's intention, as bitter as holly-bark. Liam moved fast and silently, unencumbered by the heavy pack which he had left in her house. By the time the men saw him, he was walking casually towards them.

"Good morning!" he called cheerfully. "What brings you out so early?"

The men stopped. "You'll be the tinker," said one of them. "There's a pack o' rubbishy pots up there in the house."

"So there is," Liam agreed. "The place was empty, so –" He broke off in mock concern. "Is it your house? I'm sorry if – "

"Agnes Balfour stays there," said the man, "as I think you know well, tinker. Where is she?"

Liam shrugged. "The house was empty," he said again, clinging to the weak excuse.

"She is a witch," burst out a younger man. "She sent a red calf – red, mind you – and young Hugh McGuire has a broken ankle. This is Ross McGuire, his father – he'll tell you."

"A wee stone," said the man called Ross. "That's all he did, just threw a wee stone. I've a score to settle with Agnes Balfour."

"Travelling folk have no truck wi' witches," Liam said, and made to push past the men. "I'll need to get my pack from that house."

They barred his way. "You'll have seen her," Ross insisted.

"I've seen no old witch."

"She isnae old. Just a young lassie."

"Red hair on her. Like a deer."

"Like a red calf, you mean," Ross snorted.

Liam looked thoughtful. "I was down in the Borders," he said, "and I heard there of red cattle from Holland – aye, and there's a farmer in Galloway has a red bull. Callum Mitchison. You'll know him maybe?"

The men shook their heads uncertainly.

"Agnes Balfour has a bairn with her," said Ross, returning like a hound to the scent. "A young one, in her shawl."

"You'll no' find her," Liam told him. "If she's a witch, she may be away flying as an owl or running as a hare." He snapped his fingers. "I did see a hare, when I was down bathing at the pool, and a leveret with her."

"That'll be her!" said the younger man excitedly. "Let's away for the dogs and catch her!"

"Aye," said Ross. "Catch her and kill her, and the young one too, then that'll be an end to it, and we can sleep easy in our beds."

"I'll be on my way," said Liam. This time the men parted to let him through, and he went on up the track towards the house.

Agnes, crouched in the heather, knew he would be gone when she returned there. She knew, too, that he had sown the seeds of uncertainty in the men with his rational explanation of the calf, and that they would tire themselves out with a day's hunting and lose the edge of their anger. How many innocent hares would be torn to pieces this day? She, too, pressed herself to the earth like a hunted thing, and could feel herself a hare, with long ears flattened against her back and whiskers trembling at the scent of savagery.

That night, there was still warmth in the peat fire under the turves Agnes had stacked on it nearly twenty-four hours ago. She knelt and blew gently, coaxing the small red heart into stronger life, feeding it with dry twigs, and at last sat back on her heels as a thin column of smoke began to rise. Her mind was full of the image of Ross McGuire.

I must not hate, she said in careful silent words. But she knew it was too late. That morning, as the man wished death to her and her baby, she had feared him and hated him, and now she knew he was condemned. She sighed and got to her feet. There was no power in repentance. And at least Ross McGuire would not come to her door again. Neither would the others, for fear of the same fate, whatever it would be – but they would bide their time.

It was past midnight before Liam came slipping back into the house from a darkness lit only by a thin moon. He was edgy, his traveller's uneasiness at being under a roof made sharper by his encounter with the men. Agnes could feel it as he lay beside her, cold and angular and unrelaxed.

"Was it true about Callum Mitchison and the red bull?" she murmured in his ear.

He gave a short laugh. "There are red cattle on the borders, right enough, but they'll no' find a Callum Mitchison. It was a name just came into my head."

The small hope died without protest. As Liam's bony body began to warm, Agnes slid her hand inside his clothes and caressed him, but her touch seemed only to fill him with new restlessness. "I'd best be away," he said.

"Not yet. Rest a little."

Obediently, he lay beside her until the tension went out of him, but he twitched like a dog in his sleep, and was alert again as the short summer night gave up its deepest darkness. He wrapped his plaid round him at the open door, and Agnes, shivering a little, crept across the floor to stand beside him.

"You should leave this place," he said quietly. "Make a new start, where nobody knows you."

"All places would be the same," Agnes told him. His simple idea of escape would not free her from the destiny which waited. "But, Liam, one day Mari will need your help. You must not forget her."

"How could I forget my own bairn?" Liam said indignantly.

Agnes kissed him, and hid her smile. Forgetfulness was part of the skill by which he lived, and yet he meant what he said. She took the white stone from the deep, lidded crock where she had kept it since she had retrieved it from under the cherry tree, and put it into his palm. "It will help you remember," she told him. Liam's fox-brown eyes met hers briefly. "I need no talisman," he said. She should have known that he would carry nothing that he could not sell or use. He put the stone down carefully among the drying herbs, then shouldered the heavy, untidy bulk of his pack and looked round the room for what Agnes knew would be the last time for many years. "Good fortune go with you," she said.

She watched him as he went up the track with his quick, quiet tread, then Mari stirred in her rush basket by the fire and gave a spluttering cry, and Agnes felt her breasts tingle almost painfully with the milk the baby was demanding. It was a call she could not deny.

Liam looked back to wave when he reached the first bend in the path, but Agnes no longer stood in the doorway. He walked on, trying to suppress a childish sense of disappointment. Maybe, he thought, he should do the sensible thing and marry Margaret Townsley, who waited for him with her family in the dark woods of Argyll. He would never love her as he loved Agnes, but he saw again in his mind's eye the mutilated thumbs, and knew he had not the courage to stand by the witch's daughter.

*

Such happiness. Close, enfolded. The warm food flows over my tongue, filling my hunger. But there is a sharp smell about the strong being by which I am held, and a feeling of tightness and fear. There is something dangerous. My mouth cramps on my feeding and I choke a little and cry, then am held differently, patted and rocked, murmured to. I am safe again, but I know something new. Everything has changed.

*

There was a time when I was innocent, I'm sure of that; but witches, like dogs, become dangerous once they are afraid. I remember when that happened – it was on a Sunday morning. My father took me with him, as he often did, to look at the new houses standing behind their bare gardens with 'For Sale' notices planted in the brown earth, though I didn't know then what the big red letters said. He had the key to one of them that day, and we walked across dusty new floors and looked out of windows that were blobby with puttied finger-marks.

I suspected nothing. It was autumn, with rooks cawing and frost still lying white under the trees. I remember the smells that came from the closed Sunday shops as we walked back down the street, a reek of bacon from David Grieg's, clean cotton from Mrs Ponting's where there were glass-fronted drawers of folded vests and aprons, and ribbons of all colours and widths on white cardboard drums, with a paper strip that unreeled with them. Sweetness of jelly babies and the squashy pungency of tobacco crept from the newsagent's, powerfully strong leather from the shoe-shop, sawdust and the throat-catching tang of blood from the butcher's. And then there was the new shop with no smell at all. There was hardly anything in its two big windows with a door between them – a few clothes spread out flat, a glass vase, some books standing open on their edges.

Books were good friends. I had been through the flowered borders of the pale blue nursery-rhyme book, into the land where a boy stuck a feather in his cap and called it macaroni, and where Mary walked in her garden with the silver bells and cockle shells. My name was Mary. It was my garden and I knew it well, just as I knew the boy and his pony and the moonlit street where children came out to play. Books just made things real instead of leaving them as undreamed dreams.

In this shop window, one book stood in front of the others, and when I saw it, my heart jumped hard and my hands tingled. Pictures leaned out of the half-open pages, but they were like no pictures I had ever seen. There were claw-like fingers and black clothing and contorted, greenish faces, writhing smoke and liquid that was wreathed in snaking fumes, an old, pointy-hatted woman with a single tooth in her black mouth, and a cat with its fur on end and its narrow eyes blazing.

I had to see more. In that moment, I knew that the book was about the unknown bad things out there in the grown-up world. In its pages was what could happen to me if I was naughty. It was against this that I had been protected and kept close; this was the secret. For the first time, I fell into a passion of covetousness.

Reasonably, my father pointed out that the shop was not open. When we got home, I heard him telling my mother in the kitchen what had happened. She said, "That pop-up book about witches – yes, I've seen it. Good thing the shop was closed, it would frighten her to death." And my father said he supposed she knew best.

On the following Saturday, I made him buy me the book. I couldn't bring myself to touch it, though – I walked on my father's other side, so that his body shielded me from what was coming through the paper bag that contained it. He tried to smuggle the thing up to my bedroom, but my mother saw. She said, "You've bought that book." I remember his apologetic smile, but not what he said.

I had a bedside light shaped like a red toadstool. The pictures rose up in its dim pinkness as each page was turned, pointing long fingernails at me, displaying black pots and terrible faces. That night, I dreamed that I was being held down, bound, pushed towards the fire. Gleeful faces, glimpsed through snaking smoke, yelled for my death.

"I told you," my mother said to my distraught father as she tried to hush my screaming. Then her voice was close in my ear. "Mary, it's all right, it's not true, they're only pictures."

But pictures are always true. Someone has thought them, someone has seen them in the mind's eye which is for that person, a truth. Someone had enough hatred for witches to paint them in that way. At the time, I couldn't make those explanations, but I found in the morning that my mother had put the book on the top of my wardrobe where I couldn't reach it. I knew she was trying to protect me, but it was too late. Its evil seeped through all the shelves with my clothes on them and glowed with black light. I became ill, and the nights mixed with the days in an aching endless dream. The doctor came. He held my wrist with his very clean white fingers, and looked at the watch he had taken from his waistcoat pocket. Nobody said anything, but their breathing sounded very loud. The touch of the sheets on my skin was painful and I shivered although I was soaked in sweat.

That night, another world overwhelmed me. Things of huge size, as ponderous as soft mountains, were both myself and not myself; I had become a great balloon that floated above the world, yet twitched and tugged at the soul of me with hot strings. I would look down from the floating, billowing darkness and see my parents sitting by a bed that had myself in it, then with a sharp drop our positions would be reversed and I would be back in my sweating body, seeing their anxious faces above me. In a few moments I would drift away again, watching them from on high, sorry for them and yet somehow irritated by their helpless gazing.

One evening, I woke to find that I was in the double bed in the room where a gas fire was lit. The other world had gone. The fire hissed gently and the room was very warm. The bedside lamp had been draped with a blue silk shawl with long fringes that made barred shadows on the wall, like a soft cage. It was very beautiful.

They moved me back into my small bedroom when I was better. The terrible book had gone from the top of the wardrobe, but a darkness remained there, and I did not like to open or close the narrow door with its small brass key that was shaped like an empty-centred clover leaf. I knew now that I had been in danger, and that I must in future be prepared to defend myself. With the birth of that suspicion, innocence was lost.

*

Crouched by the fire, Billy looked up sharply as he heard his father's footstep outside. Hugh, lying in the alcove bed with his bandaged ankle above the covers, shrank back into the pillows and closed his eyes, feigning sleep. Billy ran to sit on the low chair in the corner, where he hoped the long-spoked shadow of the spinning wheel would make him less easy to notice. He was still sore from the beating of the previous day. His mother's hands paused in their sewing as her husband came in.

Ross McGuire latched the door carefully behind him, then came to the fire and sat down slowly in his high-backed chair. He did not spread his hands to the blaze, but leaned his head back and let out a long, shuddering breath.

"What is it?" asked his wife.

Ross did not answer, and she laid aside her work and got up to put her hand to his head. "You are burning hot," she said.

Ross ran his tongue between dry lips. "I feel cold to my bones." His voice was hardly audible.

"You need to get to your bed, right away," said Bessie. "Hugh, come out of there – you can lie on the truckle bed. Billy, help your brother, dinnae skulk there in the corner as if you'd seen a ghost."

"A ghost of my own self," Billy heard his father whisper as Hugh reluctantly pulled himself to the edge of the bed. "Ross McGuire has stood beside me this day."

Bessie gave a little gasp. Billy, too, felt his breath catch in his chest. He knew the legend; if a man saw his own presence beside him, it meant that his death was close.

"You'll be better once you've some hot broth inside you," Bessie said, over-loud in her effort to sound capable. Then she turned on the boys, and this time the boldness of her voice cracked as she shouted at them, "You see what you've done? This is the work of Agnes Balfour. I told you not to go near the witch's house!"

"It's no' my fault!" said Hugh in panic. "You cannae blame me!"

His mother looked at him. Then she said deliberately, "I can blame you. I can and I always will."

"Hugh, wheesht," Billy begged as his elder brother began to weep and bluster. "Father's no' well."

But Hugh, whose lack of good sense had for so long left him carefree and unthinking, was overwhelmed by his mother's accusation. He roared and blubbered as Billy half carried and half dragged him across the floor to the low bed where the boys slept, and gave a bellow of pain as he collapsed onto it and jolted his injured ankle. Billy turned to look at his father, sitting motionless by the fire. For all the noise in the small room, he had the impression that the man was surrounded by silence.

"We'll soon have you better," Bessie repeated as she ladled broth into a bowl from the pot over the fire. Billy wished with all his heart that he could believe it.

*

Sometimes I see myself from outside, a child in a cotton dress, stepping to and fro on the black and white tiles of the Co-op's floor. This child looks up at her mother and says, "There's a man come to see you."

The mother frowns, and the child stares down at her feet in their sandals with the punched holes in the form of a setting sun. Her face reddens.

"What sort of man?" the mother demands.

The child shakes her head. He has turned away now that nobody has answered to his knock. He walks down the path between the lavender bushes. The black cloth brushes against his black shoes as he opens the gate to let himself out.

He came again in the afternoon. "Ah, second time lucky," he said, with a smile that made deeper folds in his pink face. My mother told me to run along outside. She wore the same smile as the man.

I went into the garden and lay down on the hot grass. There was a sun-baked crack in the lawn and I pushed my hand down into it as far as I could reach. Deep at the bottom, the earth was cool and damp. It was like being on the back of some big animal, lying there.

Later, my mother called me in for tea, and made me wash my hands and put on a clean frock. When we had eaten fish-paste sandwiches and the scones and the jam sponge, the priest gave thanks and got up to leave. In the hall where sunshine came through the coloured glass above the front door, he put his dry hand on my head and blessed me.

*

"Sky."

Lying on my back in the long grass, I say the word aloud, very slowly. It has a nice feel, the hiss of air across my tongue-tip, then the check from the back of the mouth and an open, going-away sound. These sensations together make a word, and the word means the brightness above me which was the first thing I can remember. Why should this be?

"Sky."
"Sky."
"Sss-k-y."

The word becomes strange as I say it again and again, as if a magic is happening. The tall grasses lean across the blueness and cut it with their feathers. The earth presses up under my body and warmth enfolds me. The scents of leaf and pollen come streaming in with each breath and my eyes are full of the sky. I want to do something with the shivering loveliness of it all, but I can only laugh.

*

Letters and sounds and numbers filled the air at Miss Daubeny's school, swimming in the scent of stewing prunes which came from her kitchen. The child who was myself found it all very exciting, the blackboard, the cream-painted lincrusta with a pattern of acanthus leaves, the gas fire on winter days. Miss Daubeny herself was not quite a person, but a living essence of inkwell and wallchart. She wore pointed shoes with laces, and told the girls to walk with their toes turned out because it was ladylike. She will never have known that she taught the child something very different from tables and spelling and the weaving of raffia mats. Along with these things came the rudiments of envy, and its terrible results.

I tried hard to be good at school, because I wanted to be approved of; but wanting, I can see now, is the beginning of that slippery slope down which one will hurtle, a dangerous Cresta run designed for the strong and the single-minded.

Witches are double-minded. We are never inclined to take much notice of the tight little rules imposed by other humans, because there are larger and more subtle rules, harder to understand, but much more intimately connected with ourselves. You don't sense their presence until you break them, and then there's trouble – as I found out at Miss Daubeny's.

When other children got higher marks than I did, or seemed to be happier and better-off, I wished I could change places with them. The fact that it was physically impossible didn't seem to matter; after all, I was well used to being in two places at once, watching some event occur in the street or a garden while my body sat obediently in the classroom, looking at the mustard and cress that grew on saucers of blotting paper on the window sill. I could be Jean, whose parents had given her a gleaming red bike with a leather saddle-bag. Only Jean fell off it the next day, and knocked her front teeth out, so I was glad I was still myself. But it took more than that to show me that invasion of others is a witching sin. I envied Ian, with his two white rabbits in a hutch that his father had made for them, but he developed eczema and sat miserably scratching at his raw, flaky hands. Warwick came top in the Tables Test, and grated all the skin off his nose when he fell over in the playground. Margaret tore her new dress when she had a jammy doughnut for break-time and I had only a green apple, and Jenny who wrote so neatly spilled ink all down her white blouse. The worst was Christine, of whom I was furiously jealous because her parents were taking her to a real farm for the holidays. They didn't go because her mother contracted polio. Infantile Paralysis, it was called in those days. She died on an August afternoon when the ice cream cart was ringing its bell down the street. Stop Me and Buy One, indeed.

At last I saw that I was being warned not to envy. These catastrophes would have been mine had my wish to change places been granted. The state of being Mary Carstairs was a fixed one, and I must not challenge it. Pretending was all right, as long as I knew that I was the person who pretended.

The curious thing was that the boys did not seem to know this. They rushed round the yard at playtime, being trains or, more usually, aeroplanes, and would mow you down without any sign of realising that it was not the Hurricane or Spitfire which had left someone flat on the tarmac with bleeding knees, but the boy himself. The girls, on the other hand, congregating in the earwiggy space under the tangle of Old Man's Beard that grew across the fence, knew perfectly well that they were playing at Houses or Hospitals, having discussed it first. Perhaps women, whose bodies can double into the growing of another life, are naturally double-minded, and know it. Certainly, a lot of them find it funny and somehow touching that men believe so passionately in their games. That's why there are so few of us in the panelled board-rooms of power – somewhere along the way, we stop pretending.

When you are young, you can't stop. It's too dangerous. The school game is played with terrible seriousness, and it's only the delinquent and the stupid who dare to put up any real resistance. Sometimes I wished I was like Bobby White, who used to do chimpanzee imitations when Miss Daubeny had stood him in the corner, or even Lily, whose mouth hung vaguely open – but I withdrew the wish quickly, because I meant them no harm. That's where all the difficulties started, with the knowledge that my wishes were in some way potent. Being aware of such a thing sets you a little apart.

I wanted desperately to be ordinary. I flicked pellets as the others did, passed notes, protested innocence, declared various life-long friendships – but none of it dispelled the glass sphere through which I looked out, and neither could the playground rituals of teasing and pinching and of tickling until I wept with the agony of laughter.

Saying what other people wanted to hear became a habit. Even now it's quite hard to break it, since speaking the truth is so much more difficult. The only place where I could rest from my dissembling was in the garden, where scarlet nasturtiums sprawled over the warm bricks of the low wall and the little daisies closed themselves at dusk. Often, I would climb into the cherry tree and sit hidden in its leafiness. Where my heels marked its trunk, amber beads of resin grew, more beautiful than blood.

*

There are fish in the burn, tiny ones, no more than streaks of shadow. They move like wind-blown grass, all one way then all another. My mother comes and crouches beside me, looking at them, but she is thinking of something else. "You must learn to read," she says. "You are old enough now."

This startles me. I thought it was only very special people who could read, like the priest and the doctor. And my mother. I said, "How will I?"

"It's not hard." She picks up a short stick and turns to the smooth sand which the burn has left at its edge. "This is how you write your name." She traces four angled lines that lean together like a pair of sharp mountain tops. "This makes a sound like bees humming," she says. "Mmmm." Then comes a single mountain, with a line across it. "Aah," she tells me. "As if you were very happy about something."

"Mmm – aah."

"Put them together. Mmaah."

"Ma. That's what the lambs says to their mothers."

"Some children do, too." She is drawing an upright line with a half-moon growing from one side of it, above a slanting leg. *"Rrrr."*

I laugh. *"It sounds like Anna Dubh when she purrs."*

"So it does. And this line on its own – see? – says eee, as mice do. But it can say I as well. It's the letter you use to talk about your own self."

"Mm-aa-rr-ee. Mari!" It is pure magic.

"Now you draw them." She hands me the stick. Water seeps up through the sand to fill the lines as I make them. I murmur their sounds, then realise something. *"Look! If you say this one first, it goes aa-rr-mm. Arm!"*

"Yes it does."

I write the letters in their different order, then add the single vertical line. *"And now it says army!"* I am thrilled with this new power.

"You're right, but there's another letter that sounds almost the same." She draws in two little branches at the top of my line, using her finger, then stands up and pulls her shawl about her shoulders. *"Army."* She looks away, frowning.

"What is it?"

"I'm no' sure. Something far away as yet."

"Something bad?" As I watch her, I, too, can feel the thunder cloud that is gathering somewhere in its own place. She smiles at me, and my fears are soothed. *"It would be a dull world without storms,"* she says, knowing my thoughts, and I wonder for a moment why she insists that I must read, when there is so little need for words between us. Then I see that it is to do with the coming storm. With a new sense of purpose, I ask her if there are more letters to be learned, and she says there is one for each of the sounds of speaking. *"They can put your voice onto paper or parchment, to send to somebody far away,*

or they can be carved into stone, to last for ever."

"For ever." *The years open out beyond me, and I am filled with happiness.*

*

The years open out, backwards as well as forwards, maybe even sideways, spreading beyond what I know. They form a sea of memory with misty edges, tipping over the horizon into something else, a parallel existence which, for many years, I didn't try to understand. Sometimes, there were hints of a connectedness between the present and that other world. Darkness had something to do with it, the mystery that lurks at the edges of what the eyes can see. I was afraid of the dark, because it belonged in some way to the terrible book that still haunted my bedroom, and yet other black things were friendly, like the ebony elephants on either side of the clock on the mantelpiece. And my most beloved companion was Minna, our black cat, who could be as dark as a solid shadow under a bush or a lump of mistletoe in the fork of a tree. I knew Minna so well that I could have lived inside her skin and looked out of her pale green eyes, feeling my tongue rough-spined between my pointed teeth. There was no need to wish to be her, because she was hardly a separate creature. And so, with nothing unnatural about our mingling, I caused her no harm.

*

Rrr – rrr. Anna Dubh, Black Anna, purrs beside me as we lie in the sun.

I might have been a cat. I feel the way my claws grip and the tip of my tail twitches. I know the detail of the warm dust in my coat, and the smell of it. My whiskers filter the air, sifting a mouse's quiver of fear from the clicking busyness of insects and the squat silence of a toad. The mouse is safe until later, in the cool of night time when I will be hungry.

Perhaps I have been a cat. How strange it is not to know. There is so much I would like to know. There are books full of writing, my mother says, in which old truths are told. The priest has them.

We do not go to the church. We stay away from the village, and I know it is because the people are frightening. They are arguing among themselves about religion, my mother says, fighting over the way in which God should be worshipped. People are very mysterious. If God made all things, then all things have Godness in them. That's why we are all the same inside our different shapes, me and Anna Dubh and the grass and the sky and the warm sun. What is there to fight about?

*

The church was filled with darkness, despite the stained-glass windows and the small, hot fire of red light which meant that God was there. Blackness haloed the candle flame and hid behind pillars and under pews; it was part of the heavy fabric of cassocks and skulked under the pure white of surplices, and the marble figure of the crucified Christ glimmered meekly in this dark light, the head turned sideways like the dead chickens on the butcher's slab, their eyes closed and their red wattles bowed on their naked breasts. Why had people killed this beautiful young man? He died for our sins, Miss Daubeny told us in front of her browner and wispier Jesus in the frame with the criss-cross corners, and I wondered what sins she could mean. Perhaps the emptiness of what I didn't know was filled with evil.

Mary of the blue robe was best. She shared my name, and she was calm and beautiful, and seemed to impose no conditions. In her house, Joseph would go on planing his sweet-smelling wood, and there would be none of the long silences that went on for days and caused my father to cough nervously as he fingered the pages of his book. At such times, I would carry Minna up to my bedroom and stroke and stroke her silky fur, slowly, so that each stroke took several seconds, and eased the time away.

Sometimes, when I stand at my window now and glimpse one of the cats moving through the long grass, I remember the comfort of that stroking. I still love the touch of fur and lean muscle, but these days it is the white stone that I hold in moments of bleakness, feeling its smooth weight slowly become warm in my hand.

*

Among all the stones that lie under the clear brown water of the burn, I have never found another like the one my mother keeps on the shelf with her phials and jars. It is as round and white as a little moon. One day, my mother says, it will go back where it came from, but she does not tell me where that is. I grieve to think that it must go away. I would like to keep it safe, so I ask if it can be mine.

Her glance reproves me. How can a stone be a possession? It belongs to its own self. But she says, "It will be yours when you want to give it away."

"Who will I give it to?"

She turns from me to the fire, and makes no answer. She never tells me I am being stupid. In her silence, the words are plain. When the time comes, Mari, you will know.

*

In all the faded patchwork of things that happened, some scraps retain their colour. I saw my father walk past the house one night. He didn't pause, just went straight on. He came back after a few minutes, and bent down to look at the number on the gate before he opened it. "These wretched little houses are all the same," he said. My grandmother gave me an autograph album, and in its sugar-almond pages, he wrote, *This above all – to thine own self be true.* My mother chose Burns:

O wad some Pow'r the giftie gie us
To see oursels as others see us!

The words sadden me now, written in her delicate, edgy hand. She was always uncertain, perhaps because of her orphaned childhood, sent home from India to the coldness of Edinburgh. Or perhaps she was simply double-minded.

At about that time, she left the church. The priest came to the house and there was a fierce argument. Then he swept out, and my mother cried. Years later, she explained that she couldn't condone the support of the Church for Franco's regime in Spain – but I don't think she was capable of faith. She equated it with helplessness, and found it frightening. My poor mother – she never learned the witching skills, so she found the world full of opposition.

My grandmother came from Scotland for a visit. This wasn't unusual, but on this particular occasion, she took off her hat with a certain flourish, and as she carefully replaced its long pins, excitement filled the room. "I have just seen Tom," she announced, then added to me, "your grandfather, darling."

My mother said, "But he's in India."

"Home for a month." Nana was quietly triumphant. "He's been staying with Jessie in Helensburgh."

"Who's Jessie?" I asked.

"His sister." But they were not listening to me. They stared at each other, and my mother said, "You mean he's in London at this moment?"

"Yes. He was on the same train as me. Wasn't that odd? We met in the restaurant car. I'd just sat down and he asked if he could join me. It was rather full, you see. And then he saw who it was."

"You could have brought him here," said my mother, and I was suddenly painfully sorry for her.

"He was going for a hospital appointment. Just a check-up, he said, nothing serious. He looks older, of course, but he hasn't put on any weight. He sent his love. He'll be down to see you."

"Did you know he was coming home? Had he written?"

"Heavens, no. We haven't had any communication for years."

I watched Nana as she talked. I could see why my father called her The Gypsy Queen. Her bushy hair was grey now, but her eyes and eyebrows were still black, and she held her chin high, like someone who relished danger. A highwayman, I thought. She had given me a pistol once, just a tiny one a few inches long, but heavy and wooden handled, with a steel knob you put your thumb over to pull the hammer back. But on that visit, she had stolen my sgian dhu kilt pin with its amber thistle head, no doubt to give to someone else. She was wonderfully wicked, my grandmother.

Tom never came to see us. It had not been "just a check-up", but a consultation about a growth in his throat. They kept him in hospital for an exploratory operation, and the night before it, he clipped his fingernails and toenails carefully. "It'll save you time tomorrow when you lay me out," he said. They thought it was a joke, but he died under the anaesthetic, before an incision had been made.

*

A tinker-man comes. I see him making his way to the house, but he does not see me, for I am up the hill with the wild ponies. The pots and kettles which dangle from his pack make a clinking noise, hollow and plaintive. My mother is down there in the garden, gathering herbs, but when she sees the man, she runs to meet him.

The pony mare butts at me, blowing with her sweet breath. She does not move away when I put my hand on her neck. I can feel the energy that runs through all her big muscles and bones, and the scent of her is lovely.

"Mari!" My mother's voice is clear in the empty hillside.

She wants me to meet the man. I would rather stay with the ponies, but I call back and start to move down through the heather.

"Mari," says my mother as I climb over the wall, "this is Liam. He is your father."

The man seems dark against the sun in the sky. The edges of his hair and beard are lit by its shining, as if he is a man of fire. He holds out his arms to me, but he is too big and too glowing, and I step back.

"We have been a long time on our own," *my mother says, as if excusing my behaviour.*

The man laughs and puts his arm round her shoulders, and they turn to go into the house.

The ponies are moving away across the hill. I wish I could be like them, living anywhere and everywhere, not having to stay in one place.

My mother and the man called Liam are in the house for a long time. I sit on the wall and wait, and their voices murmur. When my mother comes out with Liam, she looks as if she has been crying. I let the man take my hands, for the sun is behind me now, and he is no longer fiery, just dark. His eyes are light brown, and they stare into mine as if they are trying to be steady, but they shift and flick like the young trout in the burn. "One day, Mari," *he says,* "you must come and visit me, and meet your wee brother, Jamie. Will you do that?"

I nod, but his words are puzzling. The metal pans clink together as he shoulders his pack, and I know it is a sound I will remember. He kisses my mother. "I'll not forget you," *he says. Then he walks away up the track with a long, easy stride, and does not look back, though my mother watches him until he is out of sight.*

There is great perplexity. "If I have a wee brother, he must be your bairn," *I say to my mother.* "So why is he not here?"

She says, "You will understand when you are older." *Then she turns away and goes back to the house.*

The sun is almost touching the hill's edge. I wish she had not called me down from the ponies. It seems now that I was younger when I stood with them, not knowing there could be this nameless anxiety.

*

If you are brought up by a wise mother, as I think Mari was, then you know that within you is the thinker of thoughts and the feeler of sensations, and that this central being combines with the outer one which people see, so that the two are comfortably one. If I ever write a primer of simple witchcraft, I will have to stress the importance of that uniting; without it, you are working against yourself.

School generally has a devastating effect on witching children. It requires them to be uniform in mind as well as in clothing, navy-blue bees who will think hive-thoughts and strive for the aims that are hive-decided. The double minded can't do this. We watch ourselves pretending, and are no more real bees than a pantomime horse can eat grass. And the others know this, and attack the impostors within their midst.

At eleven years of age, you don't know you're a witch. All you want is for the torment to stop, and to be accepted. For this, you will hide your private self, bury it deep so that you appear to be as single and simple as the others; and for many, it dies. I was no different. I read books about jolly girls of the Upper Fourth who won through by being good sports, and tried instantly to be unfaithful to my inner self. I smiled, I pretended I didn't mind that everything I had was systematically stolen and that whatever room they told me to go to was not the right one for our lesson, I would willingly have buried the awkward, painful self which stood and watched my own performance. But it was no good. That central consciousness already knew that it was stronger than the performer, and my pantomime only made me more and more ludicrous.

At breaktimes, I stood against a wall for its scant comfort, either in the milky-smelling dining room or outside, according to whether it was raining. Outside was slightly better. I used to look at the tuft of grass that grew beside the drain, under a black-painted down-pipe that was square in section, but one day it was gone. Tidied up.

Girls used to walk round the playing field with their arms round each others' waists, six or seven of them abreast. There were elm trees by the railway embankment. This would go on for seven years, my parents said, then if my exam results were good enough, I could go to University. It was like being in a tunnel, with not even a pin-prick of light at the end, and it never occurred to me that I could do anything about it.

*

I am picking marigolds. Their branching stalks are easy to break at the joint, and I like the soft, woody feel of them. Some of the flowers are dark orange, bright as barley-sugar, with fudgy brown centres, but most are paler, the colour of shortbread or of the strong cheese that keeps through the winter. Later, the brown segments of their seed-pods will be like little half-moons, but it is too early yet to let the plants set their seeds, for we need the flower-heads to make into healing salve.

Suddenly, it is all so intensely real that it seems like a waking dream, sharper than actuality. The orange petals, the warm air which enfolds them and me, the sensation in my fingers and lips and eyes and skin and every part of me, all mixed with the sky and the distant sea – it is magic, happening at this moment.

In a little while, the sharpness fades, but I am still full of wonder. I turn to go into the shadowed house, to see if my mother knows what has happened.

There are no words.

She holds out her arms, and we embrace. Between us, the marigolds shine.

*

Marigolds, Miss Dean announced, distributing a flower to each of the desks with their sloping drawing-boards. My specimen had a chocolate-brown centre and deep orange petals, and it held its head up like a dog swimming.

I liked Art – it was the one thing at school that occupied all of me, including the inner spectator. As my pencil followed the lines of the arching stalk and the open-eyed orange face, I was happy. Then Miss Dean held up my drawing to show the others, and remarked in her gloomy voice that it was a real interpretation and not just a copy. She was so tactless. I saw the glance that ran between the girls, and knew I would pay for that praise. Recklessly, I made it worse by asking if there were any better brushes. The school brushes were such misused things, balding and stiffened from being ground into jamjars of dirty water – they made a multiplicity of lines instead of just one. Miss Dean fished in her desk drawer and gave me a brush with firm, soft hairs, as poised as a cat's whisker that tapers to nothing. Sable, she said. And it was her own property, so please return it afterwards.

The way the lovely brush released an even film of colour was enchanting. The end of the lesson came too quickly, but Miss Dean said I could stay and finish my picture if I liked, only she was on yard duty. And she picked up her whistle on its loop of red braid, and followed the others out.

It was the first time I'd been alone in the school, except for the times when I'd stood in panic in the empty corridor and wondered where to go. This was wonderfully peaceful. Dust motes floated in the slanting light, and the room was quiet. I put in the last shadows under the petals and washed the lovely brush carefully. As I was replacing it in Miss Dean's drawer, I heard footsteps pounding up the stairs that led to the art room. Lorna and Christine and Evelyn burst in, and stopped when they saw me.

"Oh, quite the little favourite, aren't we," said Lorna.

Christine wandered over to my desk. She picked up the rubber that was lying beside the water pot and tossed it to Evelyn. Lorna jumped for it, and they began to play Pig-in-the-middle. I rushed to save my picture, but it was too late. The desk was jolted, the water-pot knocked to the floor, and the drawing slid from its board and landed face down in the dirty pool. A foot trod on it.

In that fury-charged moment, I was a single, concentrated thing, as complete as a tiger. I screamed that I hated them, hated them, that I couldn't bear it any more. My fists were clenched and tears were pouring down my face. I rushed out of the room and down the stairs, out of the door, across the tarmac and the grass, flung myself against the railing beyond the elm trees, started to climb it. The railway cutting lay on the other side, it was an escape, the shining lines led to somewhere else, I could run and run.

My school skirt hooked itself on a spike, and the girls caught up with me, their hands grabbing, hauling me back as a train thundered past. "Oh, God," Lorna said, "you weren't going to, were you?" Her face was white.

I couldn't stop crying. I tried to push them away, but they were too strong. Then I realised they were hugging me, not just holding. Christine began to cry as well. "We didn't mean to upset you," she said. "It was only fun."

After that, they declared themselves to be my friends, and we walked with our arms round each other's waists, round and round the playing field.

*

People are frightening. I am not scared by anything else that moves on the hill, not even the adders which dart so quickly across the warm earth under the heather. A boy was bitten by one of them last year, and his leg swelled and turned blue, and his mother came running up to our house, begging for help. She took the herbs my mother gave her and hid them under her shawl, then ran away fearfully, scared that she would be seen. But the boy was better in the morning.

There are never any thanks for my mother's healing. People come furtively, needing her help, but afterwards, when a septic wound is clean or a fever has given way to calm sleep, they say the cure was due to their own good nursing or to a simple bought in the market, or to nature itself.

Women are not supposed to have skill in these matters, my mother says, for it usurps the power of the leech and the apothecary, and of the priest himself, who claims on behalf of God to know that sin runs in the veins of humankind, erupting in boils and aches and sickness. That is why people are afraid to admit that they sought help from Agnes Balfour, and why it is always in the darkness of night that a gift is left at the door – a bag of oatmeal, perhaps, or a freshly-killed rabbit.

I fear them because they fear us, and their fear is manifest as hatred. Even though they smile when they come to the house, they walk in a black halo of hostility, and the deer on the hillside raise their heads sharply as if they can smell it, and run away with bobbing tails. They never run from us. The heron in the burn feels it, too, swivelling his long-beaked head to stare, then lifting himself up with slow strokes of his wings to hide in the distant trees.

We must not hate, my mother says. Our own hatred is our chief danger, for it will cause us to do harm, and life is dangerous enough without that. As it is, some illnesses cannot be cured, but she dare not state the truth that death is coming, or she will be accused of wishing it. Everyone, she says, seeks a scapegoat rather than recognise that life is a temporary state. And the witch is easy to blame. My mother waits calmly for the accusation to be made. I am not like her. I watch the hillside as warily as a hare, and feel my heart thump in terror if a man or a woman comes climbing up from the village. I would like to run and run.

*

Although the girls adopted me as theirs, it was with curiosity, as if I was an odd pet, not quite civilised. It was a convenient role. I became the class fool, the one with an irreverent comment for every occasion. Teachers shook their heads regretfully, and I came in for some blistering sarcasm from those who thought I was a cheeky brat. They should have been grateful; at least I disguised my hatred.

Often, I took refuge in being ill. They were genuine sicknesses – the long silver line in the thermometer proved it – but it's so easy to be ill if you want to. Just withdraw your energy, move slowly, breathe only with the top part of the lungs, and the waiting bacteria will colonise obligingly.

The days in bed had so many attractions. My mother became a hospital sister again, as she had been before her marriage. She stood with her hands behind her back when the doctor came, professionally correct, and provided lemon barley water in a jug covered by a beaded circle of muslin. She brought calves' foot jelly, and spoonfuls of brown medicine offered with a steady hand. I loved her so much at those nursing times.

People came to our back door sometimes, wanting a burned hand dressed or a whitlow lanced. There was a carpenter once, whose shoulder was full of splinters from a plank that had slipped. Doctors were expensive then, unless you were on the Panel, paying your sixpence a week, and many people fell into the trap of genteel poverty. There was a furtiveness about the way these visitors came tapping at the door – and some risk for my mother, too, for if anything went wrong, the medical men would be quick to accuse her of illegal practice. But she was careful and scrupulous, and her patients did well.

*

One day, my mother says, I will find a human being who seems wonderful to me, but I cannot imagine it. She told me the purpose of the white cloths which she washes and hangs over the bushes when the moon is new. She said it might be sore sometimes but I should be proud of that, as it showed that I could have a child. There is no love without pain, she said. All things must balance. I was confused, and asked her if I would have a baby when the bleeding started. "Only when you know a man," she told me, "and love him enough to let his body into yours. You will want it to happen, more than anything you can imagine."

It feels important, being grown-up enough to know this secret, but I hope it will not spoil the happiness. When nothing moves in the clear evening light except the twittering swallows in the sky, there is such joy that I want to dance like the midges in the warm air.

*

My childhood ended very suddenly, on a summer night when my father had gone for his usual "breath of fresh air", round to the George and Dragon. It was late June, but rain was falling, and the sitting-room felt damp and chilly without a fire in it. The smell of ironing came from the kitchen. I sat in an arm chair, reading Hans Andersen's tale of the princess who wove shirts of nettles to rescue her brothers who had been turned into swans. She ran out of time, and the youngest brother was left with a swan's wing instead of an arm. But it was the rejected swans I mourned for, gliding on their lake with small gold crowns on their heads. Why could the girl herself not have been part of the same enchantment, to fly with a great whistling of wings over the castle wall and away through the pink evening sky? I would rather have been a swan than a lumping, graceless human being.

Just then, my mother came in with a booklet, and said, "Now you're at the big school, there are certain things you ought to know. Otherwise you might get garbled versions from the other girls." The booklet was called 'A Preparation for Womanhood'. My mother hesitated for a moment, then went back to the kitchen and got on with the ironing.

PART TWO

A packet of sanitary towels now sat on the dark top shelf of my wardrobe, bringing with it a sense of furtiveness and guilt. I was no longer the child who laughed from a cloud in Blake's *Songs of Innocence* or trotted by the river like Grahame's Mole. All that was lost.

In the new ugliness, the misery of school sharpened again. The self I tried to leave behind each morning when I got on the bus came wandering after me like a little ghost, looking through my eyes at the bare elm trees, singing with my voice the school's Anglican words of the Nunc Dimittis, Lord, now lettest Thou Thy servant depart in peace. Tears would have come, had I let them.

Once, Miss Dean unrolled an oil painting on canvas and displayed it silently. The colours were pale and smooth. Two calm women with heavy bare arms were inside a white place that looked like a dairy. We all stared. Someone asked, "Who painted it?" "I did," said Miss Dean. Then she rolled the canvas up and put it away. She once told Patricia Willis that she hated her. I don't know why – I wasn't paying attention.

The rest of the teachers seemed unreal, as Miss Daubeny had done. I know that it's dangerous to let yourself feel like that, because it gives you permission to dismiss people and damage them, but I wasn't aware of that at the time. I knew only that I was growing older and stronger and more impatient. And then there was the episode of Miss O'Dell.

She was a button-chrysanthemum of a woman, round pink face centred on a pug nose, and she taught what was then called Holy Scripture. For weeks, her lessons had been on the lives of the prophets, of which I remember nothing except a faint liking for Amos. Then she linked her pink hands on the desk in front of her and asked, "Now, who believes in the Garden of Eden?"

I was as cautious as a cat offered strange meat. The question was loaded, that much was obvious. It couldn't be a straight test of knowledge, because the Garden was not real in that sort of way. It belonged with the valleys wild, the White Knight, the angel Gabriel. She was asking, then, if we believed in that lovely world to which imagination holds the key. Yes, oh, yes. I saw now what it was she meant to test – this was the business of religion, wasn't it, to find a faith in what could not be known?

Almost all of them said they didn't believe in the Garden. Moya said she did, but then, she was French. And there was Barbara, who played the violin, and Angela Hunisett, who went to Sunday School in a corrugated iron hut behind the station. And me.

Miss O'Dell shook her head and smiled. Then she started explaining about Darwin, as if we didn't know all that, and I wanted to scream that Darwin was talking about something else, that it was as different as hope is from jam. The betrayal shocked me, especially coming from someone who was supposed to know about faith. She should not do that. She should not do anything.

I simply swept her aside.

It's very easy to do. That's the whole essence of the thing, the easiness; there's no effort. Just as one shrugs and says that the rain must stop, that's all (and it does), or tucks away in the mind a need to meet a certain person unexpectedly, so opposition will melt away if it is allowed to. On the day after the Garden of Eden lesson, Miss O'Dell was not at school. We never saw her again. News of her death was announced by the Headmistress at Assembly a little time later. No details were given, naturally, but Miss Dean confided in her Art lesson that the Scripture mistress had died of pneumonia. I felt a strange sense of calm, like the stillness of a leaf on water that is moving fast.

That was the start of it. The calm remained with me. I have it to this day, although I nearly lost it for a time – but that remains to be investigated. For now, I am a little horrified to look back at my teenage ruthlessness.

I tolerated no unwanted impositions. When the music mistress tried to make me play my inaccurate Purcell at the school concert, she was called on that very day to the bedside of her mother, who had suffered a stroke and was not expected to live. The mother did live – I had no quarrel with her – but the concert was cancelled. Miss Webb, whose bitter sarcasm had penetrated my defences so often, became suddenly arthritic and retired from teaching. Cross-country runs and hockey matches were so frequently disrupted by thunderstorms and broken-down buses that people began to notice, and talked of the fixture-list being jinxed. Which it was, of course. I began to feel much happier.

*

"Agnes Balfour has been at her tricks again," said Bessie McGuire as she sat between her sons Billy and Hugh in the heather, resting from the peat-cutting at mid-day. They were eating the bannock she had brought with her.

"How has she?" asked Billy.

"Jenny McIver passed her yesterday and, daft lassie, she gave no answer when the woman wished her good day. Now, that was a rudeness, right enough, but Jenny said the look she got from Agnes turned in her heart like a knife. And this morning the milk her cow gave had blood in it."

"Jenny McIver's cow is newly-calved," Billy argued. "Sometimes you will find blood in the milk for a day or so. This talk of witchcraft is stupid."

"Stupid or no', that cow has calved twice before, and the milk has always been good," said Hugh angrily. "Have you forgotten what Agnes Balfour did to me?"

"I have not forgotten," said Billy. His brother's foot stuck out awkwardly from the lumpiness of his badly-set ankle.

His mother frowned at him. "Sometimes I think Hugh was not the only one bewitched on that day," she said. "There are spells on the mind as well as on the body."

"Ach!" Billy flung himself back on the rough, sun-dry heather. Jackdaws circled above him, untidily black against the sparkling sunshine. They knew, he thought. They had seen it all, they or their jackdaw grandparents, seven years ago, watching two boys go up the hill to the witch's house, seeing the arc of the white stone as it dropped through the sky. Maybe they knew what the seven years were to bring. Maybe they or their jackdaw children knew what was yet to come. He closed his eyes against the sun, but it continued to burn scarlet through the screen of his eyelids. It could not burn away the memory of the girl who had sat with her baby under the cherry tree.

*

There is no point in making excuses. I have to look at what I did, and decide whether it was a misuse of witching technology. During the reckless year that followed Miss O'Dell's death, I abandoned all the caution I had learned at Miss Daubeny's little school about the dangers of wishing. This was not wishing, I told myself. I was not pushing against the natural way of things. If this effortless game had losers, it was not my fault.

There will be those who hold this to be a valid excuse for disbelief. It was just pure chance, they will argue. Ah, but . . . the witches shake their heads and smile. If chance is your business, there is no escape down that bolt-hole. And even at the time, I knew better. One of these days, a small voice inside me said, you will pay for this. Looking back, I suppose it was right.

Things came to a head when the school staged a Christmas production of T.S. Eliot's *Murder in the Cathedral*. I wanted the part of Thomas, the Archbishop. Morbidly, perhaps, his self-scrutiny and stripping-away of temptation fascinated me. When Janine Collins got the role, I swept her aside like brushing away a crumb. She died of meningitis ten days before the performance.

Janine would have made a better Thomas than I did, I know that now. She was taller, with a lean, athletic body that would have more suitably suggested the man's strong asceticism, and her voice was crisper and more incisive. As I stood on the stage, robed and cowled, speaking Eliot's sonorous cadences, her presence overshadowed me with its emptiness, and I mourned her, and felt afraid. People said it was a good performance, specially at such short notice, but something ominous had touched me. Janine's death had been a turning-point. As Eliot put it, one moment

Weighs like another. Only in retrospection, selection,
We say, that was the day. The critical moment
That is always now, and here. Even now, in sordid particulars
The eternal design may appear.

For Thomas Becket, the sordid particulars were the four knights who came to kill him. For me, the design expressed itself even more sordidly than that. After the play, I began to have cramping abdominal pains that made my hands cold and my hair damp with sweat. Because I thought it must be something to do with having periods, I said nothing. It was perfectly natural, my mother had said. She herself was very tough about pain, despite her kindness as a nurse. When she came back from the dentist, white-faced after having several teeth out, she permitted herself only a brief rest in her arm-chair by the fire before getting up to toast crumpets for tea. One did not complain. Most particularly, women did not complain about their secret bleeding. My intermittent pains went on and got worse, and all easiness deserted me. There was no more avoiding of cricket matches and music exams and the formal dreadfulness of the gymnastics competition. School became a torment again, but this time in body as well as in mind. I wanted desperately to be away from it.

One night, the pain was so bad that sleep was impossible. In the morning, I crept down to breakfast with a bent back, barely able to move. "Heavens," my mother said. She sent me straight back to bed, and the doctor came and pressed his cold hands on my stomach. Within a couple of hours I was in hospital and unconscious, having a septic appendix removed.

There was a new-born pleasure in the days that followed, as the soreness healed and I went on shaky walks from bed to bed in the bright ward. It seemed as if a debt had been paid and the slate was clean again.

*

In the fading daylight of the October afternoon, Billy McGuire paused in his digging and stared out at the sea. Its implacable grey line filled him with despair. There was no future for him in this obstinate, intractable croft which he and Hugh had inherited from their father. Hugh had sold the fat lambs for the best price he could get, but the money had been scant and the coming winter would again be pinched and desperate. Billy's hope of a warm coat could not even be mentioned. The new moorland he was trying to bring into cultivation would take months of work, and its yield would be small until it had been manured for several seasons.

These thirteen years since his father's death had been hard, specially at first, when Bessie had been on her own with two young sons. Billy knew his mother had done her best, but the croft had got into a bad state, and even now, it could barely support the three of them, let alone Hugh's wife, Janet, whom he had married in the spring. And their child was due to be born in the new year.

Hugh wanted the place to himself. It was reasonable enough – as the elder son and the greater help to his mother in the first years of her widowhood, he had the better claim to it. Since the accident which he swore Agnes Balfour had caused, he walked with a lurching, uneven gait. He was as strong as ever, but the lightness and agility of his boyhood were gone, and he was full of bitterness.

Sooner or later, Billy knew he would have to leave. Now, as he stared at the sea and felt the wind bite through his thread-bare clothes, he made the decision. Next time the recruiting sergeant came with his red face and the clatter and squeal of his fife and drum, Billy would be in the line of gaunt boys, standing straight and proud, frowning with military fierceness so that nobody would see the heartbreak of failure. He was nineteen years old. Any army would be glad to have him. War, he thought, uses up its soldiers as a fire uses peat.

The cold wind began to chill his skin, and Billy turned again to his task, raising the heavy caschrom with its angled blade and chopping it down hard into the tangle of heather and wiry grass. He struck again and again, pulling and turning the clods of wet, root-entangled soil, determined to get the strip finished in the last of the ebbing light. In his hurry, his movements became violent and unrhythmic, but he went on working, and ignored the accident which stood like a ghost of itself before him.

The tool glanced sideways off a half-buried rock and gouged across the top of Billy's foot, slicing through his boot. Aghast, he stared at the gashed leather. These had been his father's boots, impossible for Hugh to wear because of his deformed foot, Billy's only legacy. What would the cobbler charge to mend such damage? Repair might not even be possible.

The pain came almost apologetically on the back of his dismay. Blood welled up between the ragged edges of the leather. Billy cursed himself for his folly. This was an injury which might take a week or more to heal, and it would impede him from working. Hugh would be so angry.

Bessie McGuire looked up from her spinning as he came into the room, and when she saw his face she put her hand on the rim of her wheel to check its turning. "What have you done?" she said.

Billy sat down and eased his foot out of the ruined boot, then felt a wave of giddiness as the white bones looked at him through torn flesh and skin. "Stupid," he muttered.

His mother took a bowl and went out to the burn for water, leaving the door open. The wind and the sharp eddy of peat smoke dismissed his nausea, and he sat back in his father's chair and closed his eyes. The future seemed appalling.

The wound did not heal. Hugh went about the work of the croft in bitter silence as Billy limped from house to byre, doing the few tasks he could manage, or sat with his swollen, throbbing foot propped on a stool by the fire. One day Hugh burst out, "You've yourself to blame for this."

Billy did not deny it. "I should have seen the stone. I'm sorry, Hugh."

"I am not speaking of the stone," said Hugh. His wife, Janet looked up from her sewing at the tone of his voice, her brown eyes meek and alarmed, then quietly gathered up her things and went into the other room. "You began this thirteen years ago," Hugh persisted, "When you broke our agreement and told Father we had been to look at the witch."

"That's nonsense!" protested Billy – but the half-forgotten guilt of that day stirred uneasily, surrounding him with clinging cobwebs of responsibility.

"Nonsense? The very next day, when Father went to tell the woman to keep her evil ways to herself, he came home with a fever. Is that nonsense? Is it nonsense that he died of that same fever? Nonsense that I am a cripple?" Billy hated it when his brother began to rant. He listened helplessly. "A cripple, aye, just as you will be a cripple," Hugh raged on. "Agnes Balfour has bided her time, but now the two of us are struck by the same curse. And it is your fault."

Mother said it was your fault, Billy thought childishly. You were the one who threw the stone. Aloud, he said, "Father would never have us lying." And I lied for you, Hugh, his mind went on in its obstinate plaint, that is why he beat me. And he saw again the belt with its end wrapped round his father's fist, and wept again under the insistent questioning and the blows. He swallowed hard. "Besides, he never saw Agnes Balfour that day. The house was empty when he and the others got there. Euan McBride told me, and he was with them, he saw."

Hugh snorted contemptuously. "Did he see a hare or a flitter-mouse or a cat? She saw him, right enough."

The argument went on, sour and unrewarding, until at last Billy said, "You'll be rid of me soon, Hugh. Next time the sergeant comes, I'll enlist as a soldier. I've thought of it for some time."

"And the witch thought otherwise," said Hugh. "The sergeant will not want a one-legged recruit." And he went out, slamming the door behind him so hard that smoke billowed from the fire and the pans hanging from the roof-beams jumped on their pegs.

Billy stared at his swollen foot with a new fear. Was that what lay in store – the dreadful knife and the tar and the crutches? Sweat broke out on his forehead and his hands felt clammy. Maybe there was a grain of truth in what Hugh had said, and the years of unease since his father's death had been caused by the unfinished business between Agnes Balfour and himself. He had tried to put it behind him, but the sound of the white pebble falling through the cherry leaves still echoed in his ears, and he still saw the slender neck between the tumble of dark red hair.

From outside, he could hear the splintering thump of axe on wood as Hugh worked off his rage in splitting kindling. The fear which fluttered in Billy's stomach would not be stilled; it sent electric fingers of senseless energy through his body and down his limbs. He was as shocked as a creature newly dead and quivering, robbed of all familiarity. Time had run out. The witch had waited for thirteen years, and she would wait no longer. As he got to his feet and reached for his stick which stood in the corner, Billy tried to find reasons for what he was about to do. Agnes was said to be a good healer. And if she had sent the sickness to his foot, then only she could take it away again. Perhaps she was not malign. She had cured Ishbel McKinnon's wee girl of the quinsies. And when Euan McBride's brother, Douggie, had swallowed a wasp and lay choking for breath through the swelling of his throat, she had come unbidden to the door with a bunch of herbs. Infuse them and let him sip the liquid, she had said, and put the boiled leaves across his throat under a hot, wet cloth. Within an hour, he had been out of danger.

Billy put on his sheepskin jerkin and opened the door. Hugh did not look up or pause in his bringing down of the axe with vicious accuracy on log after log of the elder tree he had cut down last spring, and from the doorway of the byre, Billy could hear the quick splish-splash as his mother milked the cow.

There was something unyielding about the preoccupation of the pair of them, as if they were joining in an unspoken insistence that a time of decision had come for the younger son. He closed the door gently behind him, then limped across the yard and started on the long walk up the hill.

A girl stood in the dark doorway and watched him as he

approached. Her eyes were as black as a squirrel's under the tangle of hair, extraordinary in its brightness, rowan red.

Billy's foot throbbed with pain, and confusion throbbed in his mind with an equal rhythm. This child-woman was not Agnes. All the way up the hill, he had been nerving himself to meet the witch, and instead, this young girl stood before him like a wild thing half-inclined to run away. "I'm Billy McGuire," he heard himself say. Jackdaws wheeled and scolded, clack-clack. He was still himself, not changed into a toad or an adder. As his terror subsided, he realised that this must be the baby Agnes Balfour had held in her arms that other time, thirteen years ago.

The girl's black eyes looked into his, then at his injured foot. "Are you wanting my mother to make that better?" she asked.

"Aye. I mean if she can. Please." The words came out of him awkwardly, in humiliating contrast to the girl's simplicity. She nodded, and disappeared into the house.

A white apron glimmered in the shadowed interior, and Billy stared at it in dread as the woman came out into the daylight. He dared not raise his eyes to her face.

"Come in," said Agnes Balfour.

Billy took a quivering breath and forced himself to meet her gaze. The dark eyes were as bright as her daughter's, but there was grey in the braided red hair now, and her face had a tiredness which was somehow reassuring. "Sit down." She indicated the stool by the fire. "Mari, I'll need some hot water,"

The girl moved to tip some water into a bowl from the black kettle which hung over the fire, and as she met Billy's eyes she smiled at him. With a sudden sense of lightness, he smiled back. It was the first time in many years that he had been offered such simple friendship.

Agnes sat on the other stool before him and took his foot in her lap, deftly slitting through the dirty rags that bound it, using a razor-sharp double-edged knife, the sight of which made his heart flutter with fresh alarm. As the festering wound came into view he turned his face away, for the smell of it was bad now. Agnes looked at the injury carefully, feeling the swollen redness on either side of the oozing gash with a light careful touch. Then she got up and put a small handful of salt into the bowl of hot water which Mari held, and looked along the flasks which stood on the shelf. She selected one, unstoppered it and allowed a few drops of the clear liquid to fall into the bowl as well. Then she took it from Mari and placed it on the floor in front of Billy. "Put your foot in this," she instructed. "Carefully – the water is very hot. Dip it a little at a time until you can bear the heat."

Billy did as he was told. "You must let it soak until the water has cooled," Agnes said. "The heat of the foot will go away with the heat of the water." Then she looked at him and added tentatively, "Would you take a bowl of broth while you sit there?"

Billy hesitated – but he was hungry, and the smell which came from the iron pot by the fire was good. "I would," he admitted. "Please." He watched as Agnes ladled some broth into a bowl and cut him a hunk of bread, and wondered whether the peace which seemed to abide in this place was to be feared. Could it be a symptom of magic?

Agnes handed him the bowl and a spoon. Then she said, "You were just a wee boy when you came here last."

Billy shut his eyes as the words struck home. She remembered. With the hot bowl in his hands and his injured foot being cared for, he felt like the six-year-old boy he had been then, scared and guilty. He took a deep breath and looked up at her. "I am sorry for what happened that day," he said. "We should not have come to spy on you." He wanted to mention Hugh's throwing of the stone as well, but a perverse loyalty forbade it.

"I knew you were sorry," Agnes said. "It was only a

small thing your brother did, but the guilt of it has been heavy to bear."

She sat down on the other stool beside her daughter, who moved a little from where she sat on the floor by the fire to lay her arm across her mother's lap. Billy took another spoonful of broth, and Agnes watched him. After a while she said, "The trouble which has come on your family was not of my intending."

"Hugh thinks you put a curse on us," Billy blurted.

Mari frowned in concern, but Agnes remained calm. "Your brother is his own prisoner," she said. "In seeking someone to blame for what is in himself, he makes the bars of his cage even stronger."

"What will happen?" Billy asked nervously.

There was a trace of reproof in the response. "I am no fortune-teller. The future grows from the present, like a tree from its seed. We must be careful what we sow."

Billy felt his face redden as he tried to make sense of what she had said. Mari gazed at him with unblinking black eyes, and her hair shone like a red halo in the shadowed room. When he had finished the broth, she came to take the bowl from him, and he smiled at her again, with more confidence this time. "Thank you," he said, and treasured the two words for the transient link they formed between him and this girl.

In sudden happiness, he leaned back and stretched, for the delight of looking at Mari sent a thrill through his body. He spread his toes in the comfortably warm water – and the wound in his foot split open afresh, letting a thick yellow discharge burst out. He gasped, staring down at it, and Agnes nodded in satisfaction. "It will heal now," she said. When the water had cooled further, she knelt down and washed the wound clean, then spread a cloth on the floor and lowered Billy's foot gently onto it. Warning him not to touch it, she fetched a jar of greyish-green ointment, which she applied thickly over the open gash and the surrounding flesh. It stung a little. She covered it with several layers of clean cloth and bound the whole foot with torn strips. "Now," she said, looking up at him with his white-swathed foot between her hands, "you must not take these coverings off until the new moon rises."

"But the moon is only in its first quarter," Billy pointed out, wondering if she really meant so long a time.

"So it is," Agnes agreed. "But do as I tell you. The herbs in the ointment need time to do their work."

"Will you need to see it again?" asked Billy, and found that he was hoping for a second visit to the quiet house.

Agnes sat back on her heels. "No," she said, and her gaze was absent. "You will not come here again. It will be elsewhere."

Again, Billy failed to understand. He eased his foot back into the slashed boot and tied the laces as best he could across the bulky wrappings. "I should have brought you something for your trouble," he said with fresh guilt. Why had he not thought of it? He could have taken a pot of his mother's bramble jelly in the hope that Hugh would not find out.

"You brought your goodwill," said Agnes. "That is better than bramble jelly."

He stared at her. How did she know his thoughts in such detail? A trace of fear was back in his mind as he thanked her for the broth and the healing of his foot, and he wondered again if his instinctive liking for her was brought about by witchcraft.

Mari opened the door for him, but she did not go back into the house when he had gone out. She came after him down the path and he stopped to look at her.

"I have something for you," she said, holding out her brown fist.

"What is it?" And yet he knew. The girl opened her fingers and revealed a white pebble, smooth and opaline, almost perfectly spherical. His heart jumped as he saw it, but her black eyes were unblinking, devoid of specific intent. "You must keep it," she said, "for ever and ever." And she put the stone into his hand.

"Why?" asked Billy through dry lips.

"Because I want to give it to you. My mother said I would, one day." She reached up and kissed his mouth then, like a child again, ran back to the house and was gone.

Billy looked at the closed door for a long moment, then started down the track, his stick in his right hand and the warm stone in his left. His foot was hardly painful, and the ease of it seemed like a benediction. He turned to look back at the small house under its shaggy turf roof, hardly distinguishable in the fading light from the dark sweep of the hill. The enchantment had shifted. It smiled at him now through the face of a child who was already a woman, the inheritor of a beauty which already haunted his life. It would never let him go. He turned and walked on under the cold, clear sky.

*

I watch him go away, the big boy with the hurt foot, still limping a little as he goes down the hill. He turns and looks back at the house, but he cannot see me.

He has grey eyes, the colour of the winter sea, and his hair is brown like winter bracken. His name is Billy McGuire and I seem to have known him always. I gave him the white stone because I wanted to. He is wonderful to me.

*

At school, the talk was all about boys. I didn't understand that excitement; the gawky lads from what was called "our brother school" were all wrists and ankles and scruffy blazers, and held no magic. In the flat, well-behaved months after I came out of hospital, there was a sense of being reborn which made everything very interesting, and that was enough.

By all ordinary standards, they were strange days. The war was at its height, with frequent night raids, and we slept in the shelter that had been dug below the cherry tree. A Hurricane lamp showed up the patterns of wood imprinted on the concrete walls by the shuttering planks. Sometimes we came out in the mornings and walked across the frosted grass to a house that had no gas or water, where the floors crunched underfoot with plaster dust and the windows were broken. After a bad night, the streets would be littered with debris, the hoses of fire engines still lying snaked across them. Two children who lived in the flats above the shops were killed when their parents left it a bit late to make a run for the public air-raid shelter.

I'm embarrassed now to admit that I liked those uncertain days. The discomforts and surprises were of the kind one meets when travelling, and had the same allure. Anything might happen. It's a comfortable state, I suppose, for someone who embraces chance as a good friend.

After a while, there was a lull in the nightly raids, and it seemed safe to sleep in the house again. The comfort of a real bed instead of the narrow canvas bunk was delicious – but chance is set free when you take the risk of feeling secure, and it seized its opportunity. One night in a sudden raid, an incendiary bomb fell through our roof, cracked the rafter above where I lay, and bounced out again to land on the front lawn, fizzing. A passing Air Raid Warden put a sand-bag on it just before it exploded.

Everyone was much impressed by the luck of my escape, since the rafter had been a slim one and my head would have been the next stop. My father, badly shell-shocked in the First World War, looked at the bulging crack above my bed and put his hand over his eyes. And the effects of that event went on working. Rain dripped through the roof despite the tarpaulin stretched across the gaping hole, and the bomb repair squad said they wouldn't get round to us for some weeks yet because there were bigger jobs to see to. I caught a cold, and coughed all night in the earthy-smelling shelter where we had once again retreated. It was a friendly illness which soon turned to bronchitis, and when I started to recover, my parents sent me up to Scotland, to stay with Nana and recuperate.

So I stood on the drying green behind the small stone villa in Ayr, and looked at the sky that was full of fast-moving clouds and white sheets whip-cracking in the wind, and at the thorn trees with their east-leaning shapes, and felt purely happy. It was perfectly clear that I would not go back to London and the dreadful school; all that was over. I went into the house with the empty washing-basket and told Nana we would be coming to Scotland to stay. All of us. Perhaps quite soon.

She wasn't surprised. She looked up from stirring her little gold-edged cup of black coffee and said, "That'll be a big change for your father."

Nana herself was changing. Her eyes were still as black and bright, but her hair was pure white now, contrasting oddly with the dark eyebrows and lashes that stitched her face like a rag doll, and when we stood side by side, I was the taller. One evening in that late summer, we went to the beach and climbed down over the rocks to the sea's edge, and she put her hand on my arm for support. It was a sad moment. She was no longer in charge of me. We stared across at the peaked silhouette of Arran that broke the straight horizon with its indigo interruption, and the sky was so suffused with rosiness that it seemed almost perfumed. When we returned to the house, the telephone was ringing.

I had not wished my father to have a heart attack, had I? Not consciously – at least I am sure of that. And yet there had been the leap of impatience, the great shrugging-off of ties. What happened was a confirmation, not a surprise. "A big change, right enough," Nana said when she came back from the phone. The attack had not been fatal, but she doubted if my father would ever go back to the Bank.

She was right. He was left blue-lipped and fearful, and my mother immediately set about moving up to Ayr, out of the stress of wartime London. She had never been happy in England, and this was a heaven-sent chance to come back to an almost mythological homeland, a Jerusalem of rightful belonging. I stayed on with Nana while our house was put up for sale, hopelessly. The new houses of my father's dreams were getting old now, still with their faded 'For Sale' boards in the weed-grown gardens. Nobody would buy until the war was over.

That time of waiting for the move to happen was charged with extreme tension; it seemed as if the escape from London was along a tight-rope which might break at any minute. I didn't know what was happening about money, or how the new house would be afforded, or even whether it was to be rented or bought – my father didn't talk about such things, and my mother, I see now, was probably in a frenzy of realising her dream. Now, there's a thought. Was she, too, caught up in the active game of chance? That would explain why she and I, while loving, never shared a view of how things were. We played opposing parts.

At last the day came when the pantechnicon headed north with all our books and furniture, and my mother and father came up on the train, with Minna in a basket in the guard's van. And that night, a direct hit from a high-explosive bomb totally destroyed the London house.

It was as if the blackness which had come into it with the witching book had grown and grown until it could not longer be contained. Now there would be only rubble in the autumn rain, with here and there a barley-sugar-twisted banister and the grey guts of piping. The marigolds would lie under broken glass and splintered window-frame and the sometimes half-intact bits of roof, complete with tiles; I had seen so many bomb-sites. A letter from our next-door neighbour said the cherry-tree was untouched, funny thing, blast. I was glad about that, and saw once again how the sky sparkled through its summer leaves, though I would not be there again.

My father moved cautiously from room to room in the new house, looking out of its windows at the leafless fuchsia hedge and the muddy grass. This villa stood islanded in its own garden, and he could play the piano late at night if he wanted to, with no fear of knockings on the wall from next door. But he didn't play much any more. It made him feel tired, he said.

I started at a school in Ayr, but the place seemed oddly without significance, though it was not particularly painful. There was a strong sense of waiting for something further to happen. The balance was shifting, my mother rising like a sun in a new morning as my father sat heavily and listened for the signs of faltering in the beating of his heart. She was the one who went out now, to a job as a staff-nurse in the local hospital, to help out with the pension, as she put it. Soon, she began to talk about a house-surgeon called Donald, quoting his opinion on everything. And then she was on night-duty a lot.

Almost every day after school, I went to Nana's house, ostensibly to mow her lawn or do some little household job, but in fact to be out of our house, which seemed like an ante-room to something dreaded. Nana told me increasingly rambling stories of India while we drank tea out of her thin china cups, and turned the grey pages of the photograph album with its silk marker, looking at people from the past.

The waiting ended quite unexpectedly one afternoon when I dropped in after school as usual. "I do hope you won't mind," Nana said, "but I've taken on some help with the garden. You've been doing a wonderful job out there, but I thought the roses could do with some attention from an expert." She looked out of the window and smiled, very much the memsahib, proud of her new mali who battled with the Dorothy Perkins. "Isn't he lovely!" she said. I saw only that the boy in the garden had fair hair and wore a pale blue shirt. Nana's smile dropped a little as she continued to regard him. "To be honest," she confessed, "I'm not sure if he knows what he's doing, but he has such a nice face. Sweet William, I call him. He just came knocking on doors, looking for work." She brightened. "And besides, he's an India boy. Sent home to school, of course, and now his parents are marooned out there by this dreadful war. The convoys take weeks to get home, and so dangerous with the U-boats and torpedoes. So I asked him in for a cup of tea and we had a lovely chat. He lives with an uncle and aunt, but he'll be going into the Army soon. He's waiting for his papers."

It was as if she had a new pet. She couldn't stay for more than a few minutes away from the window. I made tea as I always did, and she insisted that I must go and ask him if he'd like another cup. I said she should ask him herself, but she wouldn't. At the time, I thought she wanted to show him off, but I wonder now if she, too, had been waiting, and was excited because she knew it was at an end.

I went out with bad grace, not sure how to address this India boy. I don't know now what I said, only that he looked up from his wheelbarrow and smiled. To this day, I can see that lift of the head and the fairness of him, the grey eyes and the straight nose and the slight unevenness of his teeth between the parted lips. "I'm awash with tea," he said cheerfully. "Couldn't drink any more just now – but thanks all the same." Then he straightened up with the handles of the barrow in his hands. The sleeves of his blue shirt were rolled up, and the roses had scratched his arms.

He said, "A bit later, maybe," because I hadn't said anything, and I nodded – yes, I remember nodding. That night, I dreamed that I ran my fingers over the lines of blood on his skin.

*

With his small son trudging at his side and two black heifers ranging ahead of him, Hugh McGuire made his lurching way up the track which led to the open moor. His misshapen ankle ached dully in the sharp early-morning air, but he ignored it. Nowadays, he noticed only brief periods when it did not ache.

The years since Billy had left to go into the army had been hard ones. While reckoning up with grim satisfaction the food his brother would have consumed had he still been present, Hugh found that he missed his help and companionship – and missed, too, the outlet for rage which Billy had provided. Their mother had seemed to lose heart after her younger son left, and within the year she had died of a growth in the stomach. There was no reason for it, Hugh had thought. She had been a strong woman, never ailing except for the toothache and chilblains in the winter. He knew who to blame. All too clearly, he could imagine the crudely-fashioned wax doll with grey hair made of rabbit fur, and Agnes Balfour's fingers thrusting the long pin into the centre of its body.

Hugh was lonely. His wife, Janet, was a good worker, and he heard her prattling away merrily to the children when she was alone with them, and yet she seemed nervous in his company, and spoke to him with a diffidence more fitting to a servant than a wife. She lay with closed eyes and clinging arms at night as he thrust angrily into her, wanting to break through to whatever passion lay so deeply hidden from him, be it only hatred. It never worked. She was as patient and enduring as a soft old mattress, and his assaults upon her merely resulted in constant pregnancy. Six-year-old Ian who stumped determinedly beside him already had two sisters and a younger brother, wee Hughie, and Hugh was secretly thankful for the wasting sickness which had killed the most recent baby before it was a week old.

They lived on thin rations. With a stern eye to the future, Hugh insisted that the best of the croft's produce must be sold so that he could re-invest in better stock. Janet made excellent butter and cheese from the milk of their five cows, and these products found a ready sale in the market at Kirkcudbright. With a dairymaid of her abilities, Hugh reckoned that there could be a lot more profit in milk – but he needed better dairy cattle. His cows, like all the local stock, were broad-chested black beasts, strong and shaggy, surviving the winters well on the open hill. Their calves made good beef animals, and most of them were bought by the drovers who herded them down the long paths to the south, to fatten on the easy pastures of England. Hugh kept his heifer calves, grumbling at the three unproductive years he had to wait before they came into season and could be put to the bull to calve the following spring. But all the talk now was of the new Dutch cattle, great red-and-white cows with long backs and deep bodies, able to calve a year earlier than the old black breed, and with massive udders that gave a vast supply of milk.

Two years ago, Duncan Kelso had brought a red bull calf from somewhere down in the Borders, and now, though still young, it was fit for service. So Hugh drove his two black heifers across the hill on the long walk to Kelso's farm, and young Ian ran behind them, waving his arms and shouting, when they paused to snatch at the grass that grew between the heather and the whin. Janet's silent glance had made it clear that she thought it a reckless expense when they had a bull of their own running with the cows on the hill, but she said nothing. Hugh set his mouth obstinately as he trudged on. A woman could not be expected to understand the idea of investment. With any luck, one or even both of the heifers would have a big, red-coated calf that would start a line of heavy-milking dairy cows. He, Hugh McGuire, would be the envy of every other crofter.

A low turf-roofed cottage stood at a little distance from the track, with a cherry tree outside its door. As he passed it, Hugh turned his head and spat. The memory of Agnes Balfour burned in his mind, even though he knew now that the red calf he and Billy had found on that fated day was most probably not the product of witchcraft. Janet's grandfather had told him that even the most unbroken line of black cattle may occasionally throw a red calf. Otherwise, he had pointed out, how could new breeds begin? It was the way of the Lord. But, calf or no calf, it was on the morning when he had ventured near the witch that Hugh had received the injury that had lamed him for life.

As he went on up the hill, a sense of being watched made him turn his head. In the darkness of Agnes Balfour's door, a young woman stood, her hair shining as red as rowan berries in the sun. A mute reproach hung in the air, and he knew she had seen him spit at the house, though the place had seemed deserted then.

He raise an unaccustomed hand to make the sign of the cross as his heart thumped in sudden fear. Was she Agnes herself, still young and red-haired through her witching magic? He went on, but felt the girl's black eyes watching him, even after the shoulder of the hill stood between him and the house.

Ian came to his side and glanced back half-fearfully. He whispered, "Was that the witch's daughter?"

"Aye," said Hugh loudly, realizing that the boy had hit on the truth. "It must be."

"She's bonny," said Ian.

Hugh aimed a cuff at him and shouted, "Never say that again!"

Ian had ducked away. Still crouching, with his arm defensively across his face, he ran away after one of the heifers and did not look back. Hugh watched him with regret, feeling again the boyhood soreness of scratched bare legs and bruised feet. He felt a wave of pity for the child who had been himself. I am the victim of an evil spell, he thought. I have been changed into a man whose fists are always clenched. It is Agnes Balfour's fault that my son watches me so guardedly. Curse her.

Walking painfully on, he repeated the last two words deliberately. Curse her. I, Hugh McGuire, hereby curse the foul witch, Agnes Balfour.

*

"He is Billy McGuire's brother."

My mother's voice comes from behind me as I stand in the doorway, locked in a horror which will not let me move. The man with the twisted foot has left hatred in the clean air of the morning, and ugliness which contorts everything. And the child with him seems unreal, like a dead rabbit whose stiffened paws are a mockery of its running over the grass. Why should this be?

Not until the man is hidden by the shoulder of the hill can I move again. My mother is staring at me, and for the first time, she seems powerless, no longer my protecting, ever-strong mother, but a thin woman whose bright hair is fading.

"We should go away," I urge her. "He is dangerous."

She smiles in sadness. "You are your father's daughter right enough," she says. "He would always fly from trouble. Thistledown in the wind."

She is right. When I was a child, I would run away up the hill if people came to the house, and crouch behind a rock where sheep shelter from the wind, to watch them unseen. Now, I want my mother to come with me, to find a place that is free of hatred. But she turns away to stir the pot that hangs over the fire.

Billy McGuire has been part of my mind ever since that day when he came up the hill with his sore foot and I gave him the white stone. The danger which comes from the man who is his brother is terribly close. My mother will accept it and endure and I should stay with her, for soon I will be the stronger and she may need me. But I want to run away.

Thistledown flies so lightly in the wind, and so far. And while it flies, it is safe.

*

That afternoon, in the small yard between the back of Duncan Kelso's house and the byre, the farmer inspected the black heifers and said, "Aye. They're both well in season. You get behind the gate, young Ian, before I let the bull out. We'll have no accidents."

Ian did as he was told, climbing up the wooden bars to hang over the top one, staring eagerly into the yard. Bellowing came from a shed of which the top and bottom half-gates were both heavily barred. Duncan knocked the latches up and pulled the top gate open, leaving the bottom one loose, then stood back beside Hugh.

The bull peered over the half-gate, blinking in the sudden daylight. His pink muzzle, with the heavy brass ring hanging between the flaring nostrils, looked astonishingly broad. His whole head was massive, with a curly crop of white hair between the long, upward-sweeping horns. He came out of the pen fast, in a flurry of strong-smelling wet straw, then stopped in the yard as if surprised by his sudden escape. He snuffed the air, then turned sharply towards one of the heifers.

"Keep well back," Duncan advised Hugh, who had advanced to look with keen interest at the bull.

"Ach, he'll not notice us when there's heifers about," said Hugh, standing his ground. Narrow-eyed, he scrutinised the bull, assessing what he would get for his money. The animal was an impressive size, standing a good six inches taller than the heifers, and he was long-backed and rangy, far different from the stocky black breed. Hugh nodded. A cow of this type would have a big frame. Those long lines in a female animal would give a generous body, deep at the hind end, with plenty of length for a big udder. "Aye," he said, "that's what I'm wanting."

The heifer threw up her head skittishly as the bull reared behind her, and trotted away. The bull came down with a heavy thud on his front feet, blowing loudly through his nostrils.

"Stupid thing she is," said Hugh. "I'll head her into the corner, then she'll stand for him." He moved across the yard with outstretched arms, urging the heifer towards the angle between the house and the byre.

"Come away, Hugh!" Duncan shouted urgently as he saw the bull whip round, distracted by the man's presence. Hugh ducked away, but was too clumsy to move fast. He had a fleeting vision of horns flashing across the sky as the bull's bulk overwhelmed him and flung him face down on the stones of the yard. The heifer, seeking escape from the corner into which Hugh had tried to herd her, turned quickly with the bull at her heels and ran past the gate where Ian still leaned over the top bar, watching. The bull followed her, but his greater weight threw him off balance on the quick turn, and he crashed broadside into the gate, splintering it from its hinges as he fell. Thrashing and snorting, he scrambled to his feet and set off after the heifer again, but Ian lay motionless below the wooden bars.

"You stupid man!" Duncan screamed as he dragged the heavy gate off the child. "Look what you've done!"

Hugh, on hands and knees, was still groaning for breath. With an arm held across his labouring chest, he managed to get to his feet. Still bent double, he stared at his son. A little blood came from the boy's mouth, and his eyes were open, staring at the sky. Then he turned his gaze to Duncan, and the farmer was shocked by its fury. "This was not my doing," he said. "You'll not blame me." But Duncan's wife, weeping helplessly over Ian and touching him with motherly hands, echoed the words of Hugh's own mother. "I can blame you," she said. "I saw what happened." Unnoticed by her or her husband, the mating between the bull and the black heifer took place on the far side of the yard.

"Mary, get me the pole-axe," said Duncan grimly. "That beast will not kill another child,"

Hugh's voice over-rode his order. "No! It was not the bull's fault. It was witchcraft." And Duncan saw, with disbelief, that the man's eyes rested speculatively on the second heifer, which the bull had now turned to.

"Witchcraft!" Mary Kelso sobbed angrily. "That's a fine excuse! It was your own greed killed your son, Hugh McGuire. Look at you – even now, you think of nothing but your money's worth. We'll take no payment for this day's work – will we, Duncan?"

"We will not," said her husband, gently helping her to her feet.

Hugh stared at the sky above the sweeping brow of the hill with bitter triumph as the red bull mated with the second heifer. He had cursed the witch, and she had fought back. She had tried to kill him, and she had cost him a son, but he himself had escaped with his life. Right was on his side. His hard-earned money was unexpectedly intact, and that was a blessing. "Thank you," he said aloud to his God.

PART THREE

The Reverend John Leddie knelt on the stone floor of his church and prayed. "Give us strength, Oh Lord, to fight against evil, in whatever form it comes." He spoke through gritted teeth, like a soldier rather than a priest, and Hugh McGuire, kneeling at his side, was stirred by a faint dislike of this official religion. His own view of God was a confused one, learned from his mother's furtive Latin mutterings as she fumbled the beads through her fingers in guilty faith. Her forbidden religion had been a mingling of fear and beauty and superstitious mystery which made this Calvinism somehow offensive in its plainness. And yet, Hugh protested in silent words, he was no Catholic. Lord Maxwell and his like could carry on their illegal observances in the safety of their rich homes, but that was a show of privilege denied to any common man.

The Minister's voice ground on, but Hugh's internal debate blocked out Leddie's words. It was not a question of belief, he told himself. Sometimes duty had to be done. One invoked the authorities, handed over the responsibility and waited for the results. If they involved unpleasant actions, that was not Hugh's fault, any more than his son's death had been. He had merely reported a case of witchcraft. This time, Agnes Balfour would have the Church to contend with.

Hugh wondered whether the Minister, who continued to pray aloud, was able to enjoy the cold pain in his knees, and whether it had been any different in the days of incense and holy statues and Confession, hushed and thick-curtained. He wondered, too, why his mother had clung so obstinately to a faith which, even in her parents' time, was becoming discredited. Surely she must have known that the priests took the offertory money for themselves and that no girl was safe from the sly-eyed, hard-drinking friars? A few of the very old still remembered how the Mass had become a mockery, with people sprawled in a drunken slumber in the pews, or talking and laughing as the holy charade was gone through.

Charade. He would not have dared to use that word, even in the secrecy of his thoughts, while his mother was alive. Her eyes would have darted to his in fearful suspicion, for she was convinced that God knew all things. Perhaps she was right. Credo in Unum Deo, Hugh said silently, I believe in One God. But must I know which one that is? His clasped fingers tightened in anxiety, then slackened again. That, too, was not his responsibility. The One God would know His own identity; and He would know, too, why Hugh McGuire knelt here, in a church devoid of comfort or beauty, enduring the ache of his crippled foot pressed hard against the stone floor. I mean no disloyalty, Oh Lord, Hugh prayed to whatever power might hear him. It is just a question of duty.

He felt a touch of contempt for the kneeling Minister whose urgent, hard-bitten words continued to pour out. There had been too much persecuting of other Christians in the name of heresy, and too much self-important praying, while the running sore of Paganism continued to stink in the land. Milk and oatmeal were left outside many a cottage door in case the Wee Folk should need sustenance at night, and it was well known that this year, as for many years, a white bull had been sacrificed on a midsummer dawn up by Applecross. The real enemy of this church was not Catholicism but witchcraft.

Hugh felt a sudden stab of fear that Agnes Balfour was watching him with her black eyes at this very moment, knowing where he was and what he thought. And what he had done. Lamb of God, he prayed urgently, Agnus Dei, I am not guilty, I merely used the channels available. You who bear the sins of the world, qui tollis peccata mundi, understand that Agnes Balfour killed my son. She must be punished.

"Amen," said John Leddie.

"Amen," Hugh echoed. He was getting stiffly to his feet when the mocking answer to his prayer clanked like a cracked bell in his brain. Agnes Dei, it said, and somewhere behind it was a smile at the blasphemous pun.

Hugh gasped and stumbled, and the Minister put out a quick hand to catch him by the elbow. "Does your foot trouble you?" he asked kindly.

Hugh shook his head, then half-lied in confusion. "Aye, sometimes." He was deeply shocked that the outrageous mixing of the witch's name with that of Jesus Christ should have occurred in his own consciousness. Then he understood. From up there in her turf-roofed house, he knew that Agnes Balfour cackled with amusement. Yes, it was she who had put the blasphemy into his mind, she and her red-haired daughter. Even here in this church, he was not safe from her. Or maybe the One God was angry with him for his defection. Could He have used the witch for His holy purpose? That was an even more terrifying thought.

John Leddie narrowed his eyes as he watched the man stumble away from him down the aisle and grapple with the heavy latch on the church door as if in a desperate hurry to get out of the place. Hugh McGuire was a Highlander, he thought, and the Lord alone knew what went on in the minds of those wild men. It was no wonder the Lowland folk distrusted them. People had long memories of their marauding and savagery. But McGuire was no worse than the rest of them. In this south-western part of Scotland, popery was never far below the surface, and it had kept its decadent, irrational grasp on the collective imagination of the people. Leddie suspected that the corrupt Catholic priesthood had come to a tacit understanding with those pagan practisers of the black arts, leaving them unmolested so as to save themselves the troublesome job of bringing them to justice. No wonder their bellies grew fat below their unwashed soutanes.

With a grunt of discomfort, he lowered himself again on to his knees, this time to pray for the soul of Hugh McGuire. For Agnes Balfour, prayer was too late.

*

The shadowed kitchen is cold, the ashes of the fire dead in the hearth. The door stands open, as they left it when they came for her. Outside, the hill is dark against the last light of the sky. I stoop to pick up the stool which lies sideways on the floor, but one of its legs has been broken and it can no longer stand. The table is still here, but the other stool has gone. People's fear of the witch does not prevent them from looting. Anna Dubh comes to my feet and mews, and I gather her into my arms.

I saw them coming up from the village this morning, the men first, with the women a little behind them, some carrying babies, some trying to keep their young lads from yelling abuse and throwing stones, though it was only a token restraint. Their eyes were greedy with curiosity. John Leddie was at their head, striking his way up the track with his staff in his hand and his Bible held to his heart like a shield against the powers of darkness.

My mother and I clung to each other by the glowing fire, so soon to be left to burn itself out. Her cheek was warm against mine, her arms close round me, and I hid my face in her darkness as though her body surrounded me as it did before I was born.

"I will tell them you are gone away from here this long time," she said. "I will say you went to seek work in the city." She took my face between her hands and kissed me on the forehead, then enfolded me again. "God protect you," she whispered. They would have laughed to hear her call on God, she who was cursed by every church, but they

cannot usurp all faith. For a moment I was comforted, but the pain was back in the next instant when my mother said, "Go quickly, my darling. They are very near."

I clutched at her and said, "Come with me – oh, please, come with me, or let me stay with you." But I was too afraid to mean it, and my legs trembled because they wanted to run.

She pretended to be angry. "Give them my lovely daughter and waste a life's work? Get along with you at once!" And the words sent me out through the door and away up the sheep-path without even looking back, holding up my skirts to bend low as I had done in childhood, hidden under the branches of birch and broom and the yellow-flowering gorse.

And now, creeping back in the evening, I stand in the empty room. There are some things I must do before leaving the house for the rain to blow in and the ferns to take root. I spread a plaid on the table and pile onto it my few clothes and the smallest of the pans from beside the dead fire. I fold the squares of muslin I will need each month, and tear up some rags in which to tie some of our dried herbs, for it would be stupid to risk illness when the healing powers are here. Carefully, I make small, tight bundles of comfrey and marigold, arnica, feverfew, willow bark, belladonna . . . and there are some which I hesitate over. Foxglove, black hellebore, lily of the valley – these are dangerous in their strength. I will leave them where they are, and those who tamper with them do so at their own risk. But I must take salt with me, and oatmeal, and a flint for the making of fire, and my mother's sharp knife.

Outside, the chickens croon sleepily, dark blobs among the high branches of the cherry tree. They can feed themselves well enough in the summer months and before the winter comes to freeze the grubs and worms into the earth, the villagers will have been up to steal them. But Jessie, the white goat, is another matter. She was away up the hill with her kid this morning when the men came, but she comes back each evening to be milked, for she gives more than her baby needs. Now, she lies calmly in the shelter of the ivy by the wall with her nanny-kid beside her, and looks at me with her yellow, square-pupilled eyes, while her jaws move in a rapid circling as she chews the cud. If the villagers come back and find her with her young one, they will believe in their mad way that it is the witch and her daughter returned, and they will kill both of them, most likely by hanging them from the cherry tree. Anna Dubh will suffer the same fate if they find her.

I go back into the house and tie the corners of my bundle, then take the lidded can for Jessie's milk from its hook on the ceiling beam and the strong stick from its place in the corner. Anna Dubh watches, crouching on the table with half-moon eyes looking up. I stroke her head, feeling the way her ears fold down under my hand – a thing I have known since early childhood. A cat is a free spirit, I tell myself. If she chooses to stay here, I must accept it. But she jumps down from the table and presses herself briefly against my legs with her tail up. But not purring. She is ahead of me in the doorway, and Jessie stands up, arching her back in a stretch.

A small moon hangs now in the dark blue sky. It will be enough to light our way if we are careful, but not so bright that anyone will notice us out on the hill, a girl with a bundle on her shoulder and a cat running at her feet, and the white goat and kid following. I will not look back at the dark house which has been my home. I leave the door standing open.

*

William seemed charged with some kind of electric current that infiltrated every cell of my being. When he looked at me or spoke to me, I felt over-full, like some distended flexible container that cannot be touched without spilling. Our conversations were few and brief, but I remember every one of them like the poems learned in childhood, and remember, too, my awkwardness and my longing.

"What's that rose called?"

"Dorothy Perkins. She's prickly, but I like her." And he smiled. I can see his mouth still, with the strong white teeth that seemed uneven because one of the front ones lay a little across the other. He added, "Perhaps I have masochistic tastes."

I smiled back, but my face reddened because I didn't know what the word meant. I went indoors and looked it up in Nana's dictionary, then sat by the window with the heavy book in my lap and continued the dialogue, with brilliant wit and repartee. It was so much easier to talk to him when he wasn't there.

William was two years older than me. He had just left his private school, having won a place at Glasgow University to read biology, but he had to join the forces first. He had opted for the RAF. On the day his call-up papers came, Nana sent me down the garden to pick some rhubarb. I was to ask him, she said, to trim the leaves off and put them on the compost heap.

"Well, that's it," William said as he held his hand out for the thick red stalks. "Marching orders. I'm off to be a squaddie. Aircraftsman McGuire, next week." He took a clasp knife out of his pocket and opened it, and I heard the crunching slice of the blade through the thick stem. I was staring at the grass. He would never even know that I had loved him.

A leathery leaf fell with a flop, then the pink, thin-curved end. "I'd have liked to get to know you better," William said. "But with the war and everything – and perhaps you didn't want to."

"But I did!" All my anguish burst out in those words. He was going away, perhaps to be killed, and the precious time had been wasted.

Our eyes met then, and he frowned and said tiredly, "Oh, blast. I wish you'd said." He dumped the rhubarb and the open knife on the grass, then put his arms round me.

It was the first time I had kissed anyone since I was quite small, and I brought my lips together for the rosebud peck of childhood. The pressure of his mouth was a shock. The rosebud was rudely parted and his tongue found its way between my teeth. We foraged gently into each other, moved our heads a little and foraged again, then parted. "Hell," he said with a sigh. "I wish I'd known."

That was all there was to it. He went back to his aunt and uncle's house in Kirkcudbright the next day, to get ready for his posting to RAF Leuchars, on the distant east coast of Scotland. And I was supposed to return to being a schoolgirl.

Perhaps I might have done, had it not been for my mother's ripening affair with her doctor friend. She went around looking, I thought, like a cat that's had the cream, smiling privately. I can see now that she must have been very happy at that time. She looked much younger. She had lost weight since she started the nursing job, and her bushy hair was cut short in a stylish bob, "helped", as people said then, by a rinse that disguised the white hairs which were already beginning to grow in it. Her newly-complete darkness made me feel more than ever different from her, a rogue red offshoot, a throwback to the unknown woman who had been Nana's mother. She had been red-haired. My own mother exuded a musky sexuality which made me oddly aware of my breasts in the gentle hold of my first-ever brassiere. I thought constantly about William's kiss.

In the mornings, I left the house at the right time for school, but I seldom went there. I fobbed off enquiries with forged notes, and spent a lot of time in Woolworth's, fingering the lipsticks and little oblong boxes of mascara. I saved up my dinner money and bought a Max Factor Lip-gloss called Flame, and secretly put it on in my bedroom, pouting at my image in the mirror. I let my hair grow longer and cut it into a droopy fringe that fell sideways across one eye like Veronica Lake. I bought a packet of Craven A and smoked them, leaving the butts in a saucer on my dressing table where I knew my mother would find them. She made no comment. Perhaps, in fact, she hadn't come into my room at all. At that time, she seemed to be almost constantly on night duty.

Fate is quite mechanical in its working. It's the weakest point which gives way. With experience, one can learn to provide this point, harmlessly, within one's own being, a fuse that will break in tears or temporary despair, and be mended with a long look at the ever-changing sky, but it takes time and a lot of painful experiment to find this. At fifteen, sexuality had filled me with its own appalling magic, and I was losing touch with what was so plain to see – that the weak point was my father.

I heard his choking groan one night through my bedroom wall, and ran barefoot in my pyjamas to tap at his door, half thinking that my mother was there with him and would call, "Come in." She wasn't, of course. She had gone out at her usual time, just after nine o'clock. He lay alone in the double bed, and his book had dropped to the floor. One hand was still stretched out for it, but the other clutched at his pyjama jacket as if to pin down the pain which was obliterating him. He lay on his back, his jaw-muscles tense, frowning hard as if trying to face up to an important question. I took his book-questing hand and felt an almost shockingly strong current run into him from me through that contact. It was not of combat but of permission. It horrified me, because I did not want him to die, and yet we were locked in acceptance. I knew now that he must have wanted it. Through this open channel rushed my love for him in a helpless granting of his wish. He looked up at me and whispered, "Thank you." A few moments later, his back arched in a violent spasm and he gave a long, deep groan, appalling in its loudness. Then he slowly relaxed, with his eyes half-open, but he was not himself any more, just a thing. I began to cry, and knew that he stood beside me, worried by my distress and his own inability to touch and to comfort. "It's all right," I managed to tell him. I had loved him so much more than I ever knew.

I don't know how long I stayed there, weeping. I put his mottled hands with their square-cut finger-nails one above the other on his chest, because I thought that's what one should do. Then I went downstairs and phoned the hospital. The Sister on the ward where my mother worked said no, Mrs Carstairs was not on duty tonight, there must be some mistake. So I left no message. I phoned our local doctor, then stood by my bedroom window waiting for his car to come. The sky was beginning to lighten. A badger shuffled slowly across the dew-silvered lawn, and I saw his narrow, striped head turn as he looked up at me, unhurried, then moved on.

*

This east coast was an alien place, Billy thought. The sea here was grey and blank, devoid of the islands which patterned the horizons of the west. Nostalgia swept over him as he thought of the tranquil peaks of Arran which he used to see from the lowland hills of his boyhood, and the sunsets which turned the whole sky rose-red and seemed to colour the very air he breathed.

He walked between the tethered horses to the burn's edge and followed it upstream to where the water ran clear, then stopped to fill his flask. He clipped it back onto his belt, then rinsed his hands in the burn and rubbed them over his face. The autumn wind chilled his wet skin. Smoke rose into the sky from the many small fires in the camp, round which men squatted. Billy could not throw off the yearning for the place of his childhood which had so suddenly assailed him, unexpected after these years in the Army. The unbroken line of the North Sea depressed him.

The love of the islands, he thought, must run deep in his family. His ancestors, the McQuarries, had come from Mull and the small isle of Iona. In those fierce times, they had fought for Donald Dubh in his hopeless claim for the Lordship of the Isles. Billy remembered how his father used to recite the legendary tale of the family's flight to the mainland, and how his grandfather had changed his name to McGuire to throw the persecutors off the scent.

Slowly he walked back to join the other men, undoing the bag of oatmeal which, like everyone else, he carried with him. There might be some meat later, if the foraging party had been successful, but the keenest edge of his hunger could easily be satisfied. Every man carried a flat metal plate under his saddle flap, and the oatmeal was quick to mix with water and shape into a bannock, hot and sustaining when it had been cooked over the fire.

As Billy tipped a small handful of meal from the bag, the white pebble which he had put there for safe keeping rolled into his palm, and the red-haired girl who had given it to him was clear in his mind again, watching him as he went away down the hill from the witch's house.

Lachlan Gibson, a man with sores on his face whom Billy had always instinctively avoided, glanced down as he passed behind Billy, and laughed. "What, do they live on stones in Ayrshire?" he asked derisively.

"It is a keepsake," Billy muttered, dropping the stone back into the bag.

Lachlan stopped. "Let me see it." Despite a reputedly debauched life – or perhaps because of it – he was fanatically Puritanical, and had a rabid loathing of anything which smacked of symbolism or mystery.

"It is no business of yours," said Billy, ignoring the man's outstretched hand.

"Some woman gave it to you."

"She was just a wee lassie." Billy tightened the strings of the bag, realising as he did so that Mari Balfour would be a woman by now. But then, in his dreams she had always been more than a child.

His involuntary smile irritated Lachlan, and his scabbed lips tightened. "That is a witching stone," he said. "I saw it. A pagan thing, rubbed by the hand of some female to give it power."

"It is not." The white stone had been given with innocence, and it was not to be defiled by Lachlan Gibson's ugly suspicion.

"Let me see it," Lachlan insisted again, and made a sudden grab for the bag. Billy pushed him away, but Lachlan was galvanised with righteous fury, thrusting Billy aside as he dived for the bag. Billy hit out wildly with the fist which still grasped a handful of meal, and Lachlan punched him in the face. Then they were fighting like dogs. Billy found his hands slippery with the blood which poured from his own nose and from a cut over Lachlan's eye. There were shouts and jeers from the other men, and then an incisive command from above them. "Stop that!"

Captain Lennox stood tall against the sky, his drawn sword glinting in the last of the sun. Lachlan hunched himself away from Billy. "The Papist bastard attacked me," he said thickly.

The oatmeal lay spilled across the grass, and in the midst lay the white pebble beside the open bag. Both men made a grab for it, but the officer was faster, covering it with a quick stamp of his booted foot. He stooped and picked the pebble up. "You were fighting over *this*?" he asked incredulously. He stared at the two men for a puzzled moment. Then he turned and flung the stone high above the grazing horses, to fall among the heather at the moor's edge.

Billy's fists were clenched and a shudder ran upward through his body, contracting his skin so that, had he been an animal, the fur on his back would have risen in a furious, bristling ridge. Mari Balfour's red hair burned like the setting sun in his mind, and with his eyes half-shut against its light, he heard his own voice coming out of him in a howling sing-song which shocked him even as he heard it. Still on all fours, he raised a hand and doubled its centre fingers so that its two outer ones spread like horns in the age-old gesture used to ward off the Evil Eye. In the Gaelic which he had almost forgotten during these Army years, he cursed Lachlan Gibson for having caused the loss of the one thing he held dear – cursed his body and mind and soul, cursed the sight of his eyes and the quickness of his hand and the strength of his limbs and the seed of his loins, cursed Lachlan Gibson and all those yet unborn who might ever have hoped to be his children.

The men listened with averted faces, and a few furtively sketched the sign of the cross in the need to invoke a power more ancient and potent than the official new religion.

Captain Lennox did not understand the words which came pouring from Billy McGuire, but he was sharply aware that the savagery of the chanting voice and the outstretched fingers was the sort of thing that had to be stamped out, and quickly. He called for the guard, and as Billy's utterance came to an end, his arms were pinioned behind him and he was jerked roughly to his feet.

Billy knew he would be flogged. The man-made penance must be accepted as part of his contrition for this act of evil-wishing; his reckoning with God would be a longer, slower business "Do it now," he said exultantly, his soul still half-free of his body, flying in the hot current of his fury. The sooner the better, before cold sobriety set in.

"You shall have your pleasure," said Captain Lennox drily. He had seen many floggings, and had never known a man to enjoy one yet.

*

My mother was strangely angry that I had been present at my father's death. She cried a lot in those bleak, shocked days, but she would not speak to me, and then one morning she turned from the kitchen sink in response to something I'd said, and screamed that I'd stolen her husband from her. After my birth, she said, he was never the same. And I had even stolen his dying. Her doctor friend, Donald, came to the house often. He organised the funeral and was tactful and self-effacing. There was no reason to hate him, but I did.

Through the weeks that followed, I still left the house at the appropriate time in the mornings, but there was no longer any pretence at going to school. Now that my truancy was permanent, I abandoned the shops for fear of being seen, and headed away from the town. I walked for miles. Once, when my mother asked why my shoes were so muddy, I said I had been playing hockey. An occasional letter arrived from the school, but I intercepted it. At eight in the morning, my mother was either out or still in bed, so it wasn't difficult. I didn't bother to write back. There was no point in trying to avert whatever was to happen.

It was a time of intense loneliness. Sometimes I went into the church, pushing my way through the blue baize door into its spicy darkness, but I was not sure any more that God resided there. It had begun to seem that I could find Him more easily in the wide, rain-washed sky.

Nana, quite suddenly, became forgetful. It began with a more frequent repetition of the old stories, sometimes the same one two or three times on end, and then she was surprised to see me each time I came, greeting me like a rare visitor even though it was barely twenty-four hours since I had last sat by her fire.

After a while, she began to call me by the name of her dead sister, Alice, and asked why the dhobi-wallah had not brought the clean washing. Hindi crept back into her conversation, though I can only remember now that she called her wardrobe an almirah. One day I found her hunting for the house mongoose because she said it had eaten the bills she had to pay. I understood in a way that her confusion dated from my father's death. It must have seemed so topsy-turvy to her that a man of the younger generation should step off into darkness out of turn.

*

Most of the women awaiting trial for witchcraft were stupid old crones, Danny Boyle thought. He disliked their presence in the prison, the sound of their mumbling and crying and the thick, old-woman smell of them. Some merely rocked and wept, but as he took them their broth and bread each day, he caught glimpses here and there of a hatred which made the skin crawl on his back. Some among them had crazed eyes which were not of normal humanity, and one or two gave out a concentrated malevolence which frightened him. He would be glad when this witch-trial was over, and the jail had returned to the decent masculinity of normal crime.

But the Balfour woman was different. She sat apart from the others, huddled by the wall with her head turned to its stones as if for comfort. Danny looked at the dark red hair braided above the nape of her neck, and wanted to see the averted face. She was hardly older than himself, in her late thirties, maybe, and there was an air of blameless reserve about her, as innocent as the scent of primroses in the foetid cell. Or perhaps, Danny thought, she was a witch of deeper cunning than the others, casting a spell over him even as he stood and watched her.

Cautiously, he approached the woman, tapping his fingers on the heavy bunch of keys at his belt. She did not look up. Danny bent towards her, clearing his throat, but even this did not break into her stillness. A faint breath of her body-smell came to him, and he was seized by a desire to slip his hand over the white neck and turn her face towards him. "Is there anything you're needing?" he ventured in a whisper. He did not want to be mobbed by a gaggle of importuning old women. "I can get things sometimes."

Her head came up instantly. "I want pen and paper," she said.

Her black eyes looked into his with none of the timid fear which he saw on every other prisoner's face – nor even, Danny thought resentfully, with the awareness of a man's presence which any normal woman should feel. She looked at him simply as the potential supplier of her needs.

Danny stood upright. This was not good enough. He had made his offer as the opening move of a more subtle game than the mere granting of requests. He eyed her speculatively. "So you can write," he said.

She made no answer, and he flushed slightly at the unspoken rebuke. A woman who could not write would hardly ask for pen and paper. He gave a masterful jerk of the head towards the door and stood back to let her go out before him.

Agnes waited while he relocked the cell door, hugging her shawl round her arms in the dankness of the passage. Then she followed him to the guard room where a fire blazed in the hearth. Surely, Danny thought, she would at least hold out her hands to the warmth? But her gaze went at once to the heavy oak table where sharpened quills and an inkwell stood ready for use.

Danny's pique increased. "So I am to do you a favour?" he remarked.

She looked at him and waited.

"And what favour can you do for me, Mistress Balfour?" Danny demanded, and found to his infuriation that it was his own cheeks which turned hot at the suggestion.

The woman's shoulders drooped a little, but she met his gaze steadily. "As you know well," she said, "I have nothing with which to bargain except my body. But my use of that is almost finished, so it may as well do me this last service." Her indifference to him was unshaken. "May I write my letter first?"

Danny shrugged. He pulled out a chair for her as she wrote. He tried to appear unimpressed as her hand moved quickly across the page in line after line of fluent words. Danny himself had learned little more than the spelling of his own name.

"This must be sealed," Agnes said, looking up when she had finished.

"The things are here," said Danny. He indicated the wax and taper. "And who is the letter for?"

The woman hesitated, and he seized his chance. "They say you have a daughter," he remarked, and had the satisfaction of seeing her look frightened. Then she was controlled again. "My daughter will not come to this place," she said firmly. "No. This letter is for anyone to read who cares to know the truth. It does not matter who is the first. But you must promise me something – the seal is not to be broken until after my death."

Danny shrugged. "So be it." He fumbled a little over the sealing of the letter, partly because of his unfamiliarity with the process, but also because this calm talk of death unnerved him. He did not like to think that this woman who sat before him would soon be as dead as a flayed ox hanging in the killing-house. Even worse, if they burned her, the braided hair and the dark eyes and the steady hand which now offered him the letter would be no more than charred ash and bone. Suddenly, the room seemed overpoweringly stuffy and nausea swam over him. He rubbed his forehead on his sleeve and swallowed hard.

"Will you keep it for me?" Agnes asked him. "Until – afterwards?"

Danny's face was very white. "Who will I give it to?"

Agnes gave a faint shrug. "There will be someone in charge. Give it to him."

"I'll do that." He buttoned the letter inside his jerkin and smoothed his hands down the faded leather, wishing he did not feel so sick.

"Thank you," said Agnes.

There was a pause. She stood with her hands at her sides, waiting, he realised, for him to exact his payment for the favour he had done her. Danny toyed for a moment with the thought of how he could boast of taking his pleasure with the bonny young witch, but his nausea persisted, and besides, the faces of his friends were suddenly aghast in his mind. "You lay with the sorceress?" They backed away, leaving him standing alone, isolated in his contamination. Danny blinked. None of that was real. Where had the vision come from? He was not a man given to imagination. He eyed the woman who stood so compliantly before him with a new suspicion. Had she put the warning in his mind?

"The writing of your letter has taken too long," he said roughly. "The other guard will be here soon to start his duty. There is no time."

Agnes gathered her shawl round her shoulders, but she did not turn away. Danny walked past her to the door and opened it, then stood back to let her go out. He followed her at leisure down the cold passage which led to the cell, and was still not sure how she had eluded him. He should have had a drink inside him, then it would have been a different story. As it was, he could not even mention it for fear of being laughed at. He had been cheated of the pleasure of boasting about it to Robbie Kerr when he came on duty. But that would not be for an hour and a half. By that time, Danny thought, he might have got over this strange feeling of humiliation.

*

There are brown trout in the shadowed water under the

bank. My fingers make no ripple as they go in, down and down, then drift with no more intent than a piece of dead wood, coming gently to the fish from below. Touching one, I feel the tingle of contact between us, and a regret for what I am going to do, even though my hunger makes it necessary. The trout is still, enjoying the stroking of his flank as a horse enjoys rubbing his neck on a rough tree, and in the next instant I have him behind the gills and he is out of the water and quickly dead, for a sharp knife is more merciful than drowning in air.

And now, having eaten, I stand at the burn's edge and stare at the great beech tree which grows on the far bank, for in these last three days it has become a kind of companion, older even than my grandmother's grandmother, and wiser than Jessie or my dear Anna Dubh. Wiser and more enduring.

The food is warm inside me and I should be contented. What is wrong? The morning is suddenly uneasy although the wisp of smoke from my fire rises steadily between the yellowing leaves of the trees to a clear sky.

In the next instant, the world is full of terror. My heart pulses wildly, and it is hard to breathe because of its violence. I am shaken by a storm of weeping. In its midst, my mother's presence is strong, distressed by my grief, comforting and enfolding me, and I know she is complete now, a finite invulnerable thing which I will carry in my soul for ever.

There is a terrible sense of guilt. While her life was approaching its end, I was occupied in catching a fish. I let her die, I offered no resistance.

The weeping goes on and on, and yet, within it, thoughts chase like mice through a dark house. Why had it come so suddenly? A legally-ordered death such as that of a woman convicted of witchcraft is a slow affair, with beating of drums and reading of pious words. There is time enough, in all that ceremony, for the condemned one to set the air quivering with her dread. But I felt no dread. There was no warning of a scaffold with its loop of rope dangling against the sun, or of that worse thing, the careful pyramid of faggots. Why did I not share in her preparation for what was to come? Why did I not know?

Time passes. As my mother's death slowly becomes a part of me, the beech tree burns itself into my awareness. Its body is smooth and grey, curving back from the anchorage of its roots in the bank, balancing its weight. A storm in some past winter has split away a great arm which lies in the burn where it fell, slowly blackening. The tree's flank has a jagged scar where the limb was torn away, and the pain of that gross wound is clear. I follow the lines of the tree's branches up to the sky, where the tracery of fine twigs against the brightness becomes an insistent thing, pressing into my vision, obliterating thought, a web of air and life. It starts to heal my anguish, like a spider's web laid across a wound. Do not try to understand, it says. Just accept.

Earth and air and fire and water, my mother chants in my mind, and I see that the beech tree is in truth all these things. The burn runs at its feet and in its sap, and the fire of the sun fuels the magical work of earth and air, and all of it is alive, all a part of the intelligence which is God, whom my mother invoked to protect me. She is part of that totality, and part of me. The pattern of broken sky sparkles between the leaves, and my tears come again, for the grief and the beauty.

*

As the weather worsened in that winter of loss, I went on walking, and never set foot inside the school at all. I still wore its uniform, and took a sandwich with me in the otherwise empty school bag, to eat somewhere up on the sheep paths that led across the moors, or on the tow path by the river. When it rained, I sheltered under the bridge, or ventured into the town for the warmth and brightness of its shops. The grey cardigan and gaberdine mac were not meant for an outdoor life, but I took a perverse pleasure in feeling the wind touch my skin and the rain soak through and trickle between my shoulder-blades. Enduring these things was a proof that I was myself, not a child any more, not dependent on a home or my mother.

I began to feel a contempt for the people who carried full shopping bags and got on and off buses. They were comfortable in their houses, trivialised by being so well protected. Bad weather meant no more to them than a slate off the roof or a damp patch under the doormat. I became a little malevolent because of this contempt. I pictured the way their umbrellas would blow inside out in a sudden wind, or how they would slip on the ice and drop their baskets and their precious money – and then I would watch with distant glee while these things occurred as I had seen them. Once, I was sorry for what I had done, and picked up an old woman's purse and gave it back to her. She thanked me effusively, and wondered why I shook my head and backed away.

It's almost embarrassing now to admit how senseless I was, and how ignorant, blundering about in search of anything that might prove itself to be reliably true. Teenagers still do it, of course, putting themselves through appalling trials while their parents watch aghast. How else can they learn? There is no teaching now on what to be, only on what to do – how to fit your performance into the prevailing convention. These observances have none of the thrill and shock waiting to be found in real experience.

When my mother announced that she was going to marry Donald, I managed to appear indifferent, although the shock was that of having at last fallen through thin ice. She and Donald would both leave the hospital, my mother said, and set up together in general practice, he as doctor, she as nurse and receptionist. I mustn't feel abandoned. The new house would be big enough for the three of us, I'd have my own room as before.

I said she must do as she liked, but count me out. She demanded to know what I thought I was going to do, and I said it was none of her business. Counter-accusations were hurled until we came to a sour, painful silence. I had no idea what I was going to do. Then, as naturally as a sleeping sigh, I knew I would go and live with Nana. She was getting old, I explained, and needed someone to look after her.

My mother shrugged. "Suit yourself," she said. I badly wanted her to hug me, but I didn't say so.

*

Liam Tarbert went into the tavern and dumped his depleted pack on the floor. It had been a good day. The town was crowded with folk who had come with prurient curiosity to see the burning, on this macabre fair-day. He had kept away from the main square with its screeching crowds and its drums and the thick column of appalling smoke which mounted into the autumn sky. House-dwellers were a dog-pack, Liam thought. For all their prim-mouthed respectability, they were capable of savaging one of their own kind.

The tavern was crowded and hot. As Liam waited his turn, he brooded with revulsion on what had been done this day to a cart-load of confused, hysterical old women. A few of them, perhaps, had found themselves able to exert an embittered will on others, but most had committed no crime other than that of living alone and mumbling companionably to their garden plants or their cats. Some were half-witted and so were thought possessed by the Devil, others, even more damningly, were intelligent. Nothing frightened the unthinking more than cleverness. Inevitably, Liam's mind went back to his old love, Agnes Balfour. He felt relieved that she lived so far from the town, out there on the moor's edge. With any luck, the occasional flarings of suspicion would come to nothing. One of these days, he promised himself, he would pay her a visit, and see the daughter he had sired. Perhaps Margaret would not mind now, after all these years of marriage. Wee Mari must be a grown woman. Incredible. He paid for his beer and pushed his way through the crowd, looking for somewhere to sit down. A young man with a flushed, heavy face was slumped on a bench by the fire, his legs sprawled apart.

"Move along a bit," said Liam. "There's room for two."

Danny Boyle gathered his bulk together half-heartedly, but remained in the centre of the bench. He stared up in pathetic appeal. "She made me do it," he said. "It wasnae my fault." He was very drunk.

"Move, will you?" Liam insisted. It had been a long day, and he wanted to rest his legs before taking to the road again. He eased himself onto the bench beside Danny.

"It's no' a nice thing ye've to do," the drunk man continued. "Tyin' their hands an' that. Takin' them out to the cart. We had a drink or two. It's only reasonable, a drink or two, wi' a job like that. But she made me do it."

Liam looked at him with distaste. "You're one of the gaolers."

The man was not listening. "Yesterday morning, she asked me, could she be in a cell on her own for her last night on this earth. Somewhere quiet, she said, away from all the greetin' and screechin'. So I took her to a wee cell." He shook his head and his face crumpled.

Unwillingly, Liam said, "Then what?"

The gaoler plucked at his sleeve confidingly. "You know the way it is, when you've a drink inside you and a woman standing there, just the two of you and nobody else in the room. And there had been once before when she made a fool of me, and if that wasnae witchcraft I'm no' Danny Boyle." He shook his head again. "I was drunk, right enough, but not so drunk I couldnae tell I was bein' insulted. She was like a rag doll, lettin' me do as I wanted. She had these dark eyes, but she wouldnae look at me, just away at something I couldnae see. And this rage came on me, and I shook her, wi' my hands round her neck. Soft, she was, like a rag doll. God forgive me, I didnae mean to. Red hair, she had. So beautiful."

Liam was on his feet, pinning the man against the wall by his shoulder. "What was her name?" he said in Danny's face, ignoring the spilled beer which spread across the floor at his feet. "Tell me!" He doubled his fist, and several bystanders moved aside as a precaution.

"No fighting in here!" the landlord said on his way past with a handful of empty mugs. He was a huge man.

Liam sat down, though it was hard to relax his clenched hands. "Just a joke," he said. "A wee bit of play-acting."

"Then choose your play with care, tinker," the landlord said, with a flick of the eyes towards the door which indicated that Liam could soon be through it.

When those about him had resumed their drinking, Liam put his hand under the gaoler's elbow and closed thumb and finger below the joint in a painful grip. "Tell me," he said with soft menace.

Danny writhed. His hand hung limp from his thick wrist. "Balfour," he said. "Agnes Balfour. What's it to you?" And, as Liam released him, he rubbed his elbow and added sulkily, "It was better than the fire. Maybe it's what she wanted."

Liam, in the turmoil of his thoughts, saw the force of the man's argument. Money had been known to change hands so that those tied to the stake were killed quickly with a knife between the ribs or a skilled breaking of the neck. Agnes would not shrink from seeking a more merciful and private death than the flames. She might well have used this man, in his strength and stupidity. Then something else struck him, and he turned urgently to the gaoler. "What of the child?" he asked. "Mari, her daughter?"

"She told me," Danny said in drunken triumph. "When she was writing the letter. The lassie was not to come here, she said. 'My daughter will not come to this place.' Aye, those were her very words. She made me seal the letter. She said I was to give it to whoever was in charge. But I didnae." He grinned with stupid cunning. "What if it said something bad about me?"

Liam looked at him carefully. So the man could not read. And feared the letter he had been given, for it was a thing made by the mind and hand of the witch. To break the seal might invite instant retribution. "Do you still have this letter?" he asked.

Danny fished inside his tunic and produced it, the white surface rubbed and dirty as if he had turned it again and again in his hands. "I meant her no harm," he said. "She asked me for pen and paper. I gave her what she wanted." His eyes filled with maudlin tears.

"But, as you say, what if she wrote something bad about you?" Liam suggested gently. "You granted her a favour, right enough, but what if it says you took your pleasure with her against her will, and she fears you will kill her? As you did," he added.

"God forgive me," Danny blubbered.

"Maybe the witch condemns you from her grave. She was a clever woman. She could have planned to take your life in exchange for her own." For a moment, Liam wondered if he was speaking the truth. The flicker of fear in his face threw the gaoler into panic more effectively than his words had done. "They'll not know it was me!" he cried. "I carried her back to the cell wi' the old women in it, that night, and laid her down, and it was dark in there, they'd not have seen me. And in the morning, who would take heed of their wild talk o' murder? They were for the fire, it was natural enough they'd be screechin'."

Fighting down his disgust, Liam said, "Will I read the letter to you?" Somehow, he had to get possession of this last message from Agnes.

Danny shook his head.

"It's better to know what she says of you," Liam urged him. "Or burn the thing and be rid of it."

"No!" Danny clutched the letter with renewed fear. "I cannae do that."

"Then give it to me, and if there is any blame for breaking the seal, it'll not fall on you." In the moment of Danny's indecision, Liam twitched the letter from his fingers and cracked the red wax, trying to appear nonchalant as his mind raced in the electricity of Agnes Balfour's presence. The rows of neat words were as meaningless to him as the pattern of sheep-feet on a mountain path, for he had never set foot inside a school, but his heart thumped at the skill and deliberation of them. He ran his eye down the lines and pursed his lips in a silent whistle of consternation.

"What does it say?" Danny asked, his head averted.

Stalling for time, Liam said, "I dinnae like to be the one to tell you."

"Ach, come *on*, man!" Tension and temper brought Danny's fists up, and Liam said quickly, "Listen, then. She says, 'The gaoler is a stupid man. He gave me ink and paper that I might write this, but his passions are strong, especially when the drink is in him. He will want his way with me because he did me a favour and I fear his anger, for I cannot disguise that he disgusts me. I think I may meet my death at his hands. Although I am guilty of the crime of witchcraft," Liam went on, warming to his role, "justice should be even-handed. Since it condemns me, it should condemn him also. This letter will not be read until after my death, and if I have died on the scaffold, it will have no purpose. But if I have been found dead, be it known that I died at the hands of the gaoler. I do not know his name, but he is a broad man, about thirty years of age, with brown hair, and he has a wart on his forehead, just above the left eyebrow." Liam looked up from his counterfeit reading and observed, "Why, yes, and so you have."

Danny's face was waxen, and sweat stood out in beads on his skin. "They will hang me," he whispered. "The officer was raging when they found her dead. It was Agnes Balfour the crowds came to see. The bonny young witch. There was nearly a riot when they knew they were cheated of her."

"You are lucky you met me this day," Liam told him. "I am a tinker. I care nothing for their laws and their executions. When I leave here I will be away over the hill and you will hear no more of me. Will I burn the thing and be rid of it?"

"Aye, burn it. She'll know it wasnae me."

"She'll no' blame you," Liam assured him. He got up and made his way through the crowd to the fire, where he crouched and tucked the letter up his sleeve, then poked the glowing peats to make the sparks fly upward. Returning, he dusted his hands with satisfaction. "That's it away."

"Have a drink," said Danny, lurching to his feet. "My good friend. My very good friend."

Liam shook his head, though it went against the grain to turn down free beer. Danny was too drunk to be trusted. Afraid though he was, he would doubtless start blethering to anyone who would listen of how the tinker had saved him. It was never wise to stay around when a trick had been successful – and besides, the letter he held hidden in his sleeve, with his arm pressed close against his body, tormented him with its hidden meaning. "Thank you for the offer," he said, "but I'll be away now. There is something I must do."

John Leddie, accosted in the street by a tinker whose breath smelt of beer, stopped reluctantly.

"I'll not keep you long, sir" Liam said. He thrust an opened letter into the Minister's hand. "I need to know what is written here. And you are a man of learning."

Leddie sighed. This would be some half-literate declaration of love, no doubt, or some shifty attempt to formalise a dubious bit of dealing – although that was not usually the tinkers' way.

"'To the person whose eye follows the words I now write, I ask only that you continue steadily' –" He looked up, frowning. "Where did you get this?"

"Read it, sir," said the tinker. "If you please."

"'Continue steadily to the end, and do not judge me until you have heard all. The only crime I admit is to a single lie. In this prison, I pled guilty to the charge of witchcraft, and this was a falsehood. But I remember the sore pain inflicted on me as a child, and how my mother lied to save me. Being weak, I would die without torment if I can. Save this one lie, which I confess lest it should weigh against me in the balance of my soul's worth, I am innocent. I have not wished injury to any person or creature, and I swear this before God, who will so soon judge me.'"

The Minister's face darkened. "'What know I of God?'" he read on, "'a woman unhallowed by communion? Only that the Holy Spirit of nature itself is endless, and has existed for ever, before mankind gave it a name. To the keeping of the Holy Power, I commend my soul. Signed this day, Agnes Balfour.'"

John Leddie thrust the letter back at the tinker as though it burned his hands. Heresy stared him in the face, and outrage rose in him at the woman's shameless admission of blasphemy. How dare she pervert the name of the Almighty into that of some brute Pagan spirit?

The tinker's eyes stared into the Minister's with a glint of amusement as he held out a coin in his dirty fingers. "An offering for your Church," he said.

Leddie struck the money from his hand with an angry slap and strode away down the street as if fleeing from contamination.

As he retrieved the coin from the gutter and wiped it on his sleeve, Liam found himself reflecting that even in death, Agnes had never cost him anything.

*

My mother came round to Nana's house with a letter in her hand. It was from the school. In view of their non-response to previous communications, Mr and Mrs Carstairs were required to remove Mary forthwith, since I was over the age of compulsory education.

Mr and Mrs Carstairs. Somehow, it was painful that they didn't know my father was dead. I suppose they hadn't been told, but it still hurt. My mother was raging with fury over my deception. Did I think it was fair to live at other people's expense if I wasn't getting educated? If I wanted to live like an adult, then I must accept adult responsibilities and pay my own way. Donald had offered me a home, there was no need to skulk about in this furtive way, it was utterly insulting. He deserved better than that from me.

I almost laughed, the way she defended Donald as if he was a little boy. He's grown up, I wanted to shout at her, you don't have to protect him, I'm not his enemy. But perhaps I was. So I didn't say anything, just folded my arms and stared out of the window, terrified that I'd start to cry. The square edges of the window-frame and the sky beyond it made a box that I could shut myself into. At last she went away.

I got a job at a shoe shop, and sneaked some money into Nana's purse each week to square my conscience, because she wouldn't let me give her any. She never noticed what was in her purse, though, so it was easy enough.

It was good to have a job, even though being shut up in the leathery-smelling shoe shop with its walls a brickwork of boxes made me miss the walking. I still took a packed lunch, and during the mid-day break would go out to the river and watch the sun's coming and going, or the ruffle of rain across the water. Swans stood on the mud-flats, and there was a black one among them, as strange as a fairy-tale. It never attempted to join the neck-snaking scramble for my apple-core.

One day as I walked from the shop to the river, a young airman in greatcoat and forage cap and boots came towards me with a kitbag over his shoulder, and it was William. He saw me and broke into a crashing run, and the next moment his arms were round me.

The layers of thick, rough uniform were between us, as irritating as unnecessary packaging. Is that why manufacturers wrap their goodies so intricately, that the purchaser may have the sexual pleasure of stripping and revealing the treasure that lies within? Under the greatcoat and the battledress and the shirt were those arms that had been bare in the garden, sun-burned and scratched by the Dorothy Perkins roses. Golden hairs grew on his skin. He had been on his way to my grandmother's house, he said, hoping I'd call there after school. He was sorry he hadn't written – things had been a bit hectic.

I laughed and said it didn't matter. Nothing mattered now, not even the months in which I had slowly given up hope of hearing from him again after a first, oddly stilted letter from Leuchars. Even when I had written to tell him of my father's death, there had been no reply. He said afterwards that he found it very hard to write words that had to do with feeling. Boarding school hadn't helped, where the weekly letter home was read and corrected by the house master.

Holding hands, we walked to Nana's house and let ourselves in through the back door. "Hamish!" Nana cried when she saw William. "Goodness, it's been years!" And so it would have been had he really been her brother Hamish, the one in the photograph album who went wandering in Africa in 1920 and never came back. She started poking in the kitchen cupboards, muttering to herself, and William and I exchanged glances. "It's all right, we haven't come for lunch," I said.

"There should be some smoked salmon. They steal things, you know, the kitchen staff. They always did."

Something would have to happen, I thought with the distant interest which always means that something is actually about to happen. And Mrs Scott came tapping at the back door, then let herself in, putting a cloth-covered basket on the table. "Goodness, Mary, are you home for lunch? I wouldn't have interrupted –"

Explanations were made quickly, and Nana was settled at the table with a bowl of home-made soup, taking her napkin out of its silver ring with a pattern of elephants and dancing gods. She didn't notice when we left.

I stopped at a telephone box and told Mr Scrimgeour I'd been taken ill and wouldn't be back to the shop that day, then William and I walked on together and found a small café. He had sausage and mash and cabbage, then jam suet roll. How dull that sounds now – but at the time, every second was iridescent and wildly important, trembling with inexplicable content. My uneaten sandwich and apple remained in my bag, but hunger was unimaginable. As before, William's presence filled me and I wanted nothing but to watch him and breathe the air that he breathed. I sipped a cup of tea while he ate, and once, he looked up and said, "It's sad about your gran – she's pretty ga-ga, isn't she. Seems to have happened so quickly."

Yes, I said, so quickly. His hair was cropped short except for the floppy cow-lick, and I wanted to put my hands round the back of his neck and draw his face to mine. I was jealous of the food that was going into his mouth. He was talking to me between forkfuls, about life on the base, people called Stan and Mick and Barney. Then he sat back and stirred his tea and said, "How about you – how's it going?"

I told him I'd left school, and he said, yes, I'd already said that. I said, oh, yes, sorry, so I had. I couldn't finish my tea.

We went and stood in the queue for *The Way to the Stars* in the paved alley beside the cinema, and he started to talk about Nana again. She'd been so bright and well-organised, he said. How was it that someone like that could change so drastically? I shook my head. There were worse changes, I thought. Look at my father. And suddenly the tears started to run down my face.

William was so kind. He put his arms round me and let me cry. He didn't ask the cause or beg me not to or seem embarrassed, though he probably was, even though it wasn't unusual in those days to see girls crying as they stood, perhaps for the last time, with a young man in uniform. After a while he said, "Is it your dad?" and I nodded convulsively. He gave me an RAF blue handkerchief and I mopped and blew, and then I told him about the badger in the garden and about my mother and Donald and about the long pretence of being at school, and he nodded and said it made you feel a bit confused when so much happened at once.

It was nearly dark when we came out of the cinema in the late afternoon, full of the heroic sadness of the story. "I'll walk you home," he said, "then I'll have to get the bus to Kirkcudbright." His aunt and uncle would be waiting.

Nana was asleep in front of the fire when we went in. William put his finger to his lips, and we crept back to the kitchen. "No point in waking her," he said. He wrote down his address at his new posting, a Bomber Command station in Lincolnshire. I folded it away carefully, and he picked up his kit-bag. I thought he would kiss me, but he made for the back door and I went out with him, closing off its light behind me. The minutes were running away so fast.

At the gate, he fished inside his coat, feeling in the top pocket of his battledress tunic, then turned my hand palm up and put something into it, heavy and hard and smooth, warm with the warmth of his body. In the little light that remained, I saw that it was a white stone, as round and perfect as the small moon that hung behind the bare trees. My fingers closed on it, feeling the way it fitted the size of my hand so perfectly. I looked up at him and smiled. "It's beautiful," I said. "Where did you find it?"

He shook his head. Wrong way round, he said. It had

found him. He had been up at the rifle range with the others, lying in the heather with his legs to one side as instructed, gun-butt tucked close to his shoulder, blowing on his fingers to try and warm them in the bitter wind of the east coast, and then had been aware of something beneath him, pressed uncomfortably into his ribs. He'd taken a hand off his rifle to grope for it, and was shouted at for firing late on the command. (William quite liked shooting, he confessed. When the rifle got warm, it felt like part of you.) He hadn't noticed until afterwards how perfect the stone was in its roundness, but when he did, he picked it up and put it in his pocket. "I've had it in mind since that day that I must give it to you," he said. "But it's taken some time."

The time didn't matter. It was the best moment I had ever known, doubly precious because its ending was already part of it. We clung together and kissed, and the torment of parting mounted in me and became a rage. I wanted to mingle with him completely, so that we became one thing. He groaned as his mouth pressed harder into mine, and his hand fumbled impatiently at my jersey, pulling it up and reaching inside to thrust down inside my skirt and stroke my belly, then to caress my breasts and gently roll the hard nipples between thumb and finger, first one then the other. I pushed hard against him, parting my legs so that I straddled his thigh, and at that pressure, the quaking within me became frantic. In a passion of sexual greed, I had a sudden sense of cataclysm, as delicious as a long-gasped-for-sneeze – and in the next instant, I knew I was bleeding.

It struck me motionless. From ecstasy, I was thrown into appalled indignation by this new quirk of the Curse of Eve. William noticed the sudden change, of course, and asked what was the matter. I could only shake my head. The taboo was too strong – I could not talk to any man about such things. And I did not understand it myself. My period was not due for another two weeks, but it had chosen this moment to impose its urgent and squalid demands.

Had I been able to tell him about the hot flood that was beginning to trickle down my legs, I wonder if William would have understood. Probably not. It was years before I knew the truth of it myself. As it was, the joy lay in ruins. We stood there for another few moments, then he said he really would have to be going, and I nodded. Our last kiss was almost perfunctory. I find it sad, even now, to think that he must have looked back to wave, and that he saw I had turned away and gone into the house.

*

Time must have passed. Grey light comes through the gaps in the roof. Jessie's rough hair is in my face, smelling herby-sweet, and Anna Dubh lies curled beneath my arm. If I do not move, I am almost warm, but every breath of air which creeps in under my shawl is icy cold.

In a dream which is not quite sleep, I seem again to be endlessly walking. Hunger is the enemy. His forces burn in my body, eating me in a cruel reversal of my need. There is still a little milk from Jessie, but my store of oatmeal is finished and the fat trout are gone now, away up the burn to spawn and die. I belong with the birds, a light, ragged thing, picking at the bitter berries, probing earth and tree-bark, but flightless, denied the freedom of the sky. Once, on a spring day when the clouds were chasing past and the world seemed to be falling sideways, my mother said, "There will always be the sky." But above the wet roof of this shelter, the sky is black, and in the morning, the sun will again be hidden in the weeping mist.

This has been the last day of walking. My limbs ache, and the hunger makes me as limp as a young lamb in the eagle's claws. My head seems to float in the summer of its dreams, and there is no more need to occupy this body. Dreaming is the sweet path to death, so easy in the chasing clouds and the blossom of the cherry tree.

✻

Billy McGuire had hunted long and patiently for the white stone, pacing to and fro across the moor, stopping to delve through the heather with its purple flowers drying to brown. The long scabs on his back cracked open as he bent down, renewing the pain of his flogging, but he returned again and again to the search while the unit remained encamped at the sea's edge. It was no use. Mari Balfour's keepsake had been taken from him with utter finality. Billy felt oppressed by a sense of broken trust, and suspected that his failure to find the stone was a punishment. He feared that he would never be forgiven.

One day, orders were given to move on. They rode northward along the coast then turned inland, amid rumours that they were heading for Aberdeen or Stonehaven, where Montrose was on the rampage again. When they camped that night, Billy made his decision. In the moonless dark, he loosed a young horse from the line and set it running with a slap across its rump. In a few minutes the guards were after it, glad of something to relieve the cold monotony of the night watch, and Billy slipped away, running low. He would not be missed until the morning.

Since then, he had kept on the move, working his way back across the country towards the lowland hills of his boyhood where Mari Balfour waited for him to make amends. He no longer tried to understand the compulsion which drove him – it could not be questioned. It was as absolute as the beating of his heart or the slow movement of the sun across the sky.

At first he travelled by night, but the going was slow and treacherous in the dark, and hunger soon sent him to outlying crofts where he could trade a day's work for some food and shelter. He was seldom turned away empty-handed, for most people acknowledged the fickleness of the luck which gave plenty to some and nothing to others.

And besides, a wandering stranger might always be the Broonie, that disguised spirit which tests hospitality and wreaks vengeance on a household found wanting.

Even during daylight, Billy's progress was slow. He kept away from towns and larger villages for fear of being recognised as a deserter, following the sheep-paths across the hills where he could, but more often skirting wide areas of reedy bog or climbing across rock and scree, too high for anything to grow but lichen or wind-stunted thorn. Sometimes a cottager would need his help for two or three days, carting the last of the summer-dried peat down from the hill or plucking geese to be packed in barrels of their own fat for the dark, cold season ahead. Such tasks were a fair exchange for hospitality, and he needed the food they earned, but he chafed at the delay they imposed, obsessed by the urgency of his journey. Mari was clear in his mind. He had to find her.

One afternoon, he came to a small village huddled in the lee of a hill. Billy hesitated. There was time enough to walk another four or five miles before dark, but heavy clouds lowered in the sky, threatening a storm. He ached with hunger and the idea of spending an evening sharing fire and food under a sound roof made him feel weak with longing. He walked down the path from the hill and approached the first house.

Before he reached it, a tinker woman came towards him, thin and strong as a donkey although her skirt bulged with an obvious pregnancy. She carried a year-old child on her back in the fold of her plaid, and held an armful of wicker baskets tied by their handles, and several other children trailed behind her.

"Fine strong willow," the woman began automatically as she saw Billy. "Buy one for your wife, sir."

"I have no wife," said Billy. "And no home. I am a traveller like yourself."

She gave him a glance of faint contempt. "You are on a journey, sir," she corrected. "And where are you bound?"

"First, to my brother's farm near Kirkcudbright. His name is Hugh McGuire. Do you know of him?"

The woman shook her head. "My man will ken the place, maybe. He used to walk the Galloway hills." She looked back along the street as if expecting to be joined by her husband.

"No matter," said Billy. "I've a mind to stay here the night. Someone may have news of him."

"Maybe. The village folk are great ones for talking." Again, there was a trace of contempt. "I doubt their tongues have stopped wagging yet about the witch-burning, and that was a good few weeks ago."

Billy felt the hair on the back of his neck rise. A terrible knowledge swept over him like cold water. Trying to speak lightly, he asked, "And who were they burning?"

"Poor souls half out of their wits, most of them, or so my man said. But Agnes Balfour cheated them of their flames. She got herself strangled by the gaoler."

Billy closed his eyes. The horror was no easier for his flash of premonition. A wave of sickness swam over him. "What of the daughter?" he asked, dry-mouthed. "Did they –"

"No. Nobody knows where the lassie is. She was away from the house when they came for her mother, and she's not been seen from that day to this." The woman looked at Billy with shrewd compassion. "You've a liking for her?"

"Aye." For a wild moment, Billy wanted to tell the tinker woman why he had been brought to this moment of standing in an unknown village street, but he suppressed the desire. The force of his compulsion must not be wasted in idle talking.

"Most likely she'll have found herself a bothy," said the woman. "Or a cave. She'll come to no harm." But her face was clouded, belying her words.

Panic rose in Billy. He took a shuddering breath and said, "I'll not stay here this night. I'll keep on. What is the quickest way to Kirkcudbright?" he added urgently. "Will

I go across the hill?"

"It's a long way," said the woman. "The hill, aye." She was frowning absently. "Be careful, laddie," she said with sudden intimacy. "You'll find her, but I think there is a terrible danger. A man who hates you."

"I've no money for fortune-telling," Billy said quickly.

"Nor would I ask any," the woman retorted. "But have a care. I wish you good fortune."

"Thank you," said Billy. He turned away, retracing his steps towards the hill under the darkening sky. He looked back once, and saw the tinker woman with her children gathered about her, a curiously motionless little group, staring after him. He waved, but no hand was raised in return.

The path soon narrowed to a steep series of muddy patches between the tree-roots. The woods were quiet except for the rush of the burn far below, and the darkness was increasing. The threatened storm seemed to be biding its time, but distant lightning flickered sometimes in the sky. Billy climbed fast, the breath labouring in his chest. His mind ran ahead of him into a dream of a different climb, up a hill to the turf-roofed house with the jackdaws clacking in the sky. He must set this house to rights for Mari, light a fire in it and make it warm, ready for when he found her and brought her home.

In the next instant, a stone gave way beneath him and his full weight came down on his turned ankle. Billy grabbed wildly for support, but found his hands empty as he fell down the steep slope to his right, rolling helplessly through brambles and hazel thicket and fern. He came to a violent halt against the base of an elder tree, with the taste of wet earth in his mouth and the pain of torn tendons flooding through his ankle. Cursing himself for his stupidity, he sat up, then hauled himself to his feet. He bowed his head in the habit of penance, acknowledging he had allowed the accident to happen. In a bad light, and in such terrain, it was madness to allow the mind's attention to slip away. It had brought its own punishment. He could go no further tonight, either up the hill or back to the village. All he could hope for was a dry patch of ground where he could roll himself in his plaid and get some sleep.

Suddenly he raised his head like a startled animal. With a thrill that electrified his whole being, he scented woodsmoke. Was it imagination? Wind began to rustle in the tree tops and lightening flickered more closely, and the scent was there again, acrid and infinitely welcome. Carefully, he started to work his way upwind, along the slope of the hill, step by painful step through the tangle of growth. His ankle throbbed, and to put weight on it was agony. Poor Hugh, he thought, remembering how his brother had looked up at him on that hot, enchanted day. But he was careful, this time, not to let his mind stray away. The smell of the smoke grew stronger as he struggled slowly on, his way lit only now by the intermittent flickerings in the sky, but at last he came to the edge of a steep bank and saw the paleness of the smoke itself. As he crabbed his painful way towards it, the small red glow of the fire came into sight. On hands and one foot, he went carefully down through the bracken. No need for hurry now. Whatever shepherd had lit this fire for the night would not be going away.

In the next flicker of lightning, Billy saw the outline shape of a roof, but it was not that which made the heart leap in his chest. By the same brief illumination, he had seen a white goat lying by the fire, and a girl who had jumped to her feet at the sound of his approach, a black cat clutched in her arms. As the first heavy drops of rain began to fall, he crawled across the grass towards her. "I had to come," he heard himself say. "I lost the white stone."

*

William wrote to me from Lincolnshire. It was a dry, joke-studded letter, very schoolboyish. The censor had scored out one sentence in thick blue crayon, but I didn't mind much. Officialdom was only interested in lapses of security, and I wasn't concerned about the destination of bombing raids – I just wanted some insight into how William thought and felt. He had got his commission, he wrote, and was now a Flight Lieutenant, "the lowest form of animal life". He was getting good at darts and had developed a taste for pink gin, supplies of which seldom failed in the Officers' Mess. He hoped I was all right, and sent his love to Nana. He didn't send his love to me, just ended with the words, "All the best – William."

I made excuses for him. The blue-pencilling suggested that he was involved in the nightly raids over Germany that were the subject of every news broadcast. The admission that "one of our aircraft is missing" was added as a throwaway line, as if someone had been mildly careless, but for William, it would mean empty places at the table, familiar faces gone, laughter silenced. And any night could hand him the marked card, change him into ash and a statistic. No wonder he lived from gin to gin in the short, blessed intervals of safety.

The excuses went further. In such short-term living, a girl who clung like a drowning soul to every word must seem an intolerable weight, a commitment to permanency that was a tempting of providence. I had been stupid – I should have had a lighter touch, been cheerful and undemanding, like the "good-time girls" who hung round every camp. Yes, it was my fault.

I bought green eye-shadow and bright lipsticks and a pair of high-heeled shoes at staff discount when some new stock came in, and these things, together with the constant memory of standing with William in the dark, filled me with sexiness. Walking down the street on my propped toe-tips, I was cat-whisker ready to spot a man's admiring glance, to collect every wolf-whistle as a token of success.

It was only at night, when I took in my hands the white stone he had given me, that William was confirmed again as my true love. The stone was as round as the more conventional ring, a symbol that was circular which ever way you looked at it, with no hollowness. It was itself, as I was and as he was, and I wept sometimes to think of the sad confusion of the days, and the pretending which my love seemed to demand.

On bolder evenings, I would stare at my face in the mirror, impatient with the roundness and healthy, inexperienced smoothness of it. I pushed my red hair this way and that, piled it up with my hands, turned my head to see as near to a profile as I could, sucked in my cheeks to try and look leaner and older and more sophisticated. I had read somewhere about a film star who had all her back teeth extracted so as to improve the line of her cheek and jaw, and I thrilled to the idea even though it appalled me. I plucked my eyebrows into a fine arch and wore big stud ear-rings. When my mother saw me one day, she said, "What *do* you look like?" – but that's what I had expected.

One day, a man came into the shop whose face trapped me in fascinated terror. He was older than William, and infinitely tougher. His eyes were pale blue, his cheeks grooved and weather-beaten, and he moved with the muscular wariness of a predatory animal. He barely glanced at the Utility, Government-approved shoes which were all I had in his size, and I realised that he had not come in to buy. "I've seen you about," he said. "When's your lunch-hour?" He had a strong London accent.

I hesitated for a second, then told him. William no doubt had the odd flirtation with a WAAF girl; in his single letter he had mentioned someone called Caroline, and said what good fun she was. He wouldn't mind if I, too, amused myself a little. There would be nothing serious about it – a small adventure would only serve to show how superior William was to anyone else. An hour later, I was in a cafe with the man, eating Spam rissoles and chips. With him, there was no sense of being over-full and speechless. I was very firm. I told him I had a boyfriend, and he said he'd be surprised if I didn't, a looker like me. But there was no harm in talking, was there? I agreed.

He was not what my mother would have called a "nice" man; that was a part of his attraction. Although he exuded crudity and danger, these very things made me safe in knowing I would never love him. There was no threat to William. This was nothing more than a good-time girl's light affair. I liked being in the man's company – he was tough and funny, and he told me dirty stories, and he never attempted to touch me, unlike horrible Mr Scrimgeour in the shop, whose hands were like fat white rats, creeping across my sleeve as if of their own accord while he went on talking about punched Oxfords and ladies' low-heeled pumps.

The man wouldn't tell me his name. He said I could call him Terry, but when I asked what the rest was, he tapped the side of his nose meaningfully. Nosey, nosey. I blushed and shut up. He said he was in something hush-hush, but I never knew the truth. Perhaps he was a criminal. One day, he remarked, "If anyone was to interfere with you – give you a hard time, like – I'd kill him." He sounded perfectly calm.

At last he asked me if I'd had it off with the boyfriend, and I said we had decided to wait until we were married. But my face flamed and he laughed. He stirred his coffee then looked at me as I leaned back with my coat open and said, "You've got lovely breasts. Don't mind me saying, do you?"

I didn't mind. I began to want him furiously. It was only sex, I told myself as I shivered inside my clothes, nothing to do with love. William wouldn't mind. The next lunch-time, the man reached in a leisured way across the table when we were at the coffee stage, and put a single finger unerringly on my nipple. I gasped and grabbed his wrist, digging my nails in, and he smiled. "How about being a bit late back to work?" he said.

He took me to a small flat above a chiropodist's surgery, double-windowed, with the High Street traffic going past outside. He lit the gas fire and dropped the spent match into an empty fish-paste pot, then pulled the counterpane roughly over the unmade bed. I was hugging my coat round me, quaking with need and yet wishing I had not come to this place. He took my hand and led me to the fire, then carefully unbuttoned my coat and slipped it off my shoulders. He moved a small tapestry footstool in front of me and kneeled down on it. Then he pushed up my yellow sweater and undid my bra and put his mouth to my breast, sucking at the nipple he held between tongue and teeth while he rolled the other one with thick, delicate fingers. The sucking and caressing went on until I was shrieking breathlessly like someone on a Big Dipper, and then he stripped off the rest of my clothes and discarded his own, and carried me across to the bed. I shut my eyes when I saw revealed the fat red thing that stood like a snake about to strike, but the fear of what was happening only added to the urgency. He ran a hand over my belly as I writhed there, and smiled his narrow-eyed smile. "Little cat in heat," he said. His hand parted my legs – oh, so willingly I let him part them – and at last his hard, heavy body came pressing down on mine, and the snake's head pushed into the quaking centre of me, and I pulled and pulled at it until I shuddered to a climax.

Afterwards, he said, "So you're not a virgin." He seemed disappointed. I told him truthfully that I'd never done it before, but he shook his head. "Don't give me that, darling. If you were a virgin, you'd be bleeding."

I didn't know what he meant. The booklet my mother had given me made no mention of the results of deflowering.

"If I'd thought you were experienced, I wouldn't have wasted all that time on the softly-softly," he said.

He never believed me, and I had no argument to offer. It

was not until many years later that I learned from a gynaecologist that spontaneous rupture of the hymen can occur, and that I had, in fact, lost my maidenhood to William, my true love. I wished I had known.

*

Billy, my love.

His hair is as wavy as the coat of a red dog. Fronds of it curl across his forehead. Under his closed lids, his eyes dart in a dream. His lashes are pale, and the thin line of his cheek leads down through the bracken-brown beard to the corner of his mouth. His lips are a little apart, and I want to follow their curve with my finger, exploring him.

Let him sleep. Each moment of watching him is a gift. The time is so precious that I must measure it carefully, noticing every second, wasting nothing. I have wrapped his swollen ankle in a compress of herbs to heal the torn ligaments and bring fresh blood to them. Blood has in it the understanding of the body's right pattern. Soon he will be well.

My joy is balanced by fear. But everything has to be paid for, and a happiness as magical as this has the right to demand a high price. I took Jessie away through the woods when he killed the white kid, which I could not have done. For a time, that young life runs in us and gives us her strength, but the parcel of her head and hide sleeps in a grave at the foot of the beech tree, and her spilt blood has lost its understanding. I share in the life she has given us, but I mourn her. And one day, I will not escape the sharing of her death.

There is no use in meeting pain before it comes. For now, this moment stretches on and on, and its perfection rises like a silent song, up through the trees and beyond the clouds to the eternal sky and the mind of God.

PART FOUR

A little after mid-summer day in the following year, I knew I was pregnant. "For Christ's sake," said Terry, "how did that happen?" After the first rash time, he had insisted that I should get myself "fixed up", as he put it, and in those pre-Pill days, I had dutifully attended a Family Planning clinic where they were surprisingly uncensorious, to be fitted with the quaintly-named Dutch Cap. And I had not been careless.

The world turned woolly-textured and nauseating, and my breasts throbbed. I dreamed of oranges, almost unobtainable in those wartime years, and felt trapped. He bought a bottle of gin and made me drink glass after glass until I vomited, then watched me as I lay in a hot bath, to make sure I did not drown, he said, although I knew he hoped to see a welcome red stain spread through the water.

The child would not be moved, and my horror suddenly turned to protectiveness. I was afraid I had harmed it, and would not take the quinine powder Terry brought for me in a folded slip of white paper. After that, he disappeared. He did not come to the shop for over a fortnight, and when I went round to his room one evening, the woman who answered the door said he had moved out. No, he had left no address.

I went on working at the shoe shop. The days shortened into autumn, but I made no plans, and told nobody what had happened. Nana's grasp on reality had slackened even further, and she almost always called me Alice, if she knew me at all, though she revealed in a lucid moment that the real Alice had died of diptheria at the age of seventeen. Somehow, that was reassuring. Though I felt sick almost constantly, at least I was not dead.

At about that time, William wrote to say that his friend, Barney, who had trained with him at Leuchars, had been killed. "Bought it" was the phrase he used. "In this mad place," he went on, "I wonder sometimes if I had any life before, or if I just dreamed it." And he ended with the words, "To my dream girl, with what I think may be love."

It was too late for tears, though I sat by the river and wept over his letter, and carried it with me everywhere. Sometimes crying overtook me in the frowsty stockroom of the shoe shop. Mr Scrimgeour did not touch me any more, but he eyed me with increasing suspicion, and I knew my days of working there would soon come to an end.

I could not tell William. I wrote back to him with a drawing of roses, and assured him that the madness would end one day. On top of his friend's death, it would have been too cruel to inflict the blow of my treachery; but it was a grotesque assurance. Madness was concentrated in me, collected there as lime-scale collects on the knob of wire wool placed in a kettle. There was no explaining it. If the mad could explain their madness, they would be sane. The rage of sexuality had swept me away and filled me with its results and here I was, podding like the fallen rose blossom into round, strong fruit.

One day in late October, I at last walked through the streets to the double-fronted house where my mother and Donald lived. The brass plate outside stated their presence, Dr and Mrs D. Fraser. I had not attended their registry-office wedding. I climbed the white steps and rang the bell, and my mother opened the door.

"Mary! Is anything wrong?"

Her surprise was understandable; it was the first time I had been to her house. As she ushered me into the big sitting room with its velvet curtains, I regretted that there had been no previous visit of a neutral sort – that I had in truth only come when something was wrong. And I don't know yet whether it really was wrong, or whether it was part of a pattern which could not be contested.

My mother was predictably furious. Didn't I realise, she said, what harm a scandal like this would do to Donald's practice, not to mention my own future? How could I have been so stupid?

Donald took a more professional view. He asked how far the pregnancy was advanced, and shook his head when I told him. Had I confessed it earlier, he said, not unkindly, he could have arranged for me to have a termination. But I'd left it too late.

I knew that. I said I was sorry, and my mother snorted and said I could have thought of that before. She was right, of course, but I didn't think in those days, I only felt. Thinking was the province of the correct and the privileged and good girls at school. I couldn't imagine yet what there was to think about.

The important thing was to get me away from the wagging tongues of Ayr, Donald said. He knew of an excellent Home for Unmarried Mothers in Edinburgh, and would book me in there as soon as they had a vacancy. I could stay until a couple of weeks after the birth. And they would, of course, arrange for the child to be adopted.

*

Margaret Tarbert trudged behind her husband along the rough road. It led, she thought, in the wrong direction. At this time of the year, with the days so short and the north wind blowing from the snows of Sutherland, it was time to be heading west, across the Clyde and up through Inveraray to the shelter of the forest where the travellers grouped together for the winter. Margaret thought with longing of the barricade, the big tent made from bent saplings, canvas-covered, where there was room for twenty people or more. She wanted the company of other women, the laughter and talk and the firelit faces. The child she carried on her back was heavy, and the one which waited its time to be born stirred uncomfortably inside her.

The older children trailed behind their parents, each of them clutching some essential article – a hank of rope, a roll of canvas, a cooking pot, a hatchet. Liam himself carried a massive pack, from which dangled bunches of willow baskets tied by their handles and clinking tinware which made him sound like a flock of belled sheep. Margaret did not waste energy in looking back at the children. There was no doubt that they would keep up, give or take some stumbling and straggling. The children of travelling people were born to walking as young swallows were born to fly.

But this was all wrong. Was Liam bewitched, that he led them towards Kirkcudbright, making for a farm belonging to the man called Hugh McGuire? They had been on this strange path even before her encounter with McGuire's brother, the young man who had seemed so haunted by the witch's daughter, but since then, Liam had looked to the dark line of lowland hills with renewed anxiety. And here they were, with the north wind at their backs, for no good reason that Margaret could understand.

"If young McGuire loves Mari Balfour, he will most likely find her," Liam had said. "And I must see her. I have a letter to give her."

Margaret had not argued. She was not in the habit of questioning her husband about his business, for their responsibilities were distinct and separate, she in charge of the children and of food provision, he making the goods they sold and doing everything which needed his greater physical strength. But now an obstinate dissent had settled in her mind, as hard to ignore as a thorn in the foot. Liam was keeping something from her. The mysterious letter rankled in her thoughts, for writing had no part of their lives – and neither did this irrational journey. She stared down at the stony ground as it went past with each footstep. Every inch of it would have to be retraced.

It was difficult to stop walking. Margaret hoped for some natural obstacle to break the rhythm of their steady stride – a burn, perhaps, where they would pause to drink, or a steepness which would slow the younger children down and cause Liam to look back at his family. And then she found herself quite suddenly enraged with her own compliance. Without any conscious decision to stop, she moved to the side of the track and sat down on the grassy bank, leaning forward because of the weight of the child on her back, her arms dangling across her bent knees. The children stopped as well, and shouted to Liam, who came back and stared in consternation at his wife. "What is it?" he asked.

Margaret did not answer him. This was too important to be rushed into. "Away and play for a while," she said to the children. "Leave your things here."

The children retreated only as far as the opposite bank, where they perched like a row of young birds, watching their mother hopefully. Margaret fished in her pack and produced a bannock which a woman in the last village had given her. She held it out to the eldest of the girls and said, "Kathy, share this out. Now, away with you all for a wee while."

"I'll take Brigid," Kathy offered, lifting the baby from her mother's back. Scrawny and maternal, she marshalled the others away, including her elder brother, Jamie, who did not question her authority.

Liam sat down beside his wife and waited.

"I want to know why we are on this road," she said.

He looked away. Margaret knew he was trying to gather his courage. Her own nervousness at this unusual confrontation buzzed in her mind like summer flies round a horse. What was it that Liam had kept so secret? Had he done some terrible thing which he dared not tell her? She could not meet his eye, but she knew she would not move until the secret was out.

Liam knew it, too. "Maybe I should have told you before we were wed," he said. "I had a mind to, but I was feared you would want no more to do with me."

So she was right. It was something terrible. Margaret's hands hung loose across her knees, but her eyes were closed in dread.

"It was a year or so before I knew you," Liam said. "I was going down to the Border country. I passed this cottage – a poor place, it was, up in the hills, quite a way from any village – and a young woman was hanging clothes on the bushes to dry. I'd not thought to stop, for I could see she had no money, but she looked at me, and there was a liking between us. She gave me a cup of goat's milk and a tattie scone, fresh-baked, and I wanted her more than anything I had ever known." He rubbed his hand over his head. "I wondered afterwards if she had put a spell on me. I wonder to this day, sometimes. But there was nothing to tell me she was a witch, except that her thumbs were scarred and misshapen. I suppose I should have known from that. She told me later of what had been done to her as a bairn, but I was deep in love with her by then. She was so bonny. Dark red hair she had, like a deer, and black eyes and a slender white neck. All that summer I stayed down in those hills to be near her. I could think of nothing else.

"And she was Agnes Balfour." There had been gossip about Liam Tarbert at the time, that he had taken up with a house-dweller. But there must be something worse. Had he made a pact with Satan?

Liam nodded. "Aye, she was." He took a deep breath. "By the next summer, she had a child. A wee daughter, Mari."

"Your child."

"Aye."

"And that was the secret you kept all this time?"

Liam stole a glance at his wife, then looked again.

"What in the name of God is there to laugh at?" he demanded.

"I wasnae laughing." Margaret took his hand. "But the birth of a bairn is no crime. I never thought I was your first woman, Liam – you were no fumbling boy. And does it matter so much who fathers a child? The lassie who bears it feels the same pain and the same love for it, whether she is married or not." Then she added in fairness, "But maybe you did the right thing, keeping the secret. When I was younger, I might have been angry, right enough."

"It was cowardice," said Liam in a moment of bleak honesty. "I was afraid to stand by her. And I was afraid to lose you."

Margaret nodded absently. It made sense. Then she asked, "What is this letter you talk of?"

Liam produced the much-folded paper. "Agnes wrote it," he said with a touch of pride. "In the prison before she died. I took it from the gaoler."

Margaret looked at the neat lines of script with baffled respect. "What does it say?" she asked.

"That she is innocent of witchcraft. I asked a Minister to read it to me."

"And that is why you want to find her daughter – to give her this letter?"

"Aye. I owe Agnes that much." Liam frowned. "But there's more. I promised her that if the bairn ever needed help, she could turn to me. And she'll be needing help now."

"She will," Margaret agreed. She thought about it, then said, "Maybe she could take to the travelling life. She's half born to it."

"Maybe she'll marry young McGuire. But I have a fear for her."

"I know," said Margaret. "You've been like a man haunted ever since the day of the burning." She stood up and called to the children who were running in the heather with the quick recharge of energy the food had given them. "Jamie! Kathy! All of you, come and get your things. We must go." There was much to think about, but it could wait to accompany their walking.

*

The routine of the house embraced me again, with its making of sandwiches for my lunch-break at work, the getting-in of coal and taking tea to Nana in bed, cooking in the evenings and conducting the disjointed repetitive conversations. There was no vacancy at the Home yet, Donald said. They normally only took girls for the last six weeks before delivery, which in my case would be February, but they had agreed to admit me in the week before Christmas, since they knew him well. It wouldn't happen, I thought – but as I made up the fire or put salt into the pot of potatoes on the stove, I felt that the days were becoming precious, like the shells one picks up on the beach when the holiday is almost over.

Both of those perceptions were correct, but one is never quite prepared for the event which has been nudging at the awareness. I was frightened when I came home one evening to find Nana huddled and quiet in her chair by the fire. She was shivering although heat radiated from her, and I half-carried her up to her room and put her to bed. She trembled and coughed, folding up her thin limbs like birds' wings as I undressed her and guided her arms into the sleeves of her nightie. The doctor diagnosed pneumonia. Half an hour later, ambulance men were gently and cheerfully taking her down the stairs she had so recently struggled up, this time on a stretcher.

I went with her in the ambulance to the hospital, then came back on the bus and phoned my mother to tell her what had happened. Then I sat opposite the empty chair by the fire, seeing the things in the room as if for the first and last time, like the landscape outside the window of a train.

When I went to visit Nana after work the next day, she was propped up in bed against a lot of pillows, busy with the laborious work of breathing. Unusually, she knew me. With perfect lucidity, she put her hand over mine and said, "Mary, dear, I hope you'll be all right –" And after another painful breath she added, " – when the baby comes."

I felt so ashamed. All this time, she had known; and known, too, that I had not told her. I'd thought she wasn't capable of grasping it, that she'd mix me up with Alice, that I'd have to explain it again and again until I began to hate her. And I'd never hated my grandmother, she was precious to me.

She tugged weakly at her wedding ring, working it past the lumpy knuckle, and gestured for me to give her my hand. She slipped the ring over my third finger. "There," she said, beginning to cough. "Better for you." The coughing overwhelmed her, and sudden colour flooded her face. A nurse hurried across, and gave me a quick frown and jerk of the head to indicate that I should go. "I'll see you again tomorrow," I told Nana, and she managed to smile.

That night, there was a knock at the door. I switched off the radio with a sinking of the heart. This would be my mother, or Donald, or both of them, with news of Nana's death. But it was William who stood on the doorstep, not in uniform this time, but wearing a sports jacket and a flat cap, and carrying an overnight bag. He thought he'd surprise me, he said as he came into the hall. A short-notice forty-eight-hour leave. And he hadn't told his uncle and aunt yet.

I stood and stared at him, numbed. He was so full of gaiety and confidence. He caught me by the waist and pulled me to him for a close embrace – and I felt the shock run through him. Carefully, he stood back and said, "You've put on a bit of weight."

His frail hope that it was just weight died in the small

space between us. I turned away and went into the sitting room ahead of him, then we faced each other. My mouth was dry. "I'm sorry," I said. "I'm so sorry."

He shrugged. "No reason why you should wait, I suppose."

I was too shocked for tears, the irony was too sharp. This was the night when my baby should have been conceived by its rightful father. He had come here for that purpose. In his first cheerful chatter at the door, he had talked of sleeping on the sofa, if my gran wouldn't mind.

"I suppose I'm lucky," William said. "Men don't get pregnant."

I couldn't resent his toughness. He was sealing himself off. I'd have done the same thing. He glanced at my finger and said, "So you've married him."

"No! It's just – Nana gave me her ring."

"What are you going to do?"

"I don't know."

"Oh, Mary." He put his hands on my shoulders. "You silly cuckoo."

I said, "What about a cup of tea?"

"If you like." He came with me into the kitchen. "Where's your gran? In bed?"

So I told him about that as well, and still I didn't cry. We took tea and biscuits back to the sitting-room and sat in armchairs on either side of the fire like a married couple, exchanging small, inconsequential snippets of news. Then we fell silent.

"You could stay," I said. "I mean – "

He shook his head and said he'd better get the last bus to Kirkcudbright. He scribbled down his aunt and uncle's address and gave it to me. Last time, when I had folded a piece of paper between my fingers, it had been before I had followed him out to the gate. "Just in case I get moved or anything," he said, then shrugged. "If you want to keep in touch, that is."

I said I did. I remember nodding, just small nods, keeping my head up so I wouldn't cry.

He hoped Nana would be all right.

I hoped so, too.

At the door, he picked up his bag and kissed me on the cheek. "Take care," he said.

"And you."

Oh William, I said as he went out into the darkness, I do love you. But the words had no sound and he didn't look back.

I shut the door. In the warm sitting-room, I saw his empty tea-cup, and the tears came in a great flood. I curled in Nana's arm chair where he had sat, nuzzling at it for some last trace of the smell of him, stroking its velour surface as if it was his fair skin, and howled aloud in my anguish.

The next day, Mr Scrimgeour gave me the sack from the shoe shop. He said he did not think I would ask him for the reason. And when I went to the hospital that afternoon, they told me Nana had died.

*

There will be emptiness. I know it now, as surely as the sea's line meets the air and the red sun goes down behind the hill. I have no power to change it.

They killed my mother for her power, although it gave her no protection. Did they not wonder why she remained a woman in their cell, instead of flying out between their bars as owl or flitter-mouse? She lives on in my mind. She is beside me, watching Billy as he stretches restless limbs and feeds the fire. Our witchcraft is no more than openness. All possibilities are in us, like the life locked in a gull's egg or the windblown seeds of grass. There is no armour we can wear against its magic, even if we wanted to. That is our power, to know the magic, and accept its pain.

*

Margaret Tarbert waited in the yard with the children while Liam went into the shadowed doorway of the byre, Inside, she could see a row of big, red-coated cows munching hay from the long rack on the wall as they stood to be milked. A woman looked up from where she sat at the nearest one, and Margaret felt a stirring of concern for the tiredness and strain which her face showed. A boy of four or five stood beside her, turning a small feather between his fingers with the absorption of childhood.

"I was wanting to speak with the master," Liam said.

"We've no need for any workers just now," the woman told him. "And if we had, it's myself you'd ask." She spared a hand from milking to restrain the cow's swishing tail and added, "My man's lame with the rheumatics, and he leaves the dealing with folk to me."

And most of the work, too, by the look of you, Margaret thought as she listened. Liam stood his ground. "You'll be Mistress McGuire?"

"Aye." Janet looked at the tinker in surprise as she leaned down to the cow's udder again. "How do you know my name?"

"My wife met with your man's brother."

"Billy?" Her thin face was lit with a smile. "How is he? It's a long while since we had news of him – he's away with the Army. Where did she meet him?"

"By Polmaddie," said Liam, and added, "but he's no' in the Army now. He was walking the hill, desperate after finding some lassie he'd set his heart on."

"I never thought he'd like the Army," Janet said, and went on milking. Liam glanced at Margaret. So the boy was not here, and neither was Mari Balfour. And they would not be welcome if they did come. Margaret felt uneasy. There was something dark about this place, brooding and angry. She caught the child's eye for a moment, and he stared at her gravely, then looked down at his feather.

"What did Billy say?" Janet asked. "Is he well? When did he leave the Army?"

"He's well enough," Liam said evasively, and Margaret wondered whether her husband had picked up some of the foreboding she had felt in her meeting with the young man. She had been careful not to tell him about the sense of danger which had hung about Billy like a dark radiance, for Liam disliked anything that might smack of witchcraft. His situation was ironic now, and he knew it. Having parted from Agnes Balfour to marry Margaret, he could not bear the idea that he might have flown from one witch to another. And yet the ability to see what was to come had nothing magical about it, Margaret mused. It was no more than a distillation of common sense.

Jamie, her eldest son, who stood almost as tall as Margaret herself, glanced round, then said in the travellers' tongue which they always used among strangers, "Someone's coming."

A man was lurching across the yard towards them, supporting his weight on two sticks. "Janet," he snapped, "what are these filthy tinkers doing here? You know I'll not have them on the place, begging and thieving."

"They've not asked for anything, Hugh," his wife said mildly, shifting her stool back from the cow and picking up the bucket of milk. "They brought us news of Billy."

"I want no news of Billy," Hugh snarled. "I have enough news of Billy with every step I take." He indicated his twisted foot with an angry shake of one stick, and almost lost his balance. Janet put out a quick hand to support him, dropping the stool with a clatter and causing the milk to slop over the edge of the pail, and the little boy who had been hiding behind her skirts flinched away in fear. Thus did the badness run, Margaret thought, from angry father to frightened son. This McGuire had spent his whole essence in building up a herd of beautiful cows, but he was no more a truly living thing than the cast skin of an adder is the snake itself. Retreating across the yard with the children, who had instinctively gathered round her, she wondered at the madness of coveting possessions. The travellers' way was better, with its ruthless burning of everything inessential whenever a camp was left. By such cauterising, greed could never spread its poison through the spirit.

Hugh's voice still sounded from the byre. "Billy is no brother of mine, nor ever was, the witch's brat. I'll not have him here, trying to get his hands on what I have bought with hard earned money. The Army knows what to do with deserters, and I hope they find him – what more does he deserve, sending us news of him through a rabble of dirty tinkers! Janet, see them off the place. And watch them, mind."

Janet obediently followed Liam as he came out of the byre and walked across the yard towards Margaret and the children, his face pale with anger.

"I am sorry," Janet said quietly as soon as they were out of Hugh's hearing. "My husband is a sick man."

"I am sorry for *you*, lady," said Margaret with dignity.

Janet glanced over her shoulder. "Wait for me down the lane," she said. "I'll not be a minute." She went into the house. Her small son stayed where he was, staring at Margaret with serious grey eyes. Then he held up his hand to her, wordlessly offering the feather. "For me?" Margaret queried, and he nodded. She took the feather and smoothed it between her fingers. "Thank you," she said. "You're a good laddie. What's your name?"

"Hughie," said the child.

So he had been called after his father, Margaret thought as they set off down the lane. But the child had redeemed the name with his innocence.

Janet came hurrying after them with a bundle clutched

in her arms. "Some clothes," she said. "Petticoats and stockings and a few things for the children." She thrust the bundle into Margaret's hands. "Thank you for the news of Billy. If you see him again, tell him I wish him well." Then she hurried back to the house with her shawl drawn tight about her arms and the boy called Hughie running at her heels.

Margaret carried the bundle until they were out of sight of the house. Then she found a rabbit hole and pushed the clothes deep into it. A gift given furtively for the purpose of relieving guilt would carry wrong-thinking with it like an infectious disease, and bring a risk of bad luck to the whole family. But she released the feather into the wind, and wished a blessing on the grave-eyed boy who had given it to her. Hugh. The name sounded again in her mind, and the child within her gave a leap as if of approval. Not long now, my wee one, Margaret said to it silently. We are going the right way at last, to the winter place where you will be born.

Then she and Liam followed the children down the close-nibbled grass to the burn which tumbled between the beech trees, and washed in the clean water.

*

I am fighting Billy for the keeping of his life, but he is too strong for me. Men live in their own minds, not in the world. He will not yield. In God is his strength, he thinks. He does not see that in himself is his God. I want to give him the world's magic, that he may respect it and live. Once the man who threatens him is dead, he could be safe.

No, my mother says. There is no safety. Do not wish, Mari. Tell him, then let it be. And her arms are already about me, for the grief that will come.

*

"We need to make a plan," said Billy. "Then the days will have some shape to them. I need to know what I am doing."

Mari looked at him with her eyes narrowed against the woodsmoke and said, "There is shape enough in the days. We are together. What need is there to do anything but find food and keep warm?"

"I've no more oatmeal, and it is two days since I last snared a rabbit. Winter is coming." Why did she not share his anxiety about these things? "What are we to live on?" Billy demanded. "You will not let me kill the goat, even though she gives hardly any milk now. We must do something, Mari, or we may starve in this place."

"And we may not." She turned her face away from him and laid her head on her hugged knees, so that he saw only the tumbling mass of her red hair. "We should wait," he heard her say. "There will be a death. The danger will pass."

"There is no need to run from danger," Billy said. "In the Army, danger was my business. I know when eyes are watching me." And I know how to kill, he added silently, in more ways than she can imagine. He got up and stretched, raising clenched fists above his head, feeling the shudder of unused energy run through his body. In his mind, he was already returning from a successful trip to the village, having found work and earned money and bought food – maybe even some trinket for her. He could not go on lying at her side like a tame bull.

"You must not go looking for trouble," said Mari, with her face still averted.

Billy frowned. In these last days, she had been strangely inward and preoccupied. She would smile at him when he asked if she was happy, and twine her arms round his neck, seeking his lips with hers, but she closed her eyes when she did this, as if she did not want to meet his gaze. She seemed obsessed with danger. But then, he reminded himself, she was with child. All pregnant women were strange in their fancies, or so it was said.

The thought of the coming child made him doubly restless. She would need his care. She should be in a better place than this. Perhaps Hugh would take them in – brotherhood must surely count for something. He had mentioned this possibility to Mari, but she had said in her remote way that it would not happen. How could she be so sure? Hugh's wife, Janet, had always been a kindly woman; if Hugh was difficult, she would put in a word for them. But it was a long journey down to Kirkcudbright, and they would need some money if they were to travel so far. "I'm a good worker," he said aloud. "I can turn my hand to any trade." Mari did not move, and he put his hand on her shoulder. "There is no blame in what I am doing," he told her. "God will be with me."

This time, she raised her head and looked at him. "If you go to the village," she said, "you will not come back."

He shrugged irritably. The coming back was the point of it all. It would be like finding her again, a second experiencing of a dream come true. Women did not understand how necessary dreams were, he thought. They lived on a practical level, without the grand imaginings of men. He had loved Mari most in the years of their separation, because in that dream-time she had been perfect, doing and saying nothing that did not accord with his own desires. The perfection had still been there in the first hours of their meeting, but after that, it had begun to tarnish a little in the damp air of reality. An absence and a new encounter might let him see her in all her shining glory again.

He bent down and kissed her. "You and your tinker's blood," he said lightly. "Imagining danger where there is none. Running from your own shadow." Straightening up, he flexed his shoulders impatiently and took a deep breath of the damp, cold air. "I am not like you, Mari. I believe in myself. Wait here a few days while I go to the village or wherever I can find work, and you will see. When I come back, I will bring you your heart's desire."

"You have done that already," she said. And her black eyes stared into his without the glimmer of a smile.

*

Did I imagine danger where there was only good intention?

Yes, perhaps. But then, it would be so simple if danger came only from ill-wishers. On the day after Nana's death, Donald and my mother came round to the house to tell me I could not go on living there alone. My mother and I embraced when she came in, and wept together, but I wished she had not felt it necessary to point out that the house would be put up for sale and that vacant possession would be needed.

That's when the net began to tighten. Donald cleared his throat with some pomposity and said that in view of the circumstances, I could of course come and stay with him and my mother until such time as other arrangements could be made. He was sure I would be discreet. Meanwhile, he would get in touch with the Home and see if they could further advance the date of my admission.

After they had gone, I washed up their coffee cups slowly, trying to see what to do. Like a reluctant swimmer who has been chivvied along to the edge of the diving board, I wanted just a little more time of warmth and deep breathing before the jump.

The following evening, Donald phoned. The Home would take me on Sunday week, he said – but my mother had gone down with shingles. A very nasty attack, on the left hand side of her face. Where it had pressed against mine as we kissed, I thought with mild interest. In view of the circumstances, Donald said again, the funeral would not take place until my mother was better. And I, of course, would be safer to remain where I was, for fear of infection.

Nana's mischievous ghost smiled at my side, and I suddenly knew she had never liked Donald. It's funny how the dead reveal themselves.

In the days I had been given, I slept late in the mornings and wandered round the house as the days shortened into winter darkness, slowly detaching from it until I became a stranger, an idle burglar with no intention to steal.

I stood with the white stone in my hands, rotating it gently, trying to see its meaning. William had given it to me as a love-token. Or had he? The way it had forced itself on him seemed insistent rather than loving. Maybe it should be his to keep. For several of the dwindling days, I came back to it, and pondered.

*

He has gone away, and the sky is empty, the bare trees and the cold earth are empty. Soon there will be a place, unknown to me, where his body will mingle with the roots of ash and elder, and the small creeping things of the soil will slowly make him theirs. It is not yet, but I know he will not come back through the forest, alive and triumphant as he was in his dreaming.

His dream is a mockery now, shivering in the space between the trees. I will not have the strength to go on living here alone. I needed him to help me find sticks for the fire and hunt for food. Without him, hunger takes a wolf-step closer, knowing that there comes a time when there is no more energy to resist it.

I must stay alive. The child within me needs my body and my living spirit. Billy spoke of his brother and the farmhouse in Kirkcudbright, but I saw only my fear of the twisted man who followed two black heifers and a frightened child up the hill. He, too, seems empty. Perhaps I should not trust this certainty. Do what you have to do, Mari, my mother says. I cannot stay here.

*

I wrapped the white stone in the handkerchief William had lent me, so long ago now, it seemed, when we stood in the alleyway waiting for *The Way to the Stars*, and I had wept. The grey-blue colour of it made a cotton sky for the small, heavy moon. Then I tore a sheet of azure paper from the pad which Nana would no longer use, and wrote on it, YOU ARE MY TRUE LOVE.

It was not a big parcel. When I had taken it down to the Post Office and watched the woman lick the stamps and stick them on, I turned away. Somehow, I didn't want to see her drop it in the sack that hung from the edge of the shelf behind her.

I went home and put some clothes into a small bag, together with half a loaf, my week's cheese ration, three rashers of bacon and the remains of a packet of tea. There was a little sugar, too, which I put in a screw-top jar to keep dry. I had my pay-off money from the shop in my purse, and the scrap of paper William had given me with the address of his aunt and uncle in Kirkcudbright. Mr and Mrs Naismith, they were called. He hadn't written their first names.

"I'm sorry I won't be at your funeral," I said to the spirit of Nana which was watching me with curiosity. She didn't seem to mind. You must do what you want, she said, I always did. I went out into the November stillness and locked the door behind me, then dropped the key back through the letter box.

Snow was wandering thinly down as I got off the bus. I went into a newsagent's shop and asked if they knew where Mr and Mrs Naismith lived, and the man said, "Up the hill on the right." He was nursing a mug of tea in both hands. He and his wife watched me as I went out. "Craigmuir," he added, and I looked back and thanked him. Yes, that was the name of the house, written in William's firm capitals.

The hill was a long one, leading away from the town, with a view across fields to the distant sea, lead-grey under a leaden sky. It was getting dark. I didn't know what sort of a place I was looking for. A cottage, probably, with a long garden full of Brussels sprouts and leeks, where William had learned his skill with growing things. I had found no entry under Naismith in the telephone directory. That wasn't unusual, but it suggested old-fashioned people, content to live in their own locality, having no truck with new-fangled inventions. It had been rather a relief that I couldn't phone first, to ask if I might come and see them, and perhaps stay for a while. What if they had said no? My first step would have been denied to me.

At the top of the hill, I walked past stone pillars on either side of a broad drive, then came back, not sure if I had seen it or dreamed it. Chiselled into the heads of each one were the dignified Roman letters which spelled the repeated name, Craigmuir.

I laughed. What else can you do when you are standing in the snow, confronted by a mistake that undoes every notion of a plan that you have made? For a moment, I felt angry with William. He should have told me. It was deceitful, hiding such grandeur under his air of modest simplicity. He had laid me open to humiliation. How could I go trailing up to this mansion with my wet coat and my shabby rexine bag? Then my indignation faded. It was not his fault. I could have asked him about his family, instead of mooning over him and being unable to speak. Now, I had to deal with the results of my folly, and I didn't know how.

A car approached, slowed down, and turned past me into the drive. In its cowled wartime headlamps, the whirling snow and the bases of great tree trunks were fleetingly clear as it went away along the gravel. My confusion ebbed. William's aunt and uncle were probably perfectly nice people, grand or not. There was no need for this sense of dread. I followed the car. It swept round in a wide circle and stopped outside the house.

From a distance, I watched a man and woman get out. He came round to give her his arm, and she stooped a little to pick up the hem of her long dress, then they went up the steps to the front door. Light gleamed briefly as it was opened to admit them. The thin snow that powdered the gravel was striped with the tyre tracks of several cars, though only one other was parked outside the house. Taxis, perhaps, had come and gone. Absurdly, I tiptoed across the gravel as if stealth would make me less offensive, and rang the bell.

"Yes?" An elderly maid stood there in a crimped cap and white apron. She held a heavy blackout curtain a little aside so that she could see my face from the light in the hall.

"I wondered if I could see Mr or Mrs Naismith," I said. "I'm a friend of their nephew, William." Did her eyes flick to the solidness of my waist? I rushed on, "I'm sorry I didn't phone first, but I couldn't find – "

"The number is ex-directory," she said. "Are Mr and Mrs Naismith expecting you?"

"Not exactly. I just thought – "

"If you will give me your name, Miss – ?"

"Carstairs. Mary Carstairs."

A man swept the curtain aside from behind her, careless of the light that blazed out. He was in full evening dress. "What is it, Ellen?"

"A young lady, sir. Miss Carstairs. She says she knows Master William."

"Right, thank you, Ellen." He took her place. "Now, my dear, it's very kind of you to look us up, but we're busy with guests this evening. William's away in the RAF, you know."

I said yes, I knew, but he was looking past me to another car which had just drawn up.

"Some other time, then, right? When the lad's here. I'm

146

sure he'll be delighted to see you." Then his voice lifted as he called, "Cameron! Come along in. And Marion. Terrible night, isn't it?"

I went away, and the snow thickened, falling in big, fluffy flakes between the trees.

*

I tie up my bundle again. There is less than there was. Winter is coming, and I wear all the clothes I have so as to keep the cold wind from my skin. There are none to be carried. The salt is all gone, and even the herbs are fewer, for I used some of them in the healing of Billy's ankle.

He will not need me again, but his child holds my life in its transparent fingers. I could have freed myself from its sweet tyranny; among these dried leaves tied in their muslin, there are some that have that power. But I will not. I feel the eggshell hardness of the baby's skull as it presses on the inside of my hip, and remember the white stone which I gave to a limping boy all those years ago, because he seemed wonderful to me. The wonder possesses me still, and I am as distracted by it as the poor hedge sparrow whose baby cuckoo takes all her strength. As distracted, and as enchanted.

*

Perhaps the most seductive enchantment is one's own. Why else should it have seemed that I was committed to an unknown future that had no substance beyond a wild idea of freedom? And yet, as I stood in the falling snow, outside the pillars of the house called Craigmuir, there was no question of going back. There never had been. That's why I had dropped the keys to Nana's house through the letter-box behind me. So I turned right, away from Kirkcudbright and the bus station, and started out along the lane. My footsteps creaked in the layer of untrodden whiteness.

On that long walk, the cold became my enemy. As the lane climbed to higher ground, the wind drove the snow hard across the open fields, and a kind of vagueness set in. I began to dream of warm hearths and the soft drop of glowing ash through the grate, the shimmer of coal caverns. Someone – was it myself? – leaned forward, a hand to the shawl about her shoulders, to stir the fragrant broth above the fire.

The sound of a distant aeroplane brought me sharply back to wet feet and the snow that mingled with each breath. William could be up there somewhere, crouched over flickering navigation lights in a sheepskin jacket and leather helmet. The picture rocked with gunfire as it had in *The Way to the Stars*. William, is it warm in an aeroplane?

He smiled. He was above the clouds, I below, moving across the earth with insect-steps, snowed upon, unable to see the moon.

At last, the lane emerged at a T-junction with a wider road. Two softly-indented tracks showed that a car had passed this way, but a long time ago. I turned left, heading towards what I hoped was the north, into the blinding whiteness. Snow blew into my face and settled on my half-shut eyelids and formed a blanket down the front of my sodden coat, and with a slow shock like physical sickness, I realised that I might be out here for the rest of the night.

During my daytime walking, there had always been other people about, even though I hadn't needed them. Several times a passing driver had stopped and asked if I wanted a lift. I'd never accepted these offers, but they had been there in the background, part of the pattern. On this night, I hadn't imagined that I would walk for hours and hours with melting snow creeping down my back and my feet numbed and frozen in their leaking shoes. But then, neither had I recognised the difference between a working weekday and a blizzard-swept night, or how the wartime petrol rationing meant that even those cars whose owners were still permitted to use them made only one or two necessary journeys each week. They spent a lot of their time tucked away in a garage, or sharing some straw-lined byre with a tractor and a couple of horses, warm and dry.

A seductive sleepiness crept over me at the thought. There would be the smell of sweet hay. I could curl up and rest. Even in this white eiderdown, I could curl up –

My knees buckled sharply, and I was in the snow on all fours, the bag fallen ahead of me. I desperately wanted to lie down and go no further.

So, we'll go no more a-roving
So late into the night.
Though the heart be still as loving,
And the moon be still as bright.

I don't know why Byron's lines should have come into my mind at that moment. My mother used to quote them.

For the sword outwears its sheath,
And the soul –

Stumbling to my feet, I begin to laugh, although it turned to a kind of sob. The wretched man was complaining of sexual exhaustion, that was all. He wanted a break from romance – he couldn't go on.

And neither could I. My legs were shaking and my breath hurt in my chest, and for the first time, I felt afraid for the part of me that was another being, waiting trustfully to be born.

Struggle is so over-rated. It's when you give up that things begin to happen. I went on slowly, for the sake of preserving a little warmth, but there was no resistance any more. The fear ebbed.

When I heard the purring tinkle of snow-chained tyres behind me, I didn't look round at first. It could be a mirage of the imagination – I wanted to be sure it was real. But the small van drew to a halt beside me, and a woman looked through the open crack of the door and said, "You'd best get in, dear, this is no night for walking."

I tried to say something, but no words came.

*

Billy made his way down the hill towards the village. Despite his hunger, there was an exhilaration about being on the move again. He had come to feel irritated by Mari's calm acceptance of the way things were. She seemed to test herself through endurance, as if she found it good to be able to ask for less and less. Why could she not see the world as being full of potential, the way he did? For those with energy and courage, all things were possible.

His mind went back to the Army days as he forged confidently downward through the tangled growth of hazel and dry bracken and the trailing lengths of bramble. Although he had hated its restrictions, there had been something well-earned about stepping forward from the line to receive the pay-day coins, salute, step smartly back and then spit on the money for luck before stowing it safely away. As he waited for his back to heal from the flogging, he stood with a few miserable others and watched, for his pay had been docked as an additional punishment for the fight with Lachlan Gibson.

Billy's fists clenched involuntarily as he thought of it. To the end of his days, he reflected, he would never forgive the man he had cursed, even though it was the loss of the white stone which had triggered him into leaving the Army and making the long journey back across Scotland. Even though it had led him to Mari. He had meant every word of the curse he had uttered, and it had taken devastating effect. A sore at the corner of Lachlan's mouth had erupted into a great weeping ulcer and he had begun to lose control of his limbs, walking with a splay-legged gait as if his feet were uncertain how to meet the ground. But the man had been sick for a long time, Billy told himself defensively as he felt a small pricking of conscience. With that scabbed face and the red eyes, anyone could see it. Lachlan Gibson had the pox. Dose him as they might with quicksilver and the ash of the willow tree, his days in the Army had been numbered, and his days of life not much longer.

It was not my fault, Billy said to himself. The curse only made it happen faster. He tightened his lips obstinately and without repentance, for the slow, enduring anger of the Highlander ran in his blood, and there could be no stepping back. Lachlan had most likely been discharged by now, to end his days somewhere down on the Borders where his people came from, for he had never married.

Emerging from the woods, Billy paused, looking down at the houses of the village. He thought of the tinker woman who had spoken to him when he was here on that other day, and envied the travellers' ability to know which houses would be welcoming and which would not. But there was nothing magical about it, he told himself. They simply passed on their experience by means of marks and signs. He himself had learned something of the same skill during his journey westward. He knew at least that the prosperous houses were the ones to be avoided. There was a better chance in the more humble dwellings, where people understood the nature of hardship. Whistling a tune, he started again down the hill.

*

The people with the van put me up on a camp bed in the living room in front of the banked-up fire, with two hot water bottles because I couldn't stop shivering. The woman told me all about how they'd been to her sister's ruby wedding. Real ham, they'd had, she said, and wee bowls of chocolates on the table after the coffee, thanks to Cousin Annie. She had this boyfriend, Dwayne, who was in charge of supplies at the American air base. "Ivy, you've had too much sherry," her husband said.

In the morning, I felt a bit stiff, but wonderfully warm and much better. My weeks of walking in the non-school days had been a good preparation for this journey – I could see that now. Ivy had draped my wet clothes over a towel-horse in front of the fire and stuffed my shoes with newspaper, so that they, too, were ready for this new day. I got the three rashers of bacon out of my bag, dampish in their greaseproof paper, but otherwise all right, and we had one each for breakfast. There were fresh rolls as well because the baker came tramping up the path with his basket over his arm. The snow had stopped, but the horse that pulled the bread cart had a sack over his back because of the cold, and his breath steamed in the frosty air.

After breakfast, the questions began. I knew they would. George and Ivy had tried to get some sense out of me last night – where I was going, where did I live, goodness, wasn't I young to be married. Nana's ring which I wore on my finger was their only source of information. All I could do was clutch the hot mug of cocoa they had given me, and shiver and shake my head, trying to keep my eyelids from closing. But this morning I had woken full of wariness, mentally concocting stories even before my limbs had undertaken their first exploratory stretch. By the time Ivy tapped at the door and came in with a cup of tea, I was ready – but there was no need for defences, not for a little while. Ivy's concern was with her own behaviour the previous night, and she poured out a torrent of apologies in case she had been inhospitable.

Oh, the complex courtesies of women! At sixteen, I was a newcomer to the subtle balance of formalities, but I instinctively counter-apologised for "imposing". We ducked and bobbed in mutual assurance until the small bruises to self-respect were smoothed and we were ready to take up the business of life again, and then she went off to set the breakfast table, leaving the way open for the questions her husband would ask.

There could be no question of telling them the truth. These kind, well-rooted people would never understand that I was travelling without any well-defined purpose, in order to let things happen. Their sense of duty would demand that I was put on some form of transport to a sensible place – probably back to Ayr. But constructing a plausible fiction was not at all easy. My grasp of Scottish geography was vague, and the place-names which flitted through my mind were more the product of family mythology than any real knowledge. Helensburgh, for instance. I had always thought it a queenly word, full of grace and dignity, but who had lived in Helensburgh? Someone to do with Nana? After a struggle, the childhood episode came back to mind, Nana sweeping into the house, full of her meeting with her estranged husband. Didn't he have a sister in Helensburgh? Jessie, was it? Never mind – Helensburgh would do. I had no idea where it was, but someone would no doubt tell me. People are always happy to set you right about facts. For the rest of it, near-truth would do. My husband was in the RAF, I'd been to see my in-laws, thought I'd found a short cut to Kirkcudbright, got lost . . . They'd given me quite a lot to drink, I'd say apologetically. Ivy would understand that.

So the questions were answered over breakfast, and when Ivy took the dishes out to the kitchen, George asked me quietly if I was all right for money. I said I was. In fact, all I had in the world was what remained of my shop pay after I had bought last week's groceries and paid for my bus fare. It would last me a few days if I was lucky, but I wouldn't be able to afford overnight accommodation. Even one stay in a bed-and-breakfast would clean me out. But I turned George's offer down as if it had been a baited trap.

I can see now that he wouldn't have expected to get his money back. He probably saw through my story, wrote me off as some young kid in trouble, was trying to be kind. But I thought he would at least expect an address if I accepted his help. Indebtedness has its obligations. So I said I was fine, and glanced at the clock on the mantelpiece, adding that I ought to be on my way. Ivy cut me some sandwiches, and George walked me to the bus stop. Any bus that came along would take me to Dumfries, he said, right to the town centre. And from there I could get the train to Glasgow. After that I'd know my way, of course. Central Low-Level to Helensburgh, no bother.

I thanked him profusely and got on the bus when it came, waving back at him through the window. But I got off at the next stop, before the conductor could sell me a ticket. I told him I'd forgotten something, and he said he'd heard that story before, but OK, just this once. Then I set off on foot in the same direction, walking carefully on the frozen snow. Buses were expensive.

In Dumfries, I sat down on a bench where there were trees beside the road, with shops set behind them, and ate the sandwiches Ivy had given me, one with cheese in it and one with fish-paste. The sky was a clear blue but it was very cold. I decided that I could afford a cup of coffee. Further down the road, a lot of lorries were parked between the bare trees, and I came to a small cafe with steamed-up windows. It looked as if it would be cheap, so I opened the door and went in. The place was surprisingly crowded, mostly with men in boiler suits and donkey-jackets, eating plates of food on tables covered with checked oilcloth. A blackboard on the wall advertised Today's Dinner – sausage pie, cabbage, mash and gravy, apple tart and custard. It smelt very good, but my sandwiches had been enough, I thought sternly. The coffee was made with a spoonful of black essence from a bottle. I took my cup to an empty seat beside an elderly man who was reading a newspaper. He sipped his tea and said without looking up, "Cold day."

"Yes, isn't it."

"You hitching?"

The question took me by surprise, then I realised that the men were all lorry drivers. What else would a girl with a travelling bag be doing here but looking for a lift? I had no destination, but the thought of the coming night worried me. It would be good to get away from this place with its snowy lanes. So I told the man I was trying to get to Helensburgh.

He put his paper down. He could take me as far as Hamilton, he said. After that he turned off for Aberdeen. But there was plenty of traffic going through Hamilton in the Helensburgh direction, heading for the west coast. He waved a hand generously. Oban, Mallaig, Ullapool.

I nodded and thanked him, trying to sound sensible and tough. Ullapool, I thought. How magical it sounded, and how far away. Perhaps that was the place I should be going to. Ullapool might be my journey's end.

*

Walking, walking. And my lovely Billy is far away, walking too, his mind set on work. But the peats are cut and stacked and the harvest in, the old hens killed and plucked. People are kind enough. They offer food and a dry bed in the barn, but he cannot come back with his stomach full and his hands empty, for to him it is a poor man who will settle for a woman's caring rather than her admiration. He thinks his luck will change, my lovely Billy. And I wait for the sky's shaking when it does.

*

The lorry-cab was warm. It shook with the vibrations of the engine, but I liked it. We were so far above the level of mere car-drivers that we seemed to be on the bridge of an ocean liner, forging across the white, hard-frozen landscape as if it was an Arctic sea. Very quickly, I settled in. The worn leather seats and the big, double-levered handbrake, the shaking gearstick and the almost horizontal steering wheel on which the driver rested his hands, wide apart, began to seem like familiar household objects in this little home that contained us. The driver seldom spoke except to utter a brief word of contempt for some car-driver of particularly blatant idiocy, and I felt very comfortable in his care. By the time he pulled the lorry into the forecourt of another transport cafe, I was tempted to say I had changed my mind and would go with him to Aberdeen. I would go anywhere for the sake of this warmth and restfulness. But I couldn't do that, not without long and difficult explanations.

I'd hoped that the driver would come into the cafe with me, but he said he'd better push on. He leaned across to pull the door shut and looked down at me. "Just ask the lads in there," he said over the engine's slow gallop. "And be careful, know what I mean? Don't pick a wrong one." Then the gallop turned into a roar and he pulled away.

Asking for a lift is very different from being offered one. I couldn't face going into the cafe – I didn't even know where to say I was going, or how long it might take to reach a place called Helensburgh, or that more dreamlike one called Ullapool. And yet, travelling was the obvious answer to the problem of where to spend the night. It would be so safe and comfortable through the dark hours, dozing in some warm, oily-smelling lorry as it forged on for mile after mile, never mind where. I walked up the road in the gathering darkness. It was not quite so cold tonight. The snow had turned crystalline and crunched underfoot, and a damp, raw wind was blowing.

A lorry lumbered out from the cafe, and as it came towards me, I turned to face it and stuck my thumb up. And it stopped. A man wound the passenger-side window down and looked out. "Wheer ye gaun, pet?" His accent was so thick that I hardly understood him. "Helensburgh," I said boldly, and added, "for a start."

"Aye, OK." He jumped down, took my bag and flung it into the cab, then helped me up, his hands on either side of my waist. Then he climbed in beside me so that I was sandwiched between him and the driver. It was a bigger lorry than the other one. With a hiss of air brakes and a shudder of the engine, we were off.

"An' efter Helensburgh?"

I shrugged. Somehow, this sandy-haired man made me feel defensive. "Ullapool, maybe."

"Ye're no' too bothered where ye go, then?"

"That's right."

He grinned and crossed his legs. There was a bunch of artificial flowers in a holder in the centre of the windscreen, and behind the cab seats was a flowered curtain. He saw me looking at it. "Tha's the bunk," he said, twitching the curtain aside to reveal a narrow, untidy bed. "Long journeys, one of us needs to sleep, ye get me."

I nodded. The bunk was the answer to all my needs, but I couldn't make use of it, not with the two men there.

"We'll be stoppin' in Dumbarton," the sandy-haired one said, and indicated the driver. "He stays there. If ye're stuck, hen, ye can use the bunk. See, we'll no' be drivin' the night."

"Could I really?" It seemed too good to be true. "If you're sure – "

The driver, speaking for the first time, said, "I'll be away home to my wife. We can give you a bed for the night, lassie, if that's what you're needin'."

It would be Ivy and George all over again, questions, apologies, lies. "No, honestly, the bunk will be fine," I said.

I blush to think of it now. The poor man was trying to give me a chance, trying to warn me. He must have seen I had never even heard of prostitutes who "work the roads". He shrugged, and went on driving.

Dumbarton arrived disconcertingly soon after we had driven through Glasgow. They parked the lorry on a piece of rough ground near the river, and the driver said to me, "Stay there a minute, dear." Then he and his mate got out, and I heard them talking. Their voices were fast and muttered, as if they were having an argument, but I couldn't make out the words. Then the driver came back and opened the door, looking up at me. "If you want to change your mind – " he said. For a moment, I hesitated.

Everything would have been different if I'd accepted his offer, and I so nearly did. He was kind, and his house would be warm. There might even be something to eat, for I was terribly hungry. The coin spun on its edge, and then fell. "I'll be all right in the bunk," I said. "But thanks all the same." And he shook his head and went away.

The sandy-haired man took his place at the door and pointed out that there was a public lavatory just across the square that I could use if I needed to. Then he added that he was off to the pub for a wee hauf, did I want to come?

I told him I didn't. I was bursting to use the toilet, but after that I wanted to come back to this small place that would be my own for the night. There was still half a loaf in my bag, and some cheese. I asked the man if they would be going to Ullapool in the morning, and he said, "Fort William. That do you?" And smiled when I said it would. "See you later, then," he said.

He came back to the cab before I had gone to sleep. I was lying down under the rather smelly blankets, fortunately with all my clothes on because of the cold – I hadn't realised how cold it would be once the engine was turned off – and was jolted into awareness as the door opened. In the next instant, his hand was on my leg and he was clambering on top of me. The whisky was strong on his breath. "Lovely, so y'are," he said.

I kicked out, struggled from under him and rolled off the bunk, landing half across the seat and half on the floor. In a floundering confusion with the gear lever, I grabbed for my bag and groped frantically for the handle of the passenger door.

"Fucksake, whit ye doin'?" he said.

I fell out of the lorry and landed on hands and knees, picked myself up and ran. "Whaur ye goin', ye stupit bitch?" The words rang out between the sleeping houses. I pelted across the roughly-rolled hardcore of the lorry park and down the road. At any minute, I thought I would hear his footsteps behind me or, worse, the lorry's engine would start up. He would hunt me down in that juggernaut, pin me against a wall, kill me. I ducked through an alleyway, across a street, down the next side turning, ran on and on until my heart was bursting in my chest and my belly ached with the weight of the child. I stood in a shop doorway and listened. There was no sound but my heaving breath, but he might still be coming after me, quietly through the streets.

Common sense began to return. He had been wearing heavy boots, his feet would clatter on the pavement. I'd hear him a mile off. But I went on walking, though more slowly so as to calm the child that lay curled inside me. An almost-full moon showed its face sometimes between the clouds and its light shone across the river that ran behind the houses on my left. It was oddly comforting, that glimpse of silvery water; very old and indifferent and reliable. The westerly wind was raw, but there was a dampness in it. A thaw was coming.

If there's no reason to stop walking, you don't – you just keep going. After a long time, I came to a town which stood back from the river behind a broad sweep of grass. The moon was further down in the sky, behind the bare branches of tall trees that grew at the water's edge. I found a glassed-in shelter with wooden benches, and there I lay down and slept.

*

Billy's senses prickled with a deserter's caution as he came into the small town. He would be watched from many a dark window, and perhaps known. But the houses were quiet, and smoke rose peacefully from their chimneys in the cold sunshine. There was no Army presence here. No danger. He smiled with a sudden access of confidence. This would be a day of new beginning.

One cottage stood back from the others at the top of a sloping path, and he stared at it with an odd sense of certainty. The place seemed tailor-made for the work he could offer. It was not derelict, but the leafless fuchsia bushes grew in twiggy abandon across its windows, and the door was cracked and rotten, needing a new weatherboard. An old man would live here alone, or a widow-woman with no family – somebody too frail to dig the stony earth or grapple with hammer and nails. Approaching the house, he saw that someone had roughly hacked down the rambler rose that had grown by the door, but even this small effort spoke of exhaustion or impatience, for the severed lengths lay where they had fallen, withered and brown among the long grass. Yes, he was needed here.

A single magpie flew up from the roof of the house at his approach, and Billy smiled to himself at the daft old superstition of bad luck. It was not luck you needed, but cleverness, he told himself. The Army, for all its faults, had taught him that. Your fortune was of your own making. He rapped on the door with his knuckles.

From inside, he heard a muffled exchange of voices, but there was a long delay before the door was opened. The woman who stood before Billy held a child on her hip, and strands of her pale hair dangled lankly round her face. A sweetish, unpleasant smell came from the room, and Billy knew at once that he had made a mistake. There was sickness here, and the house reeked of poverty and desperation. The woman said nothing, but glanced over her shoulder uneasily, as if concerned about something behind her in the dark room. Another child, maybe.

Billy felt a strong impulse to go away with his question unasked, but overruled it. "I was wondering if you're needing any work done? I'm strong and able. I can dig or chop wood – anything."

Again, there was the frightened glance back. Probably the other child getting into mischief, Billy thought, then caught a glimpse of someone throwing a blanket aside and getting up from the wall-bed. No, this would be an old mother or father, bed-ridden with the rheumatics and maybe wishing somebody would do something about the place. There could be a chance of a job yet. He leaned more confidently on the door jamb, directing his voice past the woman to the figure behind her. "I'll turn a hand to anything," he offered again. "I've been in the Army these three years."

"My brother was in – " began the woman. But her words were stopped by an inarticulate howl from behind her. There was a flurry of movement, and she screamed and ducked aside as Billy stared and could not move. Then the leaping figure was on him, and as he staggered back he saw that the red-eyed, scabrous face above the flapping nightshirt was that of Lachlan Gibson. He caught a glimpse of a curving blade flourished high above the man's head, and then a hot, searing pain burst across the side of his neck. His mouth flooded with blood and his breath bubbled in the choking stream of it, and the ground was under his back and his eyes were filled with the brilliant sky, across which was printed the image of the sickle blade.

Like horns, he thought as he struggled to pull air into his drowning lungs – and he was a boy again, rolling away down the hill.

The sound of Lachlan's crazed voice rang in the splintered sunshine. "You killed me, Billy McGuire – you and your damned curse. You and your witching stone."

The words were swept from Billy's awareness by paralysing pain, and the fight to achieve one more breath was as hopeless as if he lay fathoms deep in the sea. With a soundless sob at the pity of it all, he gave way to darkness.

*

Now I know. Here among the quiet trees your pitiful shadow comes to me, your shocked pain at the loss of your fine self comes, oh, Billy, my dead love, and I cannot comfort you.

Your bravery is gone, your brown hair and your strong hands and your eyes as grey as the sea are gone, your dreams are one with all dreams and the light of your soul is in all light, your wild dreams no more than the seagull's cry or the drift of cloud. Be at peace, lovely Billy, and hush your lamenting. Do not weep for my weeping.

PART FIVE

I woke in broad daylight. The frost had gone, and a lemon-coloured sun hung in the mist above the pearly water, but it was still very cold. I ate the last of the bread, then tipped a little sugar into my hand and licked that up as well – and, for the first time, the child inside me gave a flicker of movement, as if it, too, had woken to cramped discomfort.

There must be no more hitch-hiking for me and my unborn baby; it was too dangerous. What was the hurry, anyway? I didn't even know where I was going. But it wasn't hurry that had made me hitch a lift – I mustn't deceive myself. This was the luck-seeking journey of a stray cat. Helensburgh, Ullapool – the names were no more real than the white moon of a saucer of milk descended from some kind hand. Lulling Ullapool, lullaby.

After a while, I walked across the wet, frost-melted grass to a public toilet that stood near an empty boating-pool. Wonderfully the gas heater over the wash-basin worked. Water that comes hot from a tap is a miracle once you have left the domestic comforts behind; it's like a little homecoming. The towel was hideously dirty, but after all, this was not home, it was an unknown town somewhere west of Dumbarton.

There were no road-signs or name-boards – they had all been taken down at the beginning of the war, lest they should be of assistance to enemy spies. I felt some sympathy for the spies, landed in a foreign country with nothing to guide them. But they would at least have studied maps and photographs – they would know where they were. What I needed was to meet a spy, who would tell me in a guttural accent what town this was.

I wandered along the broad street, looking idly in shop

windows. The smell of fresh bread made my mouth water, and I went into a baker's and bought a small loaf and two potato scones. Cheese would have been good, but my ration book was registered at the shop in Ayr, so it was useless. You had to apply for Emergency coupons if you were leaving your district, but I hadn't thought of that. I ate one of the scones and walked on.

The window of a china shop was full of fragile plates and figurines and milk-jugs, and I gazed at it in amusement. This was not a place that took air raids seriously. In London, the shop windows that remained intact contained nothing but dummy packets and faded advertisements – certainly nothing breakable or in any way valuable. And then I laughed. In the centre of the display was a fluted teapot which said, in a pattern of blue, twiggy letters, 'A Present From Helensburgh'.

There was a shiver in my spy's triumph. The pattern smiled, and in something more than the lettered china. A connection was being made. My grandfather might have stood on this spot, looking into this very window, when he came to see his sister, Jessie. Jessie herself could still be alive, one of these old ladies who passed on the pavement, tweed-skirted and in a hat with a pheasant's feather.

No. She was not here. If the pattern smiled, it also shook its head. Jessie was gone; this place was not my journey's end.

I shouldered my bag and walked on out of town. Birds cawed in the bare trees and the yellow sun shone across the river. Another strip of land came into sight on the far side of the water as the road curved to the right, and I thought I must be heading northward, no longer following the Clyde but a loch that ran inland from it. After a couple of hours, I came to where this loch ended in a wide semi-circle of reeds and mud, and saw that the road divided on the far side, either to return along the far bank or go on up the hill. A wooden bench stood invitingly at the water's edge, in just the right place to sit and gaze down the loch, and I ate my remaining potato scone there, and a rather withered apple I'd bought on the way out of the town, and hunks torn from the brown loaf.

The sun was almost at the hill's shoulder by the time I started out again. It was a long climb up towards the open moor, but before I had reached the top, a small black car overtook me, then stopped. A man called through the wound-down passenger window, "Can I offer you a lift?"

No lifts, never again. But when I drew level with the car, I saw that the face which peered up at me was pink and smiling – and it emerged, over several chins, from a dog-collar and a black suit. It would be rude to refuse – and perhaps stupid, too, because on this higher ground, patches of snow lay in hollows and rock-shadows, and the light was fading.

The Minister was not a good driver. The little car bucked and stalled as he tried to start it on the hill, and he tutted mildly and called it a dratted thing, though he seemed unsurprised by his difficulties. He got it going at last, in a cloud of exhaust smoke and a smell like something burning.

I sat beside him in a turmoil of religious embarrassment. Although he wasn't an actual priest, he was not just an ordinary human being. This was God's representative, albeit of a different sort, an examiner sent to scrutinise my dubious state of virtue. But he chatted pleasantly in the manner of a professional tea-party-goer, and his elderly, brown-mottled hands on the vibrating steering-wheel seemed unalarming. He had been to a very boring meeting in Glasgow, he said, which was lucky for me, wasn't it, there being so little traffic on the roads these days. Then he asked the inevitable question. "And where are you making for, my dear?"

"Wherever you're going, really. I'm just – travelling." I didn't want to tell him any lies.

"I could take you all the way to Inveraray." It sounded as remote as Iceland. "But if you were wanting dropped off in Craggans, for instance – "

"No, Inveraray will be fine." I wondered how far it was. He didn't seem like the kind of man who would drive all night. "If that's all right."

"Yes, indeed, quite all right."

I could think of nothing else to say. The silence between us became a little awkward, and he began to hum, pom-pomming gently. Nothing religious – it was the tune to which we used to sing at school, *Please refrain from urination While the train is in the station* . . . I looked out of the window and smothered a desire to giggle.

When he got to the end of the tune, he said, "I don't think I've seen you in Inveraray, have I?"

"No." But I had to add something. "I'm just – travelling," I said again.

"And very nice, too. Where are you from originally?"

I hesitated, then said, "London."

"Goodness. You'll find it very different here, then."

"Oh, yes."

He hummed a bit more, the Toreador's Song this time, "pom, pomty pom, pom, pomty-pomty-pom" – then said, "Staying with relatives?"

"Not exactly."

"Ah. I just meant – we all know each other, you see, in Inveraray."

"Yes. You can't in London, really. It's so big."

He talked about going to London as a young man and getting lost on the Underground. He was from St Andrews himself, did I know it? No, I didn't. He said I must go there some time – a charming place, and so many young people of course, with the University. That is, before the war. He had noticed my ring. And was my husband in the Forces?

"The RAF." It wasn't a lie, was it, if you just left a rather big thing out?

"The Lord bring him safely back to you."

I ducked my head, moved by his sudden, casual prayer, and he drove on in tactful silence. When he spoke again, it was about the places we were going through, comfortably impersonal. In the gathering darkness, we rounded another loch's end and climbed a further hill. Arrocher, he told me. The Rest and Be Thankful, and up there is the Cobbler. I didn't know then whether he was talking about places or pubs, or even people, but I was grateful for his chatter. Whoever he was, I am still grateful. Down to yet another loch we went, and along its edge and over a narrow humpbacked bridge, into a town that stood guard over the still water, its buildings strangely pale in the rising moon. The Minister turned right and stopped the car in a sloping street with shops on either side. "Inveraray," he announced. "Now, my dear, can I take you to your friends' house, or wherever you are staying?"

"No, honestly, that's fine. I'll enjoy the walk." I scrambled out. "You've been very kind."

"I could easily – "

"No, really. But thank you very much."

I walked away as if with purpose, and heard the little car start up the slope with some difficulty. I didn't look back. There might have been a bed for the night in some comfortable manse, but only at the cost of revealing myself to be what he would call a lost sheep. In fact, I thought as I walked down to the railings at the water's edge, I wasn't a sheep at all, but a goat. The woolly closeness of the flock was the worst threat with its safety and certainty bought at the cost of obedience. Rather than that, I would die as a goat does, with a ready giving-in on the wild hill, where chance is open and anything may happen.

It's easy to say these things, but my bold thoughts frightened me a little that evening. Standing by the dark water on the edge of a town that might have offered shelter, shivering after the warmth of the car, the uncertainty that lay ahead was hard to embrace with any confidence. My right knee had been sore all day from the panic-stricken tumble out of the lorry's cab, and I was very tired. With just a little more money in my pocket, I might have braved the other unknown and gone looking for a bed-and-breakfast place where I could stay the night, but as it was, no alternatives appeared to exist. I turned and walked on.

Quite soon, the road swung inland from the loch, and began to climb. I had wanted nothing but to sleep, so the extra effort was almost welcome, sending my blood faster round my body, warming me into a looser stride. Once, I saw deer, sharply black against the snow that lay between the trees, and they raised their antlered heads and looked at me, but did not move.

When the hill levelled out and the walking was easier, tiredness and hunger came sneaking back, and an ache spread from my belly to my legs and my lungs, and I knew I must stop for a while. I came to a tall stone that leaned at an angle from a frozen drift of snow, and trod my way across to lean my forehead against its cold, lichened surface. Then, as the moon sailed out from between the clouds, I saw that there was a sheltered gap between this stone and a neighbouring one behind it. There was no snow there, and no grass – just a hollow of dry shale. I crept into it and drew up my knees, with my head resting on my bag. In a moment, I thought, I would get out the small remains of the loaf and the sugar that was left in the jar . . . but a kind of warmth crept through me, making my fingers seem big and clumsy, as hard to move as the shapeless things of childhood illness, when the gas fire burned in the room and the fringes of the blue shawl cast barred shadows on the walls.

*

Lichen by my cheek, rougher than Jessie's fur. Anna Dubh lies curled within my arm, and the stars move above the tall head of the stone. Billy, your brother lives too far away; if I go on trying to reach him, I will die.

He hears me. Or perhaps it is my body, with its sparrow bones and belly full of eagle child, which brings this slackening and lets the moon-truth shine. My journey will not lead to Hugh McGuire.

This stone is shouldered like a warrior, watchful and withdrawn; it will take care of me. The dream slides in, my mother turning to smile with a spoon in her hand, the other one held below it to catch the drip of broth.

The smell of rain wakes me, although the moon still shines from a cloud's edge, pointing the stone's shadow up the hill, between the white birch trees. Follow this sign. I stand, lifting the bundle, and the cat and the goat get up and stretch.

The way is steep. As the first drops blow in the wind, Jessie leaps ahead of me and stands high – on what? She is a silver goat riding on darkness. Now the moon fades and she is gone. Six paces further, and I slide into a hole, landing on this soft rubble of flaked stone, with stone above me, the roof on which Jessie stood. It is dry in here, and almost warm. This is a home. The Old Ones welcome me. This, for a time, will be my journey's end.

*

I woke to a strange sense of calmness. The air was newly mild and damp, and the road gleamed between its tree shadows. I ate what was left of the loaf, sprinkled with a little sugar, then crept out from the stone's shelter and picked up my bag.

The moonlight faded and rain began to drift in the wind, but the slope was downward now, and I kept on, head bowed like an enduring horse. After another hour or so, the trees gave way to more open country, with hedges by the road's edge, or sometimes a stone wall. It was very dark now, but I smelt the dung of animals and the sweet scent of hay. I passed the gable end of a barn and came to a farm gate that stood open and, in a further building, there was a crack of light coming from a doorway, dazzling and extraordinary, as if the war and its blackout regulations didn't exist.

I trod my way across the puddled yard towards the light, no more able to resist it than is the silly moth that batters on an evening window-pane, and looked in through the half-open door of the byre. A brown-and-white cow was lurching to her feet from a bed of straw, and she turned to lick her new-born calf which lay sprawled and wet behind her. The light came from a Hurricane lamp hung from a nail on the wall, and a young man was crouched in the cow's shadow, carefully rubbing the calf with a sack. Then he looked up and saw me.

It was a strange moment, charged with pity. The lamp-lit face was a child's, with wide-spaced eyes and an innocent mouth that hung open with surprise. Although he was thick-set and strong, the young man gave a whimper of what sounded like fear. I kept very still, because I, too, was a little afraid, and we stared at each other. Then he put the sack down and got to his feet, talking in a formless, grunting language, pointing across the yard. Someone was there whom I should speak to. I nodded and stood back to let him come out of the byre, and he beckoned me to follow him, then ran clumsily ahead. There was a babble of explanation at the farmhouse door, a further beaming of lamplight, an indication that I should come in – and I was in a warm kitchen, where an old lady sat with a bandaged foot propped on a stool. "A visitor, Davey," she said. "Well, now, isn't that nice." But Davey's main concern was not for this rain-sodden girl. He explained proudly that the cow had calved, and the woman nodded and asked, "Is it a bull or a heifer?"

"Heh – "

"That's good. Give Betsy some hay, and make sure the

water-bucket is full. You know there'll be an after-birth, don't you? She'll most likely eat it – she usually does. It'll do her no harm."

"Aye." Davey nodded, frowning with concentration, then went out.

"You can see how it is with my son," the woman said. "But he's done well. I slipped on the ice yesterday and hurt my ankle, so I've not been able to help him. But what about you, my dear? Is it a night's rest you're wanting?"

I was suddenly unable to speak. I came towards her, fishing in my bag for the half-packet of tea and the almost empty sugar jar, and put the things in her hands. Then the last strength left me, and I was weeping in her lap, and her dry hand was on my hair as the priest's had been in blessing, all those years ago.

*

Jamie Tarbert was collecting wood for the fire. Moor-land was the worst place, he thought as he ranged through the heather and dry bracken. On the shore you could find driftwood and dried bracts of seaweed, and the forest was generous in its yield, but here, you could walk a long way and find very little. It had its compensations, though. The grassy site near the burn was a good one and the girls were away to a croft on the further hill to get straw for the night's bedding, and maybe some milk or eggs.

A mass of gorse bushes stood on the hillside above him, and Jamie climbed towards it. Sometimes there was broom growing among gorse, and that was the best wood of all for the baking of bannocks, leaving them clean of any resinous smell. The ground was treacherous here, deeply rutted with clefts between the reedy grass – an easy place in which to turn an ankle. When he was small, he had often slipped down into a runnel of water, or tripped over the strong growth of whin among the heather.

Nearing the bushes, Jamie glanced up – and in the next instant, his heart was pounding with terror. Curving horns had flashed against the sky from behind the dark mass of prickles. They were gone in a moment, then reared up again in a crazy, wagging dance. Oh, God, Jamie said silently. Oh, God, oh, God. Protect me. His throat was tight with fear and his palms sweated. The devilish thing was coming closer, crashing through the gorse towards him – and then Jamie laughed. It was nothing but a white goat. Seeing him, she again reared up on her hind legs, curving her neck in goatish greeting or warning so that her horns swung against the sky.

As his fright subsided, Jamie frowned in perplexity at the goat. This was a domestic animal, not one of the wild brown creatures which lived in their own way on the highest parts of the craggy hills. So what was she doing here at this time of the year? Herds of goats were always out for the summer grazing, with a lad or lassie to look after them and take them back for the nightly milking, but the days were short now, and the goats were kept in the byres and fed on hay.

There was, as he had hoped, broom among the gorse bushes, a long, twisted branch of it, already dead and easy to part from its root. Hauling it behind him, he went on up the hill in search of more. The goat ran ahead of him. He emerged into a clearing where ancient stones lay half-buried in the turf – and stopped. At the foot of a rowan tree, a girl sat huddled on the grass. Her face was hidden from him by her unkempt red hair and the dirty shawl she had pulled tight round her shoulders. A black cat lay in her lap. Jamie stared at her in silence. She was not a traveller, or at this time of day she would be busy with preparations for the night ahead. She had not even lit a fire. He noticed the thinness of the hand which lay across the cat's black fur, and backed away a little. Maybe she had come here to die, and he should not intrude. A strange sense of fatedness hung about her.

The goat again reared up, bending her head as if to butt him, and Jamie took a quick step back to avoid her horns. His incautious movement made the cat look up, and the girl opened her eyes and saw him. She scrambled to her feet as the cat leapt away, and her red hair blew wildly in the wind. Jamie stood very still, as he would in the presence of a wild thing, and saw how she searched the hill behind him as if in fear that he had brought others with him.

The goat, seeming to understand that her owner was now aware of the stranger's presence, went to the girl and lay down, folding first front legs then hind ones, and began to chew the cud with a rapid circling of her jaws as she surveyed Jamie through golden, square-pupilled eyes. Jamie wondered uneasily whether the girl was a witch and the two animals her familiars. He stared, and the girl returned his gaze. Her eyes were dark in her gaunt face, but she seemed as innocent as a deer, he thought. And she was young – barely older than himself.

"I mean you no harm," he ventured.

She made no reply, but pulled the shawl round her shoulders again and leaned back against the tree, every movement so slow that it spoke of a terrible exhaustion. And then Jamie understood, for he knew the weakness that is brought about by hunger. "My father snared two rabbits last night," he said. "There will be a stew in the pot. I think you should come with me."

The girl's eyes closed, and a tear came from under each eyelid and coursed slowly down her thin cheeks. Jamie shouldered his broom branch and held his hand out to her. She did not take it, but as he started down the hill, looking back constantly, she followed him.

As they neared the camp, Jamie called out a warning in the travellers' cant that he was bringing a stranger, and Liam looked up from the fire in surprise. He saw his son coming down the hill with a broom-branch over his shoulder, followed by a crazy procession – a ragged girl who tottered on her feet, then a white goat, and a small black cat with a tail that stuck straight up like a foxglove spike. He went to meet them, then stopped in his tracks as his heart thumped suddenly.

The girl put back a strand of red hair from her face and looked at him with a wondering frown.

"Can it be?" whispered Liam. "Mari Balfour?"

"And you are the tinker man."

Liam took her by both hands, then folded her to him. "Lassie, I have been looking for you everywhere."

Jamie turned in wonderment to his mother, who had got up from her cooking, and she took his hand although he was almost a grown man. Together, they heard Liam say, "Mari, I am your father."

In her turn, Margaret embraced the girl, who was now weeping helplessly. "There, my pet," she said, "you are home now. You are safe. Whatever we have is yours." Mari tried to speak, but Margaret, still holding her, stroked the tumbled red hair and said, "There's no need to explain, don't trouble yourself with trying. I know all about it."

To the bewildered Jamie, who had caught the glance that flashed between his parents, it sounded as if she spoke with a kind of triumph.

*

It was providence that sent me to the farm, Mrs Dunbar said, just on that day when she had broken her ankle. We didn't know it was broken at first, but the pain and swelling were so severe that at last she admitted that the doctor had better see it, and I got on her tall, old-fashioned bicycle and rode the two miles to the phone-box at the cross-roads.

Dr McNeish agreed to come. And then, taking a deep breath to try to still the churning in my stomach, I dialled my mother's number.

"*Mary!*"

Telephones are appallingly intimate. Her fury and relief sounded in my head as if her lips were at my ear. I could hear every gasped intake of breath.

"Where have you *been*? Where are you? Do you realise it was your grandmother's funeral yesterday? How do you suppose I felt, standing at her grave and wondering if you were dead as well? Do you know the police are looking for you?"

Guilt flooded through me. "I'm sorry – "

"I should think you *are* sorry! You could have left a note or something. When the man at the shoe shop said you weren't there any more, and the house all locked up – Mary, I . . ." She was crying.

"Mum, I really am sorry."

After a pause, she said, "Well, where are you?"

"I'm at this farm."

"What farm? Where?"

"It's near a place called Furnace."

"Up by Inveraray? But that's miles away! What are you doing there?"

"Working. I've learned how to milk cows." Davey had shown me. His stubby pink hands were very clear in their language.

"Cows!" my mother said with contempt. There was another pause, and then she said, "Mary, we can't go on like this."

"No."

"When are you coming home?"

I couldn't answer at first.

"Mary – did you hear me?"

"I don't want to come home."

The pips sounded, and I put some more money in. Perhaps it gave her time to think about whether she really wanted to have me back in Ayr, because when we were reconnected, she said, "We'll have to talk it over. I think Donald can get away at the weekend – there's a locum who comes in. We'd better drive up and see you."

I panicked. "Couldn't we – just write? I mean, before we do anything else."

"*Write.*" She let the word fall like a single drip into a bucketful of bitterness, then sighed. "You'd better give me your address, then."

The letter I received was full of reproach and disappointment. She asked how she had failed me, but I couldn't tell her. The affair with Donald before my father's death was almost irrelevant; and in any case, it was my behaviour we were talking about, not hers. There was a note from Donald as well, very practical. If I went to the Home and agreed that the baby would be adopted, he would meet the necessary expenses. And when "the whole sorry business" was over, if I wanted to go to Art School or any other form of further education, he would pay for that, too. But he would not support an illegitimate child.

I wrote back and said I was happy on the farm. It was an understatement. To sit with my head pressed into the hollow of a cow's flank, smelling the sweet smell of her skin and feeling the teats fatten and refatten under the pressure of my fingers was a deep pleasure. The cows were as individual as any human being and, after a while, so were the ewes that sheltered in the lee of the wall and even the chickens, crooning on the rafters of the byre when they went to roost and arguing a little about who perched where. I liked to think of them sleeping there with their heads under their wings as I slept in my little room, all of us sheltered by stone and slate and timber.

Mrs Dunbar's ankle healed slowly, but she said nothing about being able to manage without me. Donald sent some money, but she wouldn't accept any rent – she should be paying me for the work I did, she said, in the house and outside. Neither of us raised the question of where the baby would be born; she was incurious almost to the point of indifference, and although this was a relief, it gave me no hint of what she expected.

My mother wrote to say that Donald's sister had invited them to spend Christmas in Montrose, but she gathered there wasn't much room. She needn't have worried – I wanted nothing more than to stay on the farm. There was another reason, too, why the place had become so essential to my needs and dreams; I'd begun to paint again. It had seemed to be a small skill left behind at school, but the farm had so much to look at, such a rich patterning of roofs and sky, flapping rooks and bare trees and smoke rising, brown-dappled cows and turned furrows rolling like an earth wave behind the plough as Davey guided the big horse, Cruachan, across a winter field, that I could not help but notice it and want to set it down. So I'd caught the bus into Inveraray, ostensibly to buy some baby clothes and a smock to accommodate my growing girth, and bought a sketch-block and some watercolours. There had been a purse for my mother's Christmas present as well, and, on impulse, an old book for Donald, called *Travels of a Surgeon in the Highlands*. My gifts to Davey and Mrs Dunbar would be pictures of the farm.

And William, what of William? He would have received the white stone. Had he written back to Nana's address, my mother would have intercepted the letter and sent it on – I'd specially asked her to forward any mail. But there was nothing. I tried to look steadily at the possibility that he had been killed, and rejected it. The silence was not an emptiness – almost the reverse. A tangle of hope and pain came from him and, self-centredly, I thought he was in confusion about what to do. Sometimes it was such a sharp conflict that I would go about the slow work of the farm in an ache that seemed to come from the harshness of a larger decision, as if he was tempted to give up the struggle of living. Across the divide between us, I sent him simple words. Please, William, stay alive. I ask you nothing, only stay alive. For Christmas, I drew a circle on white paper, closely cross-hatching all round it so that it stood out from darkness, and carefully lettered underneath a Christmas wish and the address of the farm. There was no need to write my name – he would understand. If he was there to do so.

Davey crooned with delight over the picture I gave him, running his finger across the painted cows as if they were real. Mrs Dunbar propped her drawing of the house on the mantelpiece and said she would get a frame for it. She would treasure it always, she said. She gave me a long scarf, knitted in secret from many colours, and it must have been she who tied a bunch of dried lavender into a little sheaf, interlaced with ribbon, for Davey to offer me on Christmas morning.

A capacious red cardigan arrived from my mother, with a book on the Impressionists from Donald. The book wasn't new, because wartime regulations forbade the printing of such luxuries, but its opulent pages were a joy. At the last moment, I had included a small drawing of the farm in my parcel to them, and my mother's letter of thanks commented that the place looked very primitive. Or was that just the way I'd drawn it?

Had I not sent that sketch, everything would have been different. But then, no single element could have been discarded without wrecking the whole pattern, I see that now. Donald was concerned, my mother said, that I might not be getting proper medical care. Who was my GP? Was I attending an ante-natal clinic? What about supplementary rations? Orange juice and cod-liver oil were important, and I was entitled to extra milk.

Buckets of milk stood in the dairy for the cream to rise, and I smiled at the thought of an extra factory-bottled half-pint – but, oh – orange juice. My mouth filled with saliva at the thought. I had longed for citrus fruit throughout this pregnancy, and the autumn-stored apples which Mrs Dunbar brought down from their attic shelves, though welcome, were not the same thing.

I went to see Dr McNeish, who took my blood pressure then disappeared into his small laboratory with the urine sample he'd instructed me to bring. I heard water running as I lay obediently on his slippery leather couch, and wondered whether he'd poured my offering down the sink, but he came back and said that was fine. Then he rubbed his bony hands together like a conjuror and felt the baby's position, pressing and pushing. The child kicked in protest, and Dr McNeish said the pair of us were as strong as horses, and I could get my clothes on. He filled in an appointment card and handed it to me across his mahogany desk, then took his glasses off and asked, with an apologetic little cough, whether I intended to have the child adopted.

I muttered that I supposed so, and my face flamed with painful colour. Dr McNeish simply said I should let him know when I'd decided, and either way, he'd do his best to help. I didn't tell him about Donald's offer and stipulation; I was trying not to think about that. I don't make decisions, even to this day; I just wait for things to become clear. But at least I had settled my mother's worries. I wrote and told her so.

Coincidence nodded sagely. Yes, quite right, that's all part of the pattern. My mother's next letter revealed that Donald had trained with Dr McNeish's son, Hector. And Hector, having grown up in Inveraray, knew the area well. He even knew the farm, and my mother was appalled that I should even think of having a baby in such an insanitary place. No bathroom, no indoor toilet, not even hot water. (This wasn't true, there was a hot tap in the kitchen that ran off the range.) No electricity, no telephone. What if there was an emergency? It was all very well for Hector McNeish's father to go bumbling on in his old-fashioned way, but I should think of the child. A new-born baby must be somewhere warm and clean.

It was a shrewd attack. Although I didn't want to admit it, there had been times during these winter weeks when, making my way to the smelly outside toilet, I had longed for tiled surfaces that could be wiped clean, and for the fragrant steam of a bathroom. The farm, for all its beauty, was a hard place. Davey was kind and loving, but he killed as naturally as any wild creature. I was used to it, but I still felt a small pang of compassion for the rabbits he tossed on the kitchen table when he had done the round of his snares. Mrs Dunbar skinned and gutted them with the same practicality she would give to the peeling of vegetables, and I had seen her break a chicken's neck with a strong downward turn of the hand, again as dispassionately as if she was wringing out a wet sheet. It was the way things had to be. I myself had learned to pluck and draw a bird, and knew I would never again look in a butcher's window without knowing the realities that lay behind the neat display.

The farm had no pets. Kyle, the black-and-white sheepdog that was so often at Davey's heels, was never allowed in the house. He stayed in his kennel in the yard. And the lean cats that hunted in the fields and the byres kept well away from humans, perhaps knowing that any nest of kittens that was found would be destroyed in order to keep the numbers down. This harshness was something I had learned to accept, but the child within me kicked restlessly, as if determined to remind me that it had its own needs, which might be quite different from mine.

I found it hard to talk to Mrs Dunbar about my mother and Donald and their views on what I should do. It seemed like the breaking of an unspoken pact. She had never looked for confidences from me, and neither had she offered any of her own. I thought she must be a widow, but she had never said so. Her conversation was never about the past, though once she could ride her bicycle again, she came back from the village full of local news and gossip. This reticence about personal things seemed to suit her as well as it suited me; perhaps she, too, simply waited to see how things worked out.

My mother's next letter acted on the trace of unease I had betrayed. Enough of this head-in-the-sand stuff, she said – if I couldn't make a sensible decision, then she would. The Home had very kindly agreed to overlook the fact that the previous arrangement had been cancelled at short notice, and were prepared to take me as from next week. She and Donald would come for me on Sunday.

It took a lot of silent rehearsal before I could tell Mrs Dunbar, in a stumbling rush of past and present facts, what was happening. She listened patiently, and at the end, she said, "You must do what you think you have to, my dear."

Secretly I was disappointed. I knew that I'd been hoping she would dismiss my mother's plan and assure me that I must stay on the farm – but she didn't.

The black car came into the yard on Sunday morning, shiny and incongruous among the startled chickens. Davey stared at it, holding out his hand to feel the warmth that came from its bonnet, then crouching down to look at the wheels, laughing when he saw his distorted face reflected in the hub-caps. "You didn't tell me about *him*," my mother muttered in my ear as she picked her way across to the house.

I had said my goodbyes to the things I loved – to the moon-white milk in the buckets, to the snowdrops in the shelter of the wall and the tracery of bare branches against the sky, to the sweet-breathed cows and to Cruachan with his gentle strength and his grave face with the cocked ears. To Kyle and to the sheep, to the fields and the walls and the prickly gorse, to the willow by the burn and the clouds that came over the hill and sent their shadows in great looping shapes before them.

Donald looked at his watch. We had better not stay for a cup of tea, he said; it was a long drive, and he had a heavy day tomorrow. So Davey brought my bag out to the shiny car, then put his arms round me and moaned, and

Mrs Dunbar kissed me and said in that short private moment between us, "Mary, you can always come back." But it was too late.

PART SIX

My mother used to say that trees were wise. I did not understand but I smiled because I loved her. I thought she must be lonely, to make a friend of trees. Now, I see her meaning.

The winter is almost at an end. Soon we will be travelling again, the children say, but Liam, whom I cannot yet call father, says we will stay here until my child is born.

I come each day to look at you, beech tree. Your body is as smooth as the grey seal, your strength immense, to bear your crown of leaves against the sky.

All my rememberings are of event and movement. Of seeing and running, of meeting and talking and touching. Yours are very different, centred on the single strand of living in this place. Your mind is not apart, housed in a brain, but in your being. You do not have conjecture, unless it is of cold to come and the need to keep your buds tight-rolled, waiting for May. The fullness of your life is in the endless running-on of now and now and now.

Despite your rootedness, you are in movement. Water comes from the deep earth into you, up through your trunk and branches and your green leaves in the summer, out to the air and blowing wind, and then it falls as rain. Round and round it goes, and seeing this circling makes me know I am alive. Watching your movement lets me measure time.

Billy sees nothing now. He is a part of time itself, and can no longer stand outside to measure it. I think perhaps we all come from time's store, and living fixes us in this strange state called Now, until we are released by death. Dreams are a slipping of the shackle.

I dream for you, my child, in these last days while we are one.

In these last days.
Last days.
Take my dreams with you, little one, and use them well.

*

I didn't know we were going straight to the Home. Somehow I'd assumed that we'd go back to Ayr first. It was a stupid idea, I can see that now. From Donald's point of view, it made sense to get the whole thing done in one day – but at the time, it took my breath away to realise that I'd been committed without any discussion, as if I was a helpless lunatic.

We drove through the hills to Tarbet and then along Lomondside, so the route was unfamiliar until we reached Dumbarton, and then strange again as we drove through Glasgow and eastward to Edinburgh, and the country became flatter and colder.

At last the car stopped outside a large terraced house on the outskirts of the city, and I was escorted up the steps to the dim hall with its black-and-white tiled floor. My ration book was handed over to a woman in a tweed skirt who wrote down my details on a card and tucked it into a filing box, with a plump smile for my mother and Donald. When they had gone, she showed me the room I was to share with three other girls, then pointed out the bathroom at the end of the corridor and told me to take a bath. Yes, now, she added in response to my query. If she had meant some other time, she would have said so. Her smile did not reappear.

I was determined not to be dismayed. A bath would be a treat – nice warm bathroom, no carrying of water from the kitchen to the tin bath in front of the fire. But I was shown into a big, cold room where a bath stood with its head to the wall like a tethered horse, and the water that gushed from the brass tap was no more than tepid. The stoking of the boiler catered only for regulation bath-times, and this was not one of them.

Everything in the Home was regulated – not just for baths, but the whole conduct of the day. Every minute was accounted for, mostly by the preservation of a rigid standard of cleanliness. Except for the tiled hall, every floor was covered with brown linoleum that had to be scrubbed every day. It never dried completely from one scrubbing to the next, so the whole house smelt cold and soapy. The chipped paintwork was wiped daily, the windows cleaned and the wooden tables scoured with stiff brushes and Vim, the water well laced with bleach so that our hands were always red and stinging. We cleaned the insides of the steel teapots with wire wool until no traces of brown remained, and peeled countless potatoes with blunt knives. We washed sheets which were sometimes blood-soaked in the deep sinks and hung them up in the yard where wires for that purpose were stretched from one high wall to the other. In the afternoons there was an obligatory period of knitting small garments while one of us read aloud from an approved book. It was *Tess of the D'Urbervilles* when I first got there, which was a depressing experience.

The sense of loss was overwhelming. I had expected that I would miss the farm, but not that I would be imprisoned in an institution which locked out the lovely world and all its surprises – or so it seemed at the time. The Home was a conveyor-belt along which we moved to the end, each girl in her turn giving birth. After that event came the final punishment. The young mothers kept their babies for a week or two and were obliged to breast-feed them until the parting. On that day, the girl would feed her baby for the last time, change its nappy for the last time, dress it for the last time in the clothes she had knitted, the bootees with ribbon through the eyelets, the dress, the matinee jacket, the lace-patterned bonnet – the Home liked its babies to go out looking nice. Then Matron would come in and take the child away. For a few days afterwards, the girl would stay in the Home, swallowing the small stilboestrol pills that were supposed to suppress the milk, though we all saw how it stained the front of her clothes with its painful oozing. Then she left, nursing nothing but her secret.

The Home was so awful that my mind ducked away from its reality. There had for years been a hint of some other place, the Mari-world, as I now think of it, but it was not until those hard-pressed institutional days that it started to become clear and strong. Its wood-smoke and blowing rain offered no easiness, but they were filled with open possibility, and gave me a haven from the lino floors and the detailed regulation of the days.

In March, when daffodils bloomed in the single flower-bed, my pains began, running long fingers from belly to back in a grip like steel. The labour room with its high bed in the centre had a rack of obstetrical instruments in a glass case on the wall, much as a garage has spanners, and the surges of torment seemed to run along their cruel shapes, in and out of the serrated jaws of huge, long-armed forceps. I prayed that they would not be used on the baby which was being pressed towards its life, and when the time came, I pushed so hard that my flesh tore and the child burst out of me in a rapid slither to which there was no resistance. "A wee boy," the midwife said, snipping and knotting. Then she put him in my arms.

He was so beautiful. Not red and crumpled as I had expected, but smooth-skinned and strangely calm, with hair which, though still wet, was thick and fair. I had dreaded the moment of seeing him in case the face which looked up should be that of his father, the man I had not loved. But my baby, against all possible reason, looked exactly like William.

*

It was such a huge effort. Days and nights and days, trapped and struggling.

Now there are only dreams. I hear her cry sometimes, the child who was part of me. They put her in my arms. Feeling her small strength, I am happy. Oh, so happy.

Dreams. I am floating, a thing of air. It is very easy. Very light. To come back into soreness and the smell of my own blood is hard. I am so tired.

Voices.

They persist. The baby's name, they say. What shall it be? My lips are heavy weights. Great machines, remote from me, needing huge power to work them. When I have breathed some more, I will try.

"Agnes."

There. The word was perfect. A gift for my daughter.

She has my mother's name.

And her mother's life.

*

After my baby was born, I could no longer find my way into the Mari-world. It still existed – I had no doubt of that – but my dream-presence there had gone. There was no way into it now except through conscious imagining, and that was very different from the simple being-there which had seemed so effortless. I was shut out from that place, firmly returned to the dreadful Home, more alone than I had ever been – except for my baby son.

There was no decision to be made. Rather than let them take my William-child away, I would have died. My mother came to see me at the Home, and stared at her grandson with careful self-control. I knew she longed to pick him up, and her denial of it made the air between us ache with tension. She said briskly, "You'll have to give him a name, won't you. Or do they leave that to the adoptive parents?"

I told her he was called David William, and she said, "Why David?" She didn't query the William part – perhaps

Nana had told her more than I thought she knew. I shrugged and said, "Just because." Feeling vulnerable makes you cautious and I hadn't forgotten her dismissive comment when she saw Davey, with his shambling gait and wide-spaced eyes.

Caution is not a strong enough word. It was just plain cowardice that made me let my mother go without telling her that I was going to keep Billy. Instead, I sat down beside the sleeping child and wrote her a letter.

*

John Leddie frowned. A rabble of tinkers at his church door was an unseemly sight, disrespectful to the Lord whose proper observance demanded at least a modicum of decent clothing, unsullied by everyday use. He advanced towards the group suspiciously.

A man stepped forward and said without preliminary, "Could you baptise the bairn, sir? If it's no trouble to you."

There was something familiar about the face, Leddie thought. But then, these people all looked alike, dark and lean and uncouth. "What is your name?" he asked.

"Tarbert, sir. Liam Tarbert. You once read a letter for me."

The words brought sharp recall. It was as if the Minister stood again amid the jangling noise of the street fair, with the sickening, insidious smoke stinging his eyes and spreading the taste of burning flesh into his throat. The written lines had been firm and fluent, strangely arrogant in their demand that the writer should be believed innocent of witchcraft. Such confidence in a woman was its own condemnation, powered as it must be by unnatural forces. He made an involuntary gesture of rejection, as if again thrusting the letter from him.

"You remember it," said the tinker.

"Yes, I remember. Where is this child?" Leddie stared

with hostility at a girl who stood among her brothers and sisters, holding a baby of several months old. Surely she was too young to be a mother? One never knew. These people bred like rabbits, great colonies of them, increasing during the dark winter months so that there were ever more of them about the roads of Scotland. He frowned at the girl and her baby.

"No, sir," said the man, seeing the direction of the Minister's gaze. "That is my son, Hugh, who is already baptised. This is the child who is new-born."

A much older woman stepped forward and put her shawl aside from the tiny infant which lay hidden in her arms. Leddie stared at the small, tranquil face and frowned more deeply. Downy hair covered the baby's head, but it was not dark, like the rest of the tribe. Every strand of it shone like burnished copper.

"Are you the mother of this child?" he demanded sternly.

The woman lifted her chin and said, "No, sir."

"Then who is? Why is the mother not here?" Maybe the baby was stolen, Leddie thought. Tinkers were widely reputed to take children as they took everything else which was not carefully guarded or locked away – and this particular lot were doubly untrustworthy, touched as they were by the taint of witchcraft.

Liam said, "The mother is dead, sir. Poor lassie, the birth was a hard one, and she took the child-bed fever. We did everything we could. We even brought the doctor to her." The Minister grunted. This, at least, was something he could check. Ian Campbell, the surgeon, would be in church on Sunday. "So I am to bury the mother as well as baptise the child?" he suggested truculently. Why could these people never tell the truth?

Liam shook his head. "It has already been done, sir. We knew where she would want to lie."

Leddie felt a guilty sense of relief. He shrugged. Whoever

the girl had been, he thought, she was probably not fit to lie in consecrated ground. "What name is the child to have?" he asked.

"Agnes," said the woman.

"Agnes Tarbert?"

"No." She looked into his face boldly. "She is not a Tarbert. She must keep her mother's name. Agnes Balfour."

"*What*?" The signature on the letter he had read burned in the Minister's mind. Possibilities whirled. There had been mention of a daughter – had she been the mother of the red-haired child that was now presented to him? And if so, why were these tinkers in charge of it?

Liam was watching him shrewdly. "The bairn is our grandchild, sir," he said. "Her mother was my daughter."

Leddie took a step back as the facts fell into place. This man had lain with the witch. That was the reason for his interest in a letter he could not read. Satanism grinned nakedly through the tinker's narrowed, unsmiling eyes.

The woman said gently, "The child is innocent, sir. And we will be away from here tomorrow."

In the silence that followed her words, the Minister struggled with his conscience. There was nothing unusual in the request for baptism itself, for these people always insisted that their children were baptised, even if it was more as a Pagan token of good luck than a genuine desire for religious commitment. But witchcraft ran in the child's very veins. By accepting her into the Church, would he be condoning heresy rather than converting it?

The tinkers waited for his decision, their eyes unblinking. Leddie sighed, then turned to push open the heavy door behind him. "You had better come in," he said.

*

When I told the Matron I was going to keep Billy, she was less outraged than I had expected. She said of course that I was a stupid, ungrateful girl and would undoubtedly pay for my folly, but even as she spoke, she was leafing through her desk drawer, which seemed surprisingly untidy. Ah, yes, she said, finding the right piece of paper. Mr and Mrs Raymond – very nice people, they had taken girls from the Home before. They offered a live-in job at their hotel. Not much pay, but then, I would be getting my keep. And they didn't mind the baby, provided I understood that I could not be with it all the time.

Montrose House Hotel was oddly like the Home, except that it had carpets and shabbily grand hotel furniture. It was again in a terrace with steps up to the front door and a basement kitchen and scullery, and the dank, high-walled garden was, Mrs Raymond said, very nice in the summer. The hotel was out near Leith docks, and apart from a few elderly residents, it attracted mostly a passing trade. Due to an arrangement which the Raymonds had with certain taxi-drivers, there was a fairly constant stream of one-night people who had arrived at the docks and were going on elsewhere the next day. Most of them were servicemen.

The work was hard, because the majority of the beds had to be changed every day. I had a tiny attic room at the top of the house with a cot in it for Billy and a bed for me, a bent-wood chair and a black-painted chest of drawers, and Billy was supposed to stay there all the time except for the four-hourly feeds. From the basement kitchen where I prepared vegetables and did the endless washing, I could not hear him cry, though I listened in constant anxiety. The other servants liked to have the below-stairs radio on, and the Light Programme chatter and music added to the impossibility of knowing whether my baby was all right.

I didn't put up with it for very long. A flash of impatience made the situation seem stupid, and that afternoon, Janice, the chamber-maid, tripped on the trailing end of an armful of dirty sheets and fell headlong down the stairs, breaking her arm. As a result, Mrs Raymond said I had better take over Janice's job, and they would get someone in to help in the kitchen. I don't know what happened to Janice – I didn't see her again.

The new arrangement was much better. As I stripped beds and cleaned rooms, I could hear if a small wail came from above me, and run up the narrow stairs to pacify Billy or give him the feed he wanted. He was a greedy baby. As if suspecting that I was using a certain amount of her time for my own purposes, Mrs Raymond said I must take on the ironing as well, but I didn't mind. I carried the laundry up to my room and did it there. Billy liked that. He was such a joy to me, with his determined little fists waving in the air and the quickness of the change from crying to contented sucking when I fed him. I had no pram, but on my rare afternoons off I would carry him out for a walk, well wrapped against the wind that blew in across the North Sea. The big treat was to find a jumble sale in some church hall where I could buy him new clothes; he was growing fast.

Letters for the residents were put on the hall table, but any for the staff were stacked behind the tea caddy on the kitchen dresser. I looked there every morning. There was one from my mother, resigned rather than angry. Had I ever thought of anyone but myself? Perhaps she was right, but it didn't seem so at the time. Mrs Dunbar sent me a five-shilling postal order to buy something for the baby, and said she hoped she would see him one day. There was nothing from William. I had asked my mother whether there had been any letters for me at Nana's house, but she said there had not. For a moment, standing there on the steps of the Home, our eyes met. She said, "No news is good news," and gave a shrug of apology for the cliché. I shrugged as well, and said, "S'pose so." It was one of our closest moments. But from William, despite all my passionate wishing, there was only distance.

*

Margaret Tarbert leaned forward to stir the broth which simmered over the fire. Her movement did not disturb the baby she held to her breast, and the child continued to suck contentedly. It was a lucky thing, Margaret thought, as she had so often done in these last months, that she had always been blessed with an abundance of milk. Her own baby, Hugh, looked twice the size of this wee one as he lay asleep in his rush basket – but then, he was nine months old, beginning to be independent of his mother's breast. Margaret sat back, looking down at the child whose young mother lay in her grave at the foot of a beech tree which grew by a burn, many miles from here.

That death would haunt Margaret for the rest of her life. Mari had been so terribly aware of its coming, despite the high fever which sent her into periods of merciful delirium, when she babbled of circles and of water and of Billy McGuire, her true love, saying he was one with time. And then she would smile, and speak to her dead mother with gaiety. And all the while, even in the cruel time of full consciousness, her hand had stroked and stroked the black fur of Anna Dubh, for the cat had never left her until the thin body had at last shuddered into stillness.

At that moment, the cat had given a single wailing cry, and had run from the place, disappearing into the woods. They had not seen her for three days, until after the grave had been dug in the quiet spot where they knew Mari had gone so often in the last days of her waiting, when the family had paused in their travelling until the baby was born. Then Anna Dubh had returned, and Margaret had found her stretched in the basket beside the red-haired child, purring as the small fingers closed in her black fur.

Now, as the cat lay at Margaret's feet, her own belly moved gently with the unborn kittens within her. Liam would want to drown them as soon as they were born, Margaret knew, but she resolved privately to keep at least one for Anna Dubh to rear. Animals shared the same anguish of emptiness as a woman whose baby is lost, and felt the same pain of the unused milk.

There was also a superstitious feeling at the back of Margaret's mind that the cat should be treated with some respect. Something of Mari lingered about Anna Dubh, as it did about the gentle goat, whose yield of milk had improved as if in gratitude for the hay they bought her with their sales of tinware and clothes pegs or as part of the payment for a day's work.

The baby released the nipple with a small, contented sigh, and Margaret smiled as she pulled her clothing across her breast. "You'll be a bonny lassie, wee Agnes," she said to her. Then she leaned down again to put the last of the sticks on the fire, hoping that the children would soon be back from their foraging for fuel. It would not be so very long, she thought, before these babies would be running on the hill with the others. Time went so fast.

*

One Friday morning when Billy was two months old (time went so fast) I sang as I cleaned the first-floor bedrooms. There was nothing to explain the happiness – but then, there never is. When a marvellous event is about to occur, you get the joy and excitement of it first, without understanding why.

I went into the front bedroom, lugging the vacuum behind me. Sun shone through the tall sash windows and the room was faintly perfumed, a satin night-dress thrown across the turned-back sheets of one of the twin beds. Mrs Raymond didn't like wasting a double room on a solitary guest, but the rest of the hotel was full. She didn't like them lingering over their breakfast either, so this visitor would be doubly unpopular. We were supposed to have the rooms done by ten, so as to get on with the kitchen work. I folded the beautiful night-dress and laid it on top of the half-packed suitcase, then stripped the bed and remade it. I cleaned the wash-basin and bent down to empty the waste-paper basket that stood by the dressing-table, noticing with some amusement that, even for a one-night stay, this woman had set out her silver-backed brushes – and my heart almost stopped.

There, at the centre of the fan-pattern made by the two hair-brushes and the two clothes-brushes, lay the white stone. Blood thumped hard in my eyes, and for a moment, the sunshine darkened. My hand reached out as if it was someone else's and I watched it pick up the stone, and then, as the familiar weight and smoothness lay in my palm, giddiness swam over me, and I sat down on the green, flower-patterned carpet.

The door opened and a tall woman stood there, tucking a receipt into her handbag. She frowned when she saw me, and said, "Goodness. Are you all right?"

I started to get to my feet. She saw the stone in my hand, and I thought for a moment that she would ring the bell and summon Mrs Raymond, but her lined, sun-tanned face was not angry. She just said in mild reproof, "I would hate to lose it."

I put the stone back in its place, very carefully, then turned to face her. "You see," she went on, "it belonged to my son."

William's mother.

Belonged. Used to belong. She meant –

"No," I said. The word could hardly be heard, and I had to clear my throat and say it again. She was frowning. I didn't know where to start. "Are you – could you be Mrs McGuire?"

"That's right. It's in the visitors' book."

"I hadn't looked. It's just – when I saw the stone – do you have a son called William?"

She didn't answer directly, though there was a quick, involuntary movement of her hands and a small sound as if of pain. Then she said, "You must be Mary. If you know about the stone."

"Yes." William and Mary, king and queen. I'd never seen us that way before.

"You lived in Ayr. With your grandmother."

"Yes."

"He talked about you so much." She sat down on the new-made bed, feeling with her hand for its surface behind her, still staring at me. Her eyes were suddenly bright with tears. "You know – what happened?"

I shook my head. She put out her hand, gently bringing me to sit beside her. "Mary, dear, William's plane was shot down over Germany last November."

While I was walking in the snow. William, is it warm in an aeroplane. And he had smiled.

"His Squadron Leader sent me a letter – as well as the one from the War Office, I mean. Poor young man, it must be terrible to have to send out these letters. He knew William had been posted Missing, Believed Killed, but it would be a mistake to go on hoping, he said. It just made the grieving worse. He'd seen the plane go down. It was burning." She paused, gathering control. "So brave of him to tell me. So kind. And he sent me the white stone and a few other things. There wasn't much."

A blue handkerchief, RAF issue, a crumpled message. A Christmas card, perhaps, though he would never have seen it. She was talking again. "My husband died last summer, you see. We were out in India."

I nodded. An India boy, Nana had said. Tears were pricking at the back of my eyes, and my throat ached. But he couldn't be dead, he couldn't be.

"So after this happened, there was no point in staying on. Things are changing. When the war is over, they'll want self-government. They think it will be wonderful, but I can see the place will be torn apart, Hindu and Muslim, at each other's throats. So I decided to come home. My ship docked yesterday."

Sitting beside her on the peach-coloured eiderdown that I had smoothed in a different world, I gripped my hands together, thinking of what I had to tell this woman who was William's mother. Mrs McGuire, I betrayed your son. She, loving him with the same fierce love I had for Billy, would never forgive me. I wanted a few more moments of her kindness, before it all had to be spoiled. Seconds went by. Then I took a deep breath and said, "There's something – " But the tears overwhelmed me.

She gave me a folded handkerchief, unsurprised. "You became pregnant, didn't you. William told me. It was the last letter I had from him. He was very upset, but I think he understood." After a pause, she went steadily on, "Did you have the baby?"

I nodded.

"And was it adopted?"

"No. It – he's here. That's why I got this job. Living-in."

"And what's his name?"

I had a long struggle with my constricted throat and quivering lips before I could answer that question. At last I managed to frame the word. "Billy."

"Oh, my dear."

I turned to her then, and she put her arms round me. Neither of us moved when my name was called from the corridor. There was a tap at the door and Mrs Raymond looked in. "Excuse me – "

"Not just now," said William's mother firmly. And, after a stunned pause, the door was shut again.

*

Mrs Raymond had to wait a long time for me that morning. When at last I came down to the basement kitchen, she was very angry. I was paid to *work* in this place, she said, not to go tattling to the guests. There were plenty more girls who would be glad to have my job, I needn't think I couldn't be replaced. And in any case it was time I thought about moving on, she added. When my illegitimate brat started running about, it was no use imagining I could go on working here. This was not a crêche.

I ended up cleaning the silver on what should have been my afternoon off, but I didn't mind – there were such wonderful things to think about. Again and again the extraordinary meeting replayed itself in my startled memory, together with Mrs McGuire's questions about William's uncle and aunt in Kirkcudbright. "My husband's side of the family," she had said. "His sister married Bernard Naismith – a wholesale butcher, very successful, very rich. Such funny people, the McGuires, either dreamy and impetuous or real go-getters." She had wanted to know my plans. I hadn't any, of course, except that I knew I couldn't stay at the hotel much longer. I'd really like to paint, I said, but that wasn't practical. Maybe I could work in a school kitchen so as to fit in with Billy once he was old enough to go to nursery school. And then William's mother had taken thirty pounds from her bag, folded the notes and put them in my hand. For paint and canvases, she said – whatever I needed. And it was not to be spent on the baby.

The six big white five-pound notes added up to more money than I had ever had in my life. While I was still trying to find the words to thank her, Mrs McGuire noted down the address of her sister Frances, with whom she would be staying until she bought a house of her own. Almost without surprise, I saw that Frances lived in Ullapool. "We'll be in touch," William's mother said – but of course, we always had been.

*

"I heard a strange thing today," said Liam.

"What was that?" Margaret looked at her husband across the dying glow of the fire. Above them, an owl hooted in the clear autumn evening, and another answered.

"Hugh McGuire died on the same day that Mari did. And at the same time, in the late afternoon. He stood up from his chair, they say, and his legs went from under him and he died without a sound. But his face was blue and his eyes were wide open."

"So they think Mari killed him?" Margaret shook her head, answering her own question. "They'll not know of her death, or they would. As it is – "

"As it is, they blame an old wife who stays nearby," Liam said. "She talks to herself and lets the wild birds fly in and out of her house, so she is their witch now."

Margaret threw a handful of sticks on the embers and drew her shawl round her shoulders as the small flames licked up. "Mari kept Hugh McGuire alive," she said broodingly. "A man as bad as that needs time to live out his own punishment."

"He was not such a bad man," Liam said fairly. "Just mistaken and afraid. And anyway," he added, "his wife will have needed him. Any man is better than none."

"No," said Margaret, and looked at Liam with eyes half-shut against a puff of wood-smoke. "The needing of a man is one thing. But the liking of him is quite another." And she laughed as her husband got to his feet and came round the fire towards her.

PART SEVEN

I went back to the farm.

The money William's mother had given me made it so easy. A bus ticket, a second-hand push-chair, art materials – they were all suddenly accessible. The return seemed triumphant. Davey was deeply fascinated by Billy, and spent hours playing careful games involving the offering of fingers and wordless rhymes and ticklings which amused the grown-up boy as much as the little one. And Mrs Dunbar said she'd missed me. Because of the days that had gone by before she had any treatment for her broken ankle, it had set into lumpy awkwardness, and she was cross with herself for finding the work of the farm and house so much harder than it used to be. I made her accept some of the heaven-sent money, though the hugeness of it seemed much less now. I was dismayed by its transience. Very quickly, I didn't feel rich any longer.

There's a skill to living without money, but it's tiring. If it goes on too long, an anaemia of the spirit sets in, and even the free beauty of natural things is deprived of joy. Towards the end of that summer, when the warmth faded and the nights were longer, I began to envy the swallows that twittered on the roof of the byre in preparation for their long journey. Going away is such a simple answer to anxieties – one simply hands them over to chance. But I was never alone now, with Billy's growing dependence on me for amusement and learning as well as for routine food and comfort. There could be no flight to the accommodating unknown.

Mrs Dunbar said one day, with a trace of severity, that it was high time I found a buyer for some of my paintings. There was no point in doing them if they were just to stand in my bedroom with their faces to the wall – and how was I to buy any more materials if I didn't sell something? She was right. I'd already run out of white and yellow ochre. But I hadn't thought anyone would buy my pictures – they were too odd and topsy-turvy. Childish, some might say. I'd never understood Miss Dean's lessons about perspective, with rows of telegraph poles going along in a straight road to the horizon. I hated the flat empty landscape in which they stood, and turned my poles into strange flowers with lots of exotic petals. She never seemed to mind. It was the patterning of things that fascinated me, and the pictures in my bedroom were a patchwork of slate roofs and stone walls, clouds and daisies and sheep and the stars of night-time. I put Mrs Dunbar in, too, with the stick she leaned on now, and sometimes Billy and I would be sleeping in a bed that floated through a dream sky and met an aeroplane that had fire coming from it, but only a small, harmless fire like the flame of a candle.

I wrapped up some pictures in newspaper and string and got on the bus to Inveraray, leaving Billy with Mrs Dunbar. Despite the weight of the bulky parcel, it was an amazing liberation to have both hands available, and to walk upright instead of leaning out from the living weight on the hip. Even to gaze about me without referring back to the small presence which watched and wanted was wonderfully restful. I felt faintly guilty about enjoying it so much, and took refuge in remembering that this was a business trip, undertaken for Billy's sake as well as my own.

In Inveraray, I went from shop to shop, pushing past the lengths of tweed and tartan rugs that hung at the door, putting my untidy parcel down on glass counters above displays of Royal Stewart shopping lists and stag-horn eggspoons and paper-knives with amber handles. The first man was the worst. He gave a short laugh when he saw my work, and said his six-year-old could do better. There were a lot of water-colour views on the wall behind him, and a notice that said Commissions Undertaken. The next people were less rude, but the answer was the same. Everywhere, I got the amused glance and the shake of the head. One woman found a used envelope and drew the telegraph-poles diagram for me, explaining that things should get smaller as they got further away. I wrapped my pictures up in their disintegrating newspaper and went out onto the sloping pavement that didn't fit the diagram at all. That was the last shop. I'd failed.

I walked on up the street, past the spot where the pink-faced Minister had left me on that cold night, round the corner, skirting the church to where the houses and shops were smaller. No tweed hung at the doorways here. I passed a junk shop – then stopped. I don't know why I was so sure. The place looked utterly unpromising, with a pile of stuff outside – a wash-stand with an electric fire on top, a bird-cage, a bust of some Roman in a laurel wreath, a hat-stand. I pushed the door open and went in. It was darkish, shelved from floor to ceiling with books, piled with furniture and jugs and cardboard boxes containing china and old mincers. There were some paintings too, mostly very old and in heavy frames, depicting Highland cattle or stormy glens, or sometimes both together. A woman was buying a toast-rack, and when she had gone out, the shop-keeper looked over his glasses at my parcel and said, "Pictures."

"Yes."

He propped them up wherever there was a ledge or a space, then stood and looked at them, with his hands in his cardigan pockets. "Did you paint these?" he asked.

"Yes."

He looked some more, then shouted, "Joan!"

A woman came out of the back room with her finger in a book and some shapeless grey knitting clutched to her chest.

"Put all that down and look at these," the man ordered. "What do you think?" She, too, regarded me over the top of her spectacles, then she turned her attention to the pictures. She took her time about it. The pair exchanged considered nods, then the woman said, "Very nice. But there's no' just an awfu' big demand for modern art in Inveraray."

"I've noticed," I said.

They were still looking at each other, coming to an unspoken decision. "We'll put your pictures up for you, my dear," the man said.

"And let you know if we sell one." His wife, or sister or whoever she was, finished his sentence for him. "Is that all right?"

I said it was all right. As I went out, the woman was carefully winding the string from the pictures round her fingers.

*

At a few months old, Agnes learned that selling was important. As she grew big enough to look over Margaret's shoulder from the shawl that bound her close, she saw that there was often a person standing in a doorway, and the importance was there, in the space between them and this person. Mostly, there would be a shake of the head and a closing of the door, and the walking would go on, but sometimes, things were given and received, and the strong back which carried her had a feeling of excitement.

The boys Agnes thought of as her elder brothers did not help in the selling. They would whittle pegs and give a hand to bend and tie the willow to make an overnight shelter, but the game of persuading money to slip from palm to palm did not excite them. Agnes, growing older, was fascinated by this test of how much effect one person can have on another. It was a kind of power. She began to give her smile straight to the eyes of the housewife who stood at the door, and felt how the space across which the smile travelled could soften. Sometimes, a coin would be put in her hand.

*

Mrs Dunbar was indignant on my behalf when I came back without having made a sale. People didn't know what they were missing, she said. But a few days later, a man drove into the yard in a long, dark green car – and all the pictures I had left in the junk-shop were on the back seat. He was very thin, with a sweet, goofy smile and wispy hair, and his name was Martin Fisher. Even at that time, arty people would have heard of him, but I hadn't, of course. He had come to visit his mother in Inveraray, but he ran an art gallery in Glasgow, and he wanted to put on an exhibition of my work. He said I was a Genuine Primitive.

Mrs Dunbar took offence at the description. "She's no more primitive than you are, my fine mannie," she told him, and he laughed. That was the nice thing about Martin, the way he would always laugh. He explained that it just meant somebody who painted entirely in their own way, without what he called "art-schooliness," and I was glad about that, because I hadn't understood him either. So he was invited in for tea, and was very complimentary about the plum jam and the baking, and Mrs Dunbar of course apologised for it being a poor offering because we'd not been expecting a guest. Apart from that, she didn't talk much, just watched and listened as he outlined his plans. I'd need a year to get the stuff together, he said, so we'd aim at an exhibition next December – ideal for the Christmas market. Oh, and he had given the shopkeeper a hundred and eighty pounds for the pictures he'd bought, so that's what they owed me, less commission. And I shouldn't pay them more than ten per cent.

I was staggered. It was so much money that I could hardly meet Mrs Dunbar's eye – but she was looking at

Martin with a farmer's shrewdness. "You'll be making a penny or two out of that," she said, and he laughed, unabashed, and said he hoped so.

Winter went by and gave way to spring, and I worked for long hours on my paintings. Billy spent more and more time with Davey or Mrs Dunbar, though I was with him at his waking and sleeping and every mealtime. I was too engrossed to miss his company except at odd moments when I heard his babbling conversations drift in from the yard – and he, muddy and happy, showed no sign of missing me. Martin dropped in occasionally, to see how I was getting on. He loved the dreaming picures with the bed in the sky. Very real, he said; life is nothing but a consensus of our dreams. He was very clever, Martin. When the summer was over and the fat lambs went away to market, he asked me for a list of people to invite to the Private View.

It was then that I realised how few friends I had. Nobody from my school days, if that's what those truant, wandering months could be called; nobody from the Home, no family. I wrote down Dr and Mrs Donald Fraser, then crossed it out. I wanted my mother and Donald to see the pictures, but to meet them for the first time in nearly two years at such a public, formal event was more than I could cope with. So my list was a short one – Davey and Mrs Dunbar, Dr McNeish because I liked him, and William's mother.

I had written to Helen McGuire, and she had answered eventually from her new house in Ullapool, saying she knew Inveraray well, and hoped I would be happy at the farm, but there had been silence after that, and she seemed to have joined William's remoteness. She would be busy, I thought, with furniture and carpets and the arranging of her silver-backed hairbrushes. But she sent a card to say she would be delighted to attend the Private View.

Dr McNeish offered to take us all in his car, and his wife

said she would baby-sit for Billy. We set out after the evening milking. I was wearing a long black skirt and a ruffled blouse which Mrs Dunbar had unexpectedly produced from a mothball-scented wardrobe, and she was in a silky dress and – astonishingly – high heels. We got slightly lost in Glasgow, because Dr McNeish said it had all changed since he was there last, so there were quite a lot of people in the gallery by the time we arrived. I didn't know any of them. Martin was beaming, because seven paintings had already been sold. The feeling of being separate came over me, as if I stood and watched myself smile and heard myself speak. Helen McGuire was not there, and I kept looking at the door, wanting to see her come in.

Davey was having a great time. He crowed with delight over the things he recognised, stroking the cows and Cruachan and the buildings with his stubby fingers. People frowned a little and moved away from him, and I took his hand. Then William's mother was across the room, and she waved in greeting. She began to make her way through the crowd. Mrs Dunbar was at my side, and I turned to her to introduce this woman whom I had so magically met – and she saw Helen McGuire and gasped. Helen, too, put a hand to her mouth, and Davey began to wail loudly in the sudden tension. Martin was at my side quickly, suggesting that we might like to move into his office.

It was no more than a cubby-hole, the floor-space so taken up with leaning canvases and portfolios that we were crammed into a close group beside Martin's untidy desk. Mrs Dunbar and William's mother both tried to speak, and then they were in each other's arms, laughing and weeping. I kept hold of Davey's hand as he moaned excitedly and tried to join them.

"But where did you *go*?" William's mother was asking. "Why didn't you get in touch with us?"

Mrs Dunbar shook her head, blotting her eyes with her handkerchief. "Helen, I did try, my dear. Heaven knows, I tried. I left that letter for you, but your father sent it back. It was all crumpled – I could see it had been read. But he said you and Frances would never forgive me. He'd asked you to write, he said, but you'd refused."

"We never had a letter." Helen McGuire's face was anguished. "We talked about it so often, Frances and I – we never understood what happened. Father just said you'd gone away."

Martin cleared his throat with a trace of embarrassment, and Mrs Dunbar said, "I'm so sorry, you'll think this is very strange. But you see – Helen is my daughter."

Yes. Of course. In the continuing remoteness, I wondered why I hadn't seen it before. The two of them were of the same spirit.

Martin gave a little tug at his embroidered waistcoat and said, "Well, I'm glad it's nothing serious," and then looked embarrassed again when we all laughed. Davey laughed, too, and bounced up and down, and Mrs Dunbar put her arm round his shoulders.

"Helen," she said, "this is Davey. Your half-brother."

That was a bad moment. After a barely perceptible pause, Helen said, "Nice to meet you, Davey." She put out her hand to him, but without deciding whether to try and shake hands or pat his arm, so the gesture was clumsy, more a poke than a greeting.

Martin went back to his guests. I wondered whether I should go, too, but Davey had a tight hold of my hand again, staring from face to face in confusion, and I didn't feel I could leave him. The two women were full of urgent questions.

"But where did you go?" Helen asked again. "We tried to get Mrs Marr to tell us – d'you remember Mrs Marr, the housekeeper? We never liked her much. But she just said you were staying with a friend. Father wouldn't say anything at all, then when we pestered him, he got angry, you know how he was. He shouted at us that you'd run away with another man. And he supposed we'd go and blab it to the whole world, he said. We didn't, of course, we never said a word, we felt so awful."

"You poor wee things. Helen, listen – "

But Helen wasn't ready to stop. "He sent us off to boarding-school, you know. Very quickly. He didn't even wait for the begining of a new term. Mrs Marr seemed to be packing our things the very next day, though I don't suppose it was. I didn't want to go, I was fifteen, I said I could leave school – but he wouldn't hear of it. Then I trained to be a nanny. That's how I met my husband. He was out in India, and his wife had died, and there was an Ayah, but he wanted his children to be with somebody British. He said he wouldn't have them growing up speaking Kitchen Hindi. He was very kind. Much older than me, but I felt sort of safe with him. Poor Peter. He died two years ago."

"Mary told me." Mrs Dunbar was quicker to grasp it than I was. Irrationally, I still grappled with the thought that I must have told her all this as well, that she should have recognised who Helen was. Everything fitted except the surname – she hadn't known her daughter's married name. "And about your son," she said. "William. My dear, I'm so sorry."

Helen nodded, and her mouth trembled a little. She and I did not look at each other. But there was something else that Mrs Dunbar had to ask. "Helen, what about your father? You said 'How he was'. Is he – "

"Of course, you don't know. He died four years ago. A stroke." She looked anxiously at her mother. "They said he didn't suffer."

Mrs Dunbar gave a little sigh. "So much to take in," she said. "So much to tell you, Helen."

But William's mother had recovered from the torrent of words that had swept her along in the first shocked minutes. "Later," she said. And with another touch of hands and an exchange of smiles, we went back into the gallery.

*

"Where is my mother?" Agnes asked.

"She is dead, my darling. She died when you were born."

"Why did she?"

"Because she was very ill."

"Can she see me?"

Margaret paused in her cutting-up of potatoes and dropping them into the pot beside her on the grass. "Maybe," she said.

"I think she can." And Agnes scanned the winter sky that was so clear between the twigs of winter trees, although the sun had gone.

*

Helen came back to the farm that night, cancelling her planned stay at a Glasgow hotel. There was quiet in the car as she and Davey and I sat close together on the back seat. The road ahead gleamed fitfully in the light of a full moon. I felt that Dr McNeish had not had much of an evening, but he'd said he enjoyed it – and I found out afterwards that he'd bought the painting of Davey and Cruachan.

In his own little room upstairs, Billy was sleeping peacefully, his fist crammed against the side of his face. Mrs McNeish said he had not woken, but he stirred as the sound of voices drifted up the stairs, and muttered something, though his eyes were still shut. I heard Helen come into the room behind me, and stood back to let her see the sleeping child. She stooped and looked at him steadily. When she straightened up, her smile was a little tremulous. We left the room quietly, and closed the door, and at the top of the stairs, she murmured, "It really is astonishing. He's so much like – our family."

So much like William.

It was true, and yet it brought me no comfort. Helen's

family was not mine, and never would be. Billy and I were impostors.

The talk round the kitchen table went on late that night, long after Dr McNeish and his wife had gone home. Davey became sleepy and went obediently off to bed when Mrs Dunbar suggested it, and then the deeper hurts and memories began to be pieced together. Helen recalled a Sunday lunch-time after her mother had left home.

"There was roast lamb," she said. "Father was called from his study to come to the table. He'd been in there for days, drinking whisky, talking to himself. The whole house smelt of whisky. It frightened us, hearing him through the door, his voice going on and on, and nobody else there. Anyway, he started to carve the meat, but his hands were shaking and the knife slipped. It clattered onto the plate. He didn't say anything, just sat back in his chair with one hand gripped inside the other. The blood was welling up between his fingers. Then he started to cry. He made this awful noise, like a child. I didn't know men could cry. Mrs Marr wrapped a table napkin round his hand and told me to phone the doctor, then she took him out to the kitchen."

Mrs Dunbar said, "Poor Harry." And there was a long pause. Neither Helen nor I spoke. We knew by now that she had run away with Angus Dunbar, but it was not for us to probe into the reasons. "He was so angry," she said, and leaned her head on her hand, pressing a bread-crumb absently with her finger, not looking at us.

"What was he angry about?" asked Helen gently. And it was then that Mrs Dunbar looked up, her face painfully red. "You've a right to know," she said. "I was expecting a baby – and it wasn't Harry's. He knew it couldn't be. We'd not been – close, you see, not for a long time. And someone had told him about me and Angus. I thought he was going to kill me."

"Davey." I hadn't meant to speak aloud, but the jigsaw piece fitted so neatly and meant so much.

"Yes, Davey. Such a disappointment to Angus, the way Davey was." She still managed not to cry. "Angus and I had been childhood sweethearts, it wasn't as if I was just having an affair. Harry knew about that, he knew my parents wanted a better match for me than a poor crofter. He'd given me the big house and the servants – he even loved me, in his way. But there was a cruel side to him. We used to buy in hay and oats for the carriage horses, you see, and when he heard that Angus Dunbar was cheaper, he had him bring the feed to the house. And it was my job to check the sacks in. He made me go down to the stables, mistress of the house. The stupid man." And she did cry then, with her hand over her face and a slow turning of her head from side to side. Helen reached out and put her hand on her mother's arm, and the touch seemed to sweep away the last restriction. The words came tumbling out, telling how she had run out into the lane on that desperate, violent night and was overtaken by Angus Dunbar driving his horse and trap back from a cousin's wedding twenty miles away, how he had wanted to go up to the house and have it out with Harry when he saw her cut and bruised face; how she stayed with Angus that night, and never went back.

"So there must have been a divorce," Helen said. "Father never told us."

Mrs Dunbar shook her head. "He wouldn't hear of it. Angus and I never married. People here know, of course, but they're used to it now." She put her hand over mine. "I'm sorry, Mary, I should have told you. It's silly, isn't it, keeping these old secrets."

I shook my head. They were so hard to tell. I got up and put the kettle on the hob in the new easiness between us, and we had more tea and made toast and ate it spread with dripping, well salted.

"Father took up with Mrs Marr, you know," said Helen, "after we moved to Ullapool. Very discreetly, of course, but we knew, Frances and I. We'd hear him going to her room." One more painful question remained to be asked. "I don't see why – forgive me, perhaps this is none of my business – why Father wasn't prepared to accept the baby as his. Being such a one for the keeping up of appearances."

"Oh, he wanted to, right enough," said Mrs Dunbar. "That was the cause of our quarrel." Her chin lifted a little, and I saw how beautiful she must have been, and how proud. "I'd not pass off one man's child as another's."

There was no hint that the words were meant for me, and I am sure they were not. But in that moment, I knew with appalling clarity that William would return, and that he would ask me to pass off another man's child as his. And I would agree.

*

Agnes stumbled through the heather, trying to keep up with Hugh. The older children were well ahead of them, making for the trees that grew higher on the hillside. Some of them already carried bundles of firewood.

Ian and Annie were climbing over an ivy-hidden wall. They disappeared into the mass of leaves and cherry blossom on the far side, and Agnes heard their voices, as sharp as bird-cries in the clear air. "Look!" "There's an old house!" Brigid scrambled after them, and then Hugh. Agnes was used to being the last. She clambered from stone to stone without real hurry, and paused as she reached the top and looked over. The turf roof of the house had fallen in, and ferns grew in the crevices of its walls. A rotting door leaned open in the dark space of the doorway, half-hidden by bramble and long grass, and jackdaws flew up from the exposed beams. "Clack!" they called, as if scolding the intruders. "Clack! Clack!"

Ian emerged from the house with the broken leg of a stool in his hand, which he held before him to push aside the leaning nettles. "There's a table in there," he said, "but we'd need an axe."

Agnes did not move. Sitting on the wall, she felt the warmth of the stone under her legs. Two white butterflies tumbled in a lazy dance above the tangle of leaves, and the sun beat down on her upturned face, its dazzle broken by the blossom of the cherry tree. With sudden intensity, she knew she would remember this moment for ever.

"What are you smiling at?" Ian asked.

"Nothing."

But he stared at her for a few moments longer, perplexed by the radiance of her face, and by the way the edges of her red hair seemed fire-touched by the sun. "You can carry this," he said, reaching up to hand her the stool-leg with a touch of disapproval. There was something uncanny about such joy.

Liam Tarbert climbed quickly up the stones behind Agnes, looking to see what his children were up to. When they saw his face, they felt impelled to defend themselves, though for no clear reason. "There's nobody staying here," Ian said. "It's all falling down."

Liam did not smile. "So it may be," he said. "But somebody stayed here once." He looked at Agnes, and saw the stool-leg which she held in her lap. "You've been in the house."

"No," said Agnes truthfully. "Ian gave it to me."

Liam turned to his son, and saw his own frown reflected in the boy's puzzled face. "It's only firewood," Ian said.

"You must look for firewood somewhere else," Liam told him. "Not here."

"Why?" asked Brigid.

"It's a long story."

"Will you tell us?" They were always eager for a story.

"Aye, tonight I'll tell you. But away you go now, all of you. Agnes, you stay here a wee minute."

When the other children had gone, Liam lifted his granddaughter down from the wall and set her astride his hip, then carried her into the cottage, edging carefully through the narrow space and being careful to keep the child's bare legs clear of the pointed nettle-leaves. In the grass-grown interior where the sun sparkled through the holes in the roof, he set Agnes on her feet and took the leg of the stool gently from her hand, laying it down beside some shards of pottery half-buried in the earth floor. He stared round the derelict room. A disintegrating table stood by the wall, and a broken pot projected from a clump of fireweed growing in the blackened hearth. Another woman with hair as red as that of the puzzled child who stood beside him had turned from the fire once, and smiled. And more than that.

"Your mother was born in this house," he said.

"Was she?" Agnes looked round with concern, wrinkling her nose at the smell of rottenness. "It's no' very nice."

"It was nice enough once." Warm, it had been, and fragrant with the scent of the herbs that lay spread on the table to dry. And good broth in the pot. Liam closed his eyes. The hand that had ladled it into a bowl for him had been slim and strong, even though the thumb of it ended in a malformed pinkness of shiny skin. Dear God, the cruelty of people.

Agnes watched him, and was quiet.

Liam took a deep breath, straightening his shoulders. "I would burn it all," he said. "Leave the place clean. But that is not the house-dwellers' way. We must let it have its own burial."

Outside, he heaved the door from where it was rotting into the grass and wedged it roughly into place, then took his granddaughter's hand. The child stopped and stared up into the mass of cherry blossom. "Is this my mother's tree?" she asked.

"Nobody can own a tree," said Liam. "She knew it well though." He looked at it for a long moment, remembering. "When she was a baby, her mother sat with her under that cherry tree."

"What was her mother's name?"
"Agnes."
"Like me?"
"Like you."
"And what was the baby's name?"
"Mari."
"And she was my mother."

Liam did not answer. Agnes looked up at him. "I'll have a baby when I'm grown up," she promised. But he did not seem consoled, and walked away through the long grass.

Running to catch up with him, Agnes paused to pick up a single petal. Held between finger and thumb, it looked old and brown-edged, and she let it flutter away again, not liking the idea that the sun-bright mass of white blossom was made of such imperfect things.

*

One summer day in the year when the war was ending, a telegram came. Hamish from the post office cycled up to the farm with it. He stood and watched while Mrs Dunbar opened the brownish-orange envelope, knowing already what the words said. She read the printed message silently, and gave a little gasp. Then her eyes met mine with the beginnings of a smile.

"William," I said, and she nodded.

The two paper strips of capital letters had not been pasted onto the form quite straight. RED CROSS FOUND WILLIAM SAFE HOME SOON LOVE HELEN. The lines seened to dance in front of my eyes. "Good news?" asked Hamish, hoping to be told more. I slipped away as Mrs Dunbar began to explain, breathless with astonishment and relief, that her grandson had been found alive.

Behind the byre, I leaned against the whitewashed stone wall. Swallows were twittering in the sky, flying high in the sunshine. Beyond the apple tree, Davy was hoeing turnips.

He moved as steadily as a grazing animal, unhurried and certain. Billy crouched beside him with a trowel, chopping at a weed with fierce determination. After a while, I went across the field to the pair of them. Billy looked up and said, "Hallo," then went on attacking the weed, but when Davey saw my face, he put his hoe down carefully and came towards me with a burbling moan of concern, arms outstretched. "Oh, Davey," I said into the warm strength of his shoulder as he hugged me, "I don't know what's going to happen."

But I did, of course – oh, I did.

Helen went to meet William in London, where he arrived on a train full of repatriated troops, among whom were the emaciated survivors of the internment camps. He was taken home by his mother to Ullapool, where she kept him like the sick child he was, fending off the enquiries of the outside world and feeding him the small spoonfuls which were all that his shrunken stomach could at first accept. She wrote frequently to tell us how he was getting on, and I grappled with the need to write a letter for this returned soldier to read. It was impossibly hard. Every combination of words had too definite and too wrong a meaning, as it always does when you don't know what you want to say. I wrote down the old refrain that sang its tune in my mind, '*You are my true love*' – and shrank from sending him that truth in case it should seem too demanding or threatening, having already been stated once. On yet another sheet of paper, I wrote, Dear William, and stared at the two words, unable to add any more.

Dear William,
  Dear William,
    Dear William . . .

The repetitions wandered diagonally until they reached the

bottom corner, leaving triangular spaces that narrowed to a point on either side. In one, I drew the circle of the white stone, and filled the darkness round it with the stars from which he had fallen in a burning machine. In the other, lower one was the curled figure of myself, hugging its knees, head averted because I could not or would not draw my own face. And this, at last, was what I put into an envelope and sent to him.

He wrote back, with thanks for what he called 'the lovely mystery'. He looked forward to meeting me, he said, as soon as his mother stopped her watch-dogging. His writing had lost its force. The letters 'o' and 'a' did not complete their circles, but hung tiredly open, and he signed his name as a sprawling 'W' followed by a couple of indeterminate uprights and a zigzag that trailed down the paper. A few days later he wrote again to suggest that he and his mother would come over for lunch the following Sunday.

All that week, I felt cold and sick with suspense. Davey killed a chicken and soup was made, together with a pie, the top glazed with a beaten egg. Mrs Dunbar made scones and a fruit cake, using every scrap of the carefully-hoarded currants and sultanas. Hamish brought a tin of apricots from "under the counter" at the Post Office store, and Davey took Billy out to pick a bunch of white marguerites, and put them in a jug on the windowsill.

On the Sunday morning, Helen's car drew into the yard a little before mid-day. And it was then that I realised the truth which grinned like a skull in the sunshine. I had not saved him. There is more than one way in which a man can die.

Helen had warned us that he was badly scarred, but it was a hardly human figure which climbed slowly out of the car, a thing of broomsticks and a yellowish turnip head, dressed in a new navy-blue suit that hung bulkily on its thinness. Mrs Dunbar enfolded him in her arms with a care that suggested he might break in her grasp, and I stood holding Billy's hand as this new moment overtook and obliterated all the old ones. William turned his face to me, and I saw that the yellowness was of stretched, shiny skin, pulled tight across the skull where the flesh had been burned away. One side of his nose ended in a shrivelled twist that left the nostril gaping large and dark and the lip pulled into a pale tightness. He smiled with the other side of his mouth, and his teeth were the same, white and a little uneven. They looked very young and fresh in his ruined face. "Hello," he said.

I went to him then, and put my arms round his bony shoulders, touching my own lips to his disfigured ones. There was no strength in him, only a fevered wasps' nest of energy. I said, "I'm glad you're back." It sounded very inadequate.

Billy began to cry, stamping his feet up and down because he was frightened, and reaching his arms up to me. I turned away to lift him up, and knew that this would be the pattern now. William needed my care, and I would not withhold it, but the child was more real to me than this undead wreckage of a man.

Later that day, the others tactfully took Billy out to try and fly the kite I had made him, and William and I were alone. He dug slowly in the pocket of the navy-blue suit and brought out the white stone. "You'd better have it back," he said as he put it into my hands with his reddened and deformed ones. "I think perhaps it wanted to be yours."

"Ours." I let the red hand take mine, and did not close my eyes as he kissed me; I owed him that much for not having let him die. I must now meet him on his own terms, and forget the boy in the garden.

As his strength began to return, William came to the farm frequently, at first with Helen, and then driving her little car on his own. I didn't know it was a skill he possessed; he had learned as a boy, he said, on a tractor at first, then running his uncle's Daimler up and down the drive at Craigmuir.

Davey didn't like William. He whined and backed away when confronted with him, and once, when they met face-to-face at the corner of the byre, Davey turned to run in such panic that he tripped, and the basket of eggs he was carrying went flying ahead of him, and the split shells and bright yolks lay glistening in the mud. He was upset about it, but although I consoled him, my deeper concern was for William, who might be hurt by the crudity of Davey's reaction. I watched the scarred man constantly, in the way one watches a new animal that has come into the house, looking at the way he walked and the stillness with which he sat at the window, his head turned a little to stare at the hill. Mrs Dunbar gave him small tasks to do, and perhaps her instinct to push him gently back to usefulness was a healthy one. I wanted only to serve him, because it seemed my responsibility to make this new extension to his life tolerable to him. With all my strength, I had wished him not to be dead, and that wish had been granted, but I saw now that my mother's accusation had been right; I had thought of no-one but myself. So I brought him cups of tea with a biscuit or a scone, and offered him gooseberries picked from the bushes outside, and ripe plums when the trees came into fruit, and when I found him shelling the peas which Mrs Dunbar had set before him, I helped him. Once, I brought him a black-tipped gull's feather with every interlaced spine of it perfectly in place, and felt warmed by his lop-sided smile. He turned it for a while in his skinless fingers, then gave it to Billy to play with, and I retrieved it later from under the table, broken and bedraggled.

At harvest-time that year, William came to stay for a week, ostensibly to help with the stacking of sheaves and the threshing, though he often had to stop because his limbs began to tremble. At such times, he stood with his head bowed and his hands gripping the long pitchfork like Millet's peasant in *The Angelus*, though from exhaustion rather than piety. On the last night, when the neighbours who had worked with us had stayed for a harvest supper, he came into the kitchen where I was washing the dishes, and asked me to marry him. And I said I would.

PART EIGHT

I hardly remember the registry-office wedding or the move to a flat in the city. I did all the necessary things in a trance of misery over the leaving of the farm for the second and more final time, but William had been awarded an ex-Service grant to go to University, and was starting that autumn on a BSc course at Glasgow. He would be studying general biology, although his only real interest was in plants. They were better than people, he said; they did not have ideas.

Secretly, I disagreed. Since plants are part of all intelligence, how can they not move in accordance with their allotted ideas? But I knew that William had learned in the most terrible of ways to be afraid of what human beings thought they could do. Even the gentle time-tables of the University were abrasive to him in their authority, and he came back from his days of study in strained silence, though his whimpering when he slept was sometimes loud enough to wake me at night. We didn't talk much. Even when he turned to me from nightmare, it was for a wordless, nuzzling comfort, an encompassing pressure of limbs rather than any sharing of his fears. He was afraid to think about them, and wanted only to be soothed back into the oblivion of sleep.

William gave no sign of resenting Billy. He treated the little boy with careful politeness, smiling sometimes but never laughing, and never allowing himself to be irritated. It was as though a tight skin had been drawn across his feelings with the same tautness that covered the burned hollows of his face, and I was constantly careful not to touch on this thin covering, for fear of what lay underneath. And so we went on in those early months, exchanging safe trivialities and playing gentle games with Billy, coming together at night in a blind, desperate groping, a hugger-mugger of need that could break easily into almost frightening violence.

I wanted so much to become pregnant. To give William a child of his own would be more than an effort at atonement; I wanted him to have a new, innocent being who could not share any blame for what had happened to him, a small human creature whom he could love. But every four weeks my bleeding came like tears of loss, and I wondered what was wrong between us. Sometimes, trying to stimulate my own excitement when William's straining efforts failed, I would even evoke the presence of that other man who, in the scant warmth of an afternoon gas-fire, would run his fingers over my skin, stroke my belly and touch me with tongue and lips, murmuring, "Do you like this, little cat? And this?"

After a while, I sent Billy to nursery school in the mornings because he showed so much interest in playing with the other children we met in the park, and began to paint again. The shapes were very different from those of the lost farm, and the colours were almost monochrome, black and umber and silver-grey in the washed light of a sky that seemed to belong to the river and the estuary rather than the city. I can see again how the underlying rise of the hill was clothed with the overlapping rectangles of tenement blocks, and within those shapes the smaller patterns that were equally rectangular – doorways and windows, paving slabs, steps, bricks, hewn stone, trams. And people in their dark clothes, vertical but irregular, their feet parting in an inverted V as they walked, mirroring the upright divisions of the bare branches of city trees.

It was not until the following summer that I felt the longed-for queasiness, and knew that I was at last pregnant. William asked, carefully, how I felt about it, and I kissed him and said it was what I had longed for. He thought about it for a while, then said he expected it would be good for Billy to have another child about. It would teach him to share. I wondered if he secretly thought that the little boy was over-indulged. Billy had always been very clear in his mind that the purpose of life was to take what you wanted from it, and any frustration of this intention reduced him to screaming fury. When this happened, William would simply get up and walk away, either to shut himself in the bedroom or go out, for a walk in the park, he said, though often he came back with whisky on his breath. I did not reproach him. He was never unkind, and he had accepted my son as his own, obtaining and signing the necessary papers without any suggestion from me. Billy was now Billy McGuire.

*

In the summer when Agnes was seven years old, Liam bought a pony, together with a covered cart – a "yoke", as the pair were known collectively. Margaret was glad, for Liam had been ill in the winter with a fever which had been slow to abate, and it had left him gaunt and breathless. Kathy, her eldest daughter, had married a Johnstone boy, Robert, and now was expecting a second child, wee Bruce being a year old. Nearly all the travelling families owned a pony or a donkey now, Margaret reflected; it was as if each succeeding generation expected life to be a little easier. She frowned when she thought of this, worried that it would bring a growing weakness and dependence on others.

Liam shared her unvoiced reservation about the relief which the yoke had given them. He would not let the children ride in the cart. "You'll be losing the use of your legs," he said. But Margaret was glad to see him walk unencumbered by the heavy pack, and nobody accused him of hypocrisy when he himself sat for a while on the shaft, with his pipe in his mouth and the reins easy in his hand that rested over his knee. At the best of times, there was never any criticism of the men of the family, for they were too precious an asset for that, and in the past year, the times had been hard. But there was strength in Liam yet, Margaret thought, and with this easing of the burden, he would recover it.

They came into Kirkcudbright one August afternoon, and separated by unspoken agreement, Margaret and Kathy and the youngest children to do some selling, Liam and the older ones with the pony and cart, to establish a camp. They knew where it would be – half-way up the hill at the river's edge. There was never any problem about finding each other. The traces of wheel-rut or footprint or patch of flattened grass were hardly necessary in their pointing of the way; the presence of the family was something that could be sensed infallibly, and the way back to that wholeness was always known.

Agnes, following behind Margaret and Kathy and Hugh, lagged behind, for she had an odd preference for being on her own. It had worried the others at first, and they would come rushing after her whenever she strayed, to bring her back into their company – but they recognised now that Liam's granddaughter was different from the rest of them in more ways than the bright colour of her hair. As a small child, she could crouch for long, absorbed minutes, watching the progress of a beetle through the grass or a worm drawing its smooth length across damp earth, and even now, though she helped readily enough with the work that had to be done, and could charm a sale from a half-hostile housewife when she chose to, she would slip away on her own as no other seven-year-old would dream of doing. When she came back, there was sometimes a private radiance about her which disarmed all scolding, disquieting though it was.

As Margaret and the others went from house to house with their tinware and ribbons and clothes pegs, Agnes stood a little behind them with her small basket, smiling sometimes, but taking no real interest. She had asked often if she could go to some houses on her own to hawk the wares, but Margaret would not hear of it. "If anything happened to you," she would say, "your grandfather would never forgive me." Sometimes, it seemed that Liam cared more for this child than he had done for any of his own, but Margaret did not mind. It had shown her a warmth in him which had come as a new blessing. But on this day, there was something she wanted to do.

When they came away from the last house in the lane, Kathy stood for a moment with her hand in the small of her back, stretching against the weight of the child she carried in her shawl and the unborn one which moved within her, and Margaret looked at her daughter with sympathy. "You rest here a wee while," she said. "I'll take the children up to the farm." Kathy sat down on the grassy bank, grateful for this unusual concession, and Margaret, with no further words, set off up the stony track with Hugh, a solid, uncomplaining boy, at her side. Agnes stared after her for a moment without moving, struck by a sense of strangeness in what her grandmother had said, casual though it had seemed. Suddenly, the time was special.

As she followed, she held out her hand to the pink campion flowers that leaned from under the hedges. Each blossom grew from a slender whitish-green pod, very neat and precise, but the petals were wonderfully ragged and careless, a pale magenta pink that glowed in the shadow of hawthorn and wild rose. She paused again to put her finger under one and tilt it so that she could look into its simple face – and in the same instant, there came the absolute knowledge that she would not see them in quite this way again. This moment was dying, even as it happened. In a sudden coldness, she ran on up the track to catch up with the others, but the new knowledge came with her like a shadow that cannot be shed from the heels.

The farmyard seemed empty as they came into it, but then a boy a little older than Hugh came round the corner of the byre with a catapult in his hand, and stopped short when he saw them.

"Would your mother be in the house?" Margaret asked him, and he nodded, taking a couple of steps sideways so that he could still watch them. Then he ran across the cobbles and in through the door of the house, leaving it open behind him. "Ma!" they heard him call, "there's tinkers!"

Margaret and the children did not look at each other. The term was often used offensively, but the boy had meant no harm. A woman appeared wiping her hands on her apron, and Margaret moved towards her. Agnes watched. There was no showing of the basket of wares, no use of the opening phrase, "You've a lucky face, lady." The strangeness intensified in the silence.

"I remember you," the woman said.

"And I you, lady." Margaret looked at the brown-haired boy who had returned with his mother to the door. "And your name is Hughie. You once gave me a feather."

He shook his head, not remembering and not sure whether to smile.

Margaret returned her attention to the woman. "You have had hard times," she said. Agnes relaxed a little. This was another common opening, a statement to which most people would assent. This hard-worked housewife was no exception.

"Aye, hard enough. My man died a while ago. And you'll have heard about his brother, Billy. You brought us news of him when you were here last. He was killed by a mad-man, crazed with the fever."

"With the pox, lady," Margaret said deliberately.

The woman flushed a little and put her hand to her throat. Taking her time, Margaret looked round her and went on, "You've a fine place here."

"My sons run it now – you'll most likely know that. They're good boys. And Hughie helps me, too, we manage well enough. I could be doing with a new skillet," she added quickly, glancing at the tied bundle of tinware which Margaret carried as well as her basket. "And I can spare a few eggs and some scones, if you would like them."

"Thank you, lady."

The woman and her son went back into the house, and Hugh whispered in the cant, "He has the same name as me."

Margaret nodded, but her eyes were on Agnes, and she said, also in their own language for fear of being overheard. "It's a good farm. Fertile land, and sound buildings. And a fine house."

Agnes stared at her in astonishment. Never before had her grandmother – or any of them, come to that – showed the slightest interest in property, except in the quick, unstated summing-up that told whether a sale might be made at that door, or a kindness shown even if there was no money for purchases. She gazed round as she was told to, but could see only the plainness of her own perplexity, now linked with the shadowing which had started at the parting from Kathy and had grown to overwhelm her when she paused on the road.

The woman came back with a pot of jam as well as the scones and eggs in a small straw basket. "There's a daud of cheese there as well," she said, and added as her eyes met Margaret's, "I am mistress in my own house now."

She paid the price asked for the skillet without quibbling, although the boy called Hughie glanced at her in surprise. Agnes, in a last obedience to her grandmother's inexplicable instruction, glanced back as they left the farm yard, and saw the woman and her son still standing on their doorstep. The boy half-raised a hand in farewell.

That evening, as the fire burned low, Liam said, "So you went to Mistress McGuire's farm the day, Agnes?"

"Is that her name? Yes, we did. She bought a skillet."

Agnes wanted this to be a normal conversation, though she knew it was not. "And she gave us – "

"Aye, she was very kind. Do you remember she spoke of Billy, her husband's brother?"

Agnes frowned.

"The one who was killed," Margaret prompted gently.

"By a mad-man."

"So they say."

And then she knew what they were trying to tell her. "Is that the Billy who was my father?" She had thought somehow that he was longer ago than that, part of the old stories that were told and the old songs that were sung.

"Yes, lassie, he was," said Liam. "The woman you saw was married to Hugh McGuire, your father's brother."

"Another Hugh." But nobody answered this. It was not names they were interested in, but something else. Liam and Margaret glanced at each other, then Margaret said, "Agnes, listen. You are of their family. If you wanted, you could have your share of that fine place."

"How could I?"

"By going to stay there. If the woman knew that Billy had a child, and that you were that child, she would most likely take you in. She's a kind enough body." Margaret spoke anxiously. "And she's starved of love."

Agnes hurled herself into her grandmother's lap. "Dinnae send me away! No' to live with the country hantle, please, please!" The pony snickered from his tethering rope at the sound of her distraught voice, and Kathy and the others shifted uneasily, for the child's distress was such an abnormal thing that every one of them felt an impulse to comfort and reassure her. Agnes clung to Margaret, shuddering and sobbing, hardly feeling the hand that stroked her hair or hearing the voices that soothed her fears and promised that nobody would make her go if she didn't want to. But, for Agnes, the ominous meaning of the day had now produced its bitter fruit. She had always known that she was different from the others, that her parents were not Liam and Margaret, that she came from some other unknown place, a cottage where weeds grew in the floor, a tree of brown-edged cherry petals, a mystery. And now, after the seven years of a fairy tale, she was to be handed back like a stolen princess to some cold palace, to live among strangers for the sake of a crock of gold.

Slowly, with kisses and hugs and the close, rhythmic rocking to and fro of Margaret's body, she was pacified, though shudders still ran through her limbs and her diaphragm jumped and hiccupped from the violence of her sobbing. Liam leaned forward and took her hand in his. "Of course you'll stay with us, lassie, we'd never send you away. But we had to tell you, Agnes, d'you not see that? When you're a grown woman, if you found out there had been this choice and you'd not known about it, you might say we'd deprived you of what should have been yours."

Agnes shook her head convulsively, and the tears kept running down her cheeks, helplessly now, not only for the lingering terror, but in mourning for the self she had been until today, and for the father called Billy whom she had never known; for the campion flowers, and the pity of it all.

*

As the months went on, things became easier between William and me. He was fascinated by his unborn child. Lying beside me, he would run his fingers over the gently-moving mound of my belly, and put his burned and deformed ear against the skin, to listen, he said, to what she was saying. He had no doubt that the baby would be a girl.

During my increasingly restless nights, I dreamed often of a vortex like the open core of water that spirals its way down a pipe, but so large that I was inside it, like Alice in her rabbit-hole, tumbling down and down to the connecting air at the far end. A birth dream, perhaps, and yet the resistance through which I travelled was not of substance but of time. I was going back, touching on that other place which I had lost and yet never able to hold the connection. At the instant of arrival, I was returned abruptly to my own self and the implacable present.

As the growing child began to press against muscles and nerves, I would wake sometimes with my feet and legs knotted in agonising cramp. The only cure was to get out of bed and stand on the floor so that the weight of my body would slowly relax the clenched tendons. At four o'clock one morning, I stood in the cold bedroom for the third time that night, trying not to disturb William as I wept soundlessly with pain and tiredness. The clinic had given me quinine pills to combat the cramp, and assured me that the drug could not cause abortion when taken in small doses, but I had seen again the folded slip of paper containing a white powder, heard again the cocky excuse that he'd obtained it on the grounds of recurrent malaria. "Been in the tropics, see." No, I could not take quinine. And now, my big toes were pulled upward by the tendons that stood out along the top of my feet, as hard as strained hawsers, and it took a long time for the agonising pain to ease. Waiting to be sure it would not strike again, I walked slowly to the window and looked out. It was snowing. I leaned my head against the cold glass and watched the wandering white flakes that came out of darkness. Four winters ago, I had walked through falling snow with a different child curled in my belly, and the man who breathed evenly in the bed behind me sailed through moonlight to devastation. Perversely, there was a nostalgia for those open, frightening days when all things were possible.

The walled garden lay dimly white under the snowing sky, and I was in memory at that other bedroom window, looking down over grass white with dew, where a badger turned his narrow head to stare at me for a strange moment, and my father's spirit stood like a naked child in its new state.

Such a waste.

His voice said the words beside me, as clearly as water dropping into a deep stone pool. I gasped and turned, but of course the room was empty but for sleeping William.

The next day, I could not settle to painting. *Such a waste.* What did he mean? A waste of what? *To thine own self be true*, he had written on the sugar-pink page. Was the self wasted unless it gave something that lived on in other minds after its own death? I wandered restlessly through the flat, looking out of its tall windows at the snow and the leafless trees, and picked up the white stone that lay now on my own dressing-table, turning its weight in my hand. The dream of the vortex was back again, a spiralling return to a half-known time, a connection.

Perhaps that was the key, the connection across time between people who had known they were alive and perhaps now knew that they were dead. Was this the business of history, which had seemed at school to be such a dry chronicle of wars and intrigues? I put on my coat and went out to the local library, where I took down volume after volume from the History shelves, but found nothing about people like my father or that other presence whom I had thought of as Mari.

William smiled when I told him what I had been doing. That was not the business of history, he said. What I wanted was my family tree. I should take myself off to Edinburgh, if the nursery would keep Billy for the whole day, and consult the Public Records Office.

*

Hugh McGuire saddled his horse and looked for the last time round the buildings he had known since childhood.

The yard lay empty in the morning sunshine. Although his brothers knew that this was the day of his departure, they had seen no reason to delay the work of the farm, and Hugh had not suggested it. He had wanted this taking of farewell to be solitary, so that his remembering of it would be what he chose. The handshakes and the unsmiling wishes of good fortune were over, and did not dilute the implacable disagreement. He, being so much younger, could claim no right to the tenure of the farm, Graham and Malcolm said. Since their father's death it had been they who had carried on the work and continued to build up the herd. The sisters were safely married. But wee Hughie had always been a mother's boy.

Janet McGuire did not stand on the doorstep to wave goodbye to her youngest son. The house was empty since her death from cancer almost a year ago, and a girl from the village came in to do the cooking and cleaning. Hugh checked the girth once more, though he knew it was tight enough. Then he mounted, and rode away out of the yard and down the stony track where the pink, untidy flowers of campion bloomed. He would not be back.

*

It was easy enough to trace my father's ancestors. Theirs were the names which appeared on the gilt-lettered boards of merchants' halls, generation after generation of respectable men who married the daughters of foundry owners or bankers, with here and there a wine merchant or a draper. But my mother's line was far more difficult. The men tended to be engineers or soldiers, the records hopelessly incomplete, often with no death certificate or record of the birth of children – but then, William himself had no birth certificate, having been born in India. He'd had to supply himself with one for entry into the university, but as he said at the time, it could be a work of fiction for all they knew. Nana's mother was a Thomson, her grandmother a Stewart – and I could get no further than that. A Townsley was mentioned, and a Reid, but with no address. Most likely travelling people, the archivist said helpfully, those being the names of well-known travelling families.

I was baffled. I thought back to Nana's reminiscences of relatives called Flossie and Jack and Jessie and Norah and Alice, and wished I had asked her who these people were instead of just listening. Such a waste . . . but in family tales, as in fairy tales, nobody has a surname.

Fairy tales. For the first time, I began to think seriously about the pattern of chance that had taken me zigzagging through all other possibilities to find, among the four million people of Scotland, William's mother and grandmother, not jointly but separately. I thought of the countless times when I had swept away opposing circumstances, and of Nana's lack of surprise when her estranged husband, thought to be on the other side of the world, sat down beside her in a restaurant car on the train from Glasgow to London. If the travelling element ran through my family somewhere and explained my love of the transient and the unknown, then so, perhaps, did witchcraft.

I went back to the library and, not without a certain distaste, looked along the shelves labelled 'Occult'. The books were for the most part extremely unpleasant. They were full of ugly suspicion and stupidity, and their cruelties sickened me. I was half inclined to abandon the whole thing, and might have done so had not the librarian started to take an interest in what he called my "researches". He said he would see what he could dig up for me, and one morning he produced from under the counter a large, leatherbound book and said proudly, "Records of Scottish Witch Trials. Primary source material."

On that morning, I found the account of the case of

Alison Balfour, and it jumped from the page as if I had seen my own name. To this day, I can't explain the surge of electricity that seemed to connect me to a woman who had died a terrible death in 1596. It was not the first time I had read about the pilliewinks and the caspie claws used to crush flesh and bone, but there was a trace of protest in the words of the unknown recorder, appalled even in those barbarous days that a child should be "swa tormentit" in order to extort a confession from her mother. For a fleeting moment, I wondered if Nana had said there was a Balfour among her Jessies and Norahs and Margarets, but because I wanted it to be true, I knew I must not believe it. I had learned at least the first principle of research, which is that you mustn't deceive yourself.

When my baby girl was born, a little after Billy's birthday, on a bright, cold afternoon in March, I called her Alison. Secretly, I had hoped that her coming would provide me with a new link to my dream place of the past, but she brought only her sweet self. And it was enough.

*

Agnes, with her basket of wares on her hip and a gently-clinking bundle of tinware across her arm, smiled as she went from house to house on the outskirts of Ayr. It was a fine day, but she was warmed inwardly as much as by the morning sun. Last night, Duncan Reid had come to her side and offered to carry the buckets of water she was bringing from the burn. There had been a brief touch of the hand as they parted, and a smile. Today, she was aware that other men glanced at her as she went with her swinging walk along the road, her red hair bright in the sunshine, but her smile was not for them.

As she came to the next house, the door was flung open and a dog released. It rushed at Agnes with a rattling snarl, and hurled itself at the skillets and pans which she raised to defend herself. For a moment, she was knocked off balance, and her basket tipped, scattering its contents on the ground. The dog snapped and worried briefly at the ribbons and spools of thread, then returned its attention to Agnes, snarling. An angry ridge of fur stood up along its back, and its limbs quivered. Forcing herself to be calm, Agnes looked into the animal's frowning eyes and spoke to it. "You've no need to do that. Lie down, now. You're a good dog. Lie down."

The dog hesitated. Cautiously, it sniffed at her hand. Its hackles subsided and it sat down, then relaxed its forepaws and lay at her feet, panting a little. The house door opened and a man came out. "Come here!" he shouted at the dog, but it glanced up at Agnes and did not move. He came closer. "What have you done to him? I'll have none of your filthy tinker tricks round here."

Out of the corner of her eye, Agnes saw a man dismounting from a horse on the other side of the road, but she dared not spare any attention from the dog and its owner. She took a step away from them, but the dog shuffled along the ground to stay with her. "Come *here*!" the man roared at it more loudly.

"If I let him come to you, you're no' to beat him," said Agnes.

"I'll do what I like."

The young man who had got off the horse came across to join them. "Is there some trouble?" he asked.

The dog's owner answered with a jumble of accusations, and while his words poured out, Agnes stared covertly at the newcomer. She had seen that brown hair before, and the grey eyes. Then, with a catch in her breath, she knew. This was Hugh McGuire, young Hughie, the boy who had held up his hand in tentative farewell, that day at the farm. His eyes met hers as the angry voice ranted on, and she saw him frown as he tried to remember.

When the spate of words came to an end, she said

quietly to the dog, "Go in now." It stood up, arching its back and yawning as if it had been asleep, and trotted obediently into the house, skirting round its owner at a careful distance. With a last suspicious glare, the man went in after it and shut the door.

Hugh turned to Agnes with recognition. "You came to the farm." Colour had risen in his fair skin.

"A good few years ago," Agnes said, fascinated by the unspoken messages he was bringing her. She saw that he had dreamed of that meeting. It came as a shock to him now, to encounter his dream and find it changed. And there was sadness in his young face as well. Something had happened. A death. Yes, the mother who had tried to pull together her scanty rags of pride. "You have had a loss," she said gently.

"My mother. How did you know?" But the question was not suspicious; he asked it with absent interest as his eyes looked into hers. There was an easiness between them.

And so there would be, Agnes thought, since she and this man were cousins. *Your father and mine were brothers, Hugh McGuire*, she said to him silently, trying by explaining it to ground the electricity they were creating. The unspoken words vibrated as if they had been voiced, and she, too, flushed with the fear that she had actually said them. She pulled her thoughts away from this dangerous ground. "Was it last September, your mother's death?" Early in the month, it would be. That's when Liam had died. There would have been a joining.

"The sixth," he said.

She nodded. It had not helped – he felt even more closely bound now. She stooped and began to pick up the scattered wares from the ground. He had been sent to give her the choice, she thought. Liam's voice was clear in her mind. *If you wanted, you could have your share.*

No, Liam, she said as Hugh McGuire bent down to help her gather up the threads and laces. *I am not of their kind.*

They straightened up, and Hugh shook the dust from the skeins he had picked up, looking down at their pale colours. "I have often thought of you," he admitted. Carefully, he replaced the wares in her basket. "Will you tell me your name?"

She hesitated. A warning quivered in the sky. "I am called Agnes," she said.

"And you'll be one of the travelling families – a Tarbert, perhaps, or a Johnstone?"

Because she liked him, she defied the warning. "I am Agnes Balfour."

She saw his face change. The high colour drained away, and he involuntarily took half a step back. "My father used to speak of you. No, it can't be." Confusion swept over him. "It's too long ago. Was there – "

My grandmother. The warning shrieked in the sunshine. Agnes turned and ran, the clattering of pans mingling with the clacking of voices and a whiff of sickening smoke. Margaret had told her what they said, and what had been done to that other Agnes Balfour.

Hugh, moving away to remount his horse, saw a twist of white lace still lying in the road. He picked it up and turned it in his fingers as memories turned in his mind. His father's anger was there again like a blackness in the bright sky. Agnes Balfour, the witch, he had said, had cursed him and his family and they would never be free of it.

In the bleakness of his dispossession, Hugh wondered if his father had been right. Witchcraft was still a power in the land. And yet, as he tucked the twist of lace into his saddle-bag and put his foot in the stirrup, he found that he was still looking down the road after the girl, and searching the hill for a last flying glimpse of her red hair. Perhaps, he thought with sadness, the liking between them was an illusion, brought about by enchantment.

Nothing moved on the hill except for the circling dots

that were crows or jackdaws. Hugh swung his leg across the horse and rode on. The recruiting sergeant was waiting.

*

Shadows were gathering in William's mind, cast by the many things he would not face. Unidentified and unchallenged, they grew bigger and bigger and more ominous, and left him little freedom in which to think and move. He felt himself surrounded by malign forces which worked behind his back in a kind of Blind Man's Buff, and he, as the Blind Man, could trust nobody. For a while, he was happy with his baby daughter, an elfin child with curling wisps of copper-coloured hair, very different from strong, fair-haired Billy – but as she grew into a little girl with her own likes and dislikes, she became part of the irritating, treacherous exterior world, as we all were. Helen was blamed bitterly for coming home from India and thus robbing him of a setting where he could have, as he put it, "been somebody". His dead father was his hero, a man uncluttered by reality, last seen by William at thirteen, before the journey to Kirkcudbright and school. Peter McGuire had been perfect – shrewd, aloof, respected, popular. William, in his own mind, was all of these things, but the people surrounding him prevented these qualities from being recognised. When I said once that I didn't think any human being could be perfect, he left the room, and I found him weeping in a corner of the bedroom. I was so cynical, he said. So destructive. He was adamant that we should have no more children.

He scraped only a pass degree. It was what he had expected, he said, working with morons who didn't understand their subject. A few days later, he announced that he had applied for the post-graduate teacher training course.

They should never have accepted him. As professionals in the education business, they should have known that a man who looked so grotesque and who was so personally vulnerable could never hold his own against adolescents who want to prove that they are tough.

But in those post-war years, there was a desperate shortage of teachers – and I suppose the interviewing committee would have found it hard to turn down an ex-serviceman on the grounds that his injuries were ugly. To my dismay, William passed his final exams quite well, and got a job as a science teacher in a High School in Shawlands, where the children were particularly confident and cocky. They baited him with a joyful intensity which soon ripened into mutual hatred.

The drinking became much worse. When he came back from school each afternoon and threw his briefcase on the floor, William would pour whisky into a glass with hands that shook, and I dared not speak to him. Billy and Alison became afraid of his unpredictable temper, and my hushing of them if they made any noise must have increased the feeling that their father was an ogre to be avoided or placated. They never saw, as I did, the moments when he sat with his head in his hands and tears running down his face, saying he hated himself.

Billy, moving to a new form in his Primary school, encountered a teacher who insisted on calling him by his "proper" name of William. He flew into one of his furies and then into a long silent sulk, after which he announced that he was in future to be known as Joe. I don't know how he achieved this, but his friends adopted the new name at once, and by the end of that term, the teachers were using it as well. I was the one who found the change difficult. I began to grieve over my small son who, despite the rejection of his adoptive father's name, grew more and more like William, always seeking some outside circumstance to blame for whatever made him dissatisfied or unhappy. And his view of himself as an unfortunate victim was much encouraged by my mother.

Having always felt a little guilty about not asking them to that first Private View, I had made sure to invite Donald and my mother to my wedding. It was an almost alarmingly good move. A reconciliation followed in the wake of my new respectability, and my mother, after one horrified glance at William, decided that she was sorry for me. She began to come to our Glasgow flat a lot, always bringing presents and sweets for Billy, who took a great liking to her. He missed Mrs Dunbar, who had looked after him so often when I was working on my paintings, and seemed to regard my mother as a substitute. Remembering how she had looked at him with suppressed longing when she came to the Home, I was more than willing to let her have contact with her grandson – and I too fell easily into thinking of her as a replacement for Mrs Dunbar, as helpful and trustworthy.

If I was being selfish, I was punished for it. One day, when Billy demanded the purchase of an expensive toy which I could not buy for him, he shouted, "If I'd been adopted I'd have had nice toys. Gran says so." I hugged him and said nobody could love him as much as I did, that's why I'd kept him with me – but he was unforgiving. He was a child who wanted the end of the rainbow and the crock of gold. I hope he has found his heart's desire. When he grew up, he went to Canada and married there, and he does not write to me now.

*

Dark, smiling Duncan Reid was everywhere with Agnes, either in her mind or in his brown-skinned presence. Her solitude was invaded by him, but she shared it willingly, for he did not seem to be a stranger. Each day, her first glimpse of him brought a small shock of excitement, like the moment of coming upon a heron standing perfectly still in the burn. With its slow, broad-winged rise into the air, the magic is dispelled, but that first instant always produces a quickening of the heart.

For a long time, Agnes was content with the seeing of him and with his taking of her hand as they walked in the woods, but increasingly, it began to seem that they were a pair, as integral as the sky and sea which, together, made the sweet line of the horizon. When he put his arm about her shoulders for the first time, she turned to him as if seeking the sun, and after that, she wanted his mouth on hers and the pressure of his body and the grip of his strong arms, more than she wanted to eat or sleep. One summer evening when they were camped near the sea, they walked together across the sand dunes in the last clear light of the sun that was setting behind Arran's hills, then turned inland a little, to where the marram grass gave way to warm hollows of rabbit-nibbled turf. They sat for a while, side by side, and Agnes felt impatience mount in her until she wanted to howl like a cat because of her need, and a small moan escaped her, with a turn of the head which Duncan understood.

As his weight came over her, Agnes was astonished by her own power. The inner centre of her being, together with its secret entrance, seemed to have an energy of its own, connected as if by living threads to her mouth and to the muscles of her legs, to her hands and the sinews of her arms and the nipples of her breasts that ached sharply for his touch. The bringing of him inside her was the filling of a great hunger, and as the devouring came to a huge, inward-pulling crisis of satisfaction, she felt complete.

They lay interlocked for a long time afterwards, almost sleeping, then Duncan raised his head and kissed her, and stroked her hair. He sighed, and was inert again. The sky above them was still light, but the birds had stopped singing.

When they came back to the camp, nobody said anything, though knowing glances were cast in their direction. Quickly, Agnes went to her own quarters. It was accepted after that that she and Duncan were a couple, although she continued to live with Margaret and the other children. After a few months, a sickness began, and Margaret said it was time that she and Duncan Reid were married.

The ceremony took place in Margaret's tent. Hands were placed on the Bible, and vows were made in Margaret's presence as the officiating person. A good meal was cooked, and the singing and dancing went on all night. When Margaret replaced the Bible in the small wooden box in which she kept her treasures, she took out a folded paper, so rubbed and worn that it was falling into several sections. "Liam would have wanted you to have this," she said as she gave it to Agnes. "It was written by your grandmother."

"Did my mother see it?" Agnes asked.

"Aye, Liam gave it to her when she came to us, before you were born. She was a clever lassie." Margaret's face softened as she thought of it. "She read that letter many times."

Agnes put the paper carefully in her own box. Sometimes she would take it out and turn it in her fingers, putting it to her nose in case a faint scent of her lost mother should still linger about it, but detecting only a trace of tobacco that reminded her of Liam. She would touch the letter to her lips, separated only by time from the touch of the hand that had written these lines of fading words. It was her most treasured possession.

*

I woke every morning from a dream of grass and sky and the closeness of others, and the return to reality was painful. My poor William wanted to escape, too, but for him the way out was through drinking, which in turn made the dreadfulness worse. Perhaps he, too, was groping his way back to some other time – to his own childhood, perhaps, since he could take no pleasure in the childhood of Billy and Alison. Drunken men so often seem like big toddlers, lurching and self-important, bringing some scrap of thought to be approved of. William sometimes reminded me of Davey when, too drunk to concentrate on anything more than keeping his balance, he would tread his way towards me with open arms, wanting the hug he would never ask for when his cautious, flinching brain was fully working.

After only three years, Glasgow Corporation retired him from teaching on what was tactfully called a Disability Pension, and he was at home all the time. It became impossible to paint. He approved of my painting, he said, how could I doubt that? But in fact, I could never leave him for more than ten minutes before he came in to ask when tea would be ready or whether I wanted anything from the shops – which meant that he was going out for another bottle of whisky, though neither of us said so. It was only by keeping him in conversation that I delayed the start of the day's drinking, and he knew it, and was increasingly truculent, cutting through the talk with an accusation that I was stupid or boring or was patronising him – and perhaps there was truth in what he said. When you start to be someone's keeper, no matter how much you love and care for them, it's hard to maintain respect. And once that tell-tale edge of pitying patience is perceived, that is the greatest hurt of all, and there's a huge desire to obliterate it, demolish it, re-establish respect even, if necessary, at the basic, humiliating level of fear.

I should have confronted William early on, kicked up a fuss about the drinking, protested that he was too good a person to do that to himself or me, but I had pitied him, and now my pity enraged him, and the pair of us were locked in fear and love, each afraid of the other's power to hurt. The whisky, both the overt bottle on the sideboard and the one he kept hidden in his school trunk in the bedroom, was expensive, and I was earning nothing. Poverty began to leave its mark on the flat, spreading a hint of squalor over the shabby furnishings and the clutter of second-hand toys. Once Alison was at all-day nursery school, I got a job. It was, with a kind of inevitability, in a shoe shop – but at least it gave me some power to deal with the Bank's ominous letters. But William, alone in the flat all day, was left with no buffer against his self-destruction.

PART NINE

On a winter night in the big camp near Furnace, Agnes, helped by Margaret and some of the other women, gave birth to a baby girl. She called her Mari, after the mother she had never known.

*

What is this? My hands grasp, and are empty. The nothing-stuff is all round. It comes into me in breaths. I am astonished.
   I am.
   I am.
   I AM.

*

With a sense of breaking and giving way, I woke beside William in the night. My hair was wet with sweat and I was still sharply aware of the smell of earth and bruised grass and of a female body and wood-smoke. I turned on my side as if tired after a long struggle, and slept.

From that moment on, everything was different. For the first time since Billy's birth, I was again in contact with the Mari-place, knowing its harsh, hungry beauty in moments when my mind flicked away from the store-room behind the shoe shop or from the pavements and windy skies of Glasgow. Once again, in a magic which I had almost forgotten, I stared at the twisted pattern of water coming from the tap or the sinewy grain of a bread-board, seeing them as new things charged with their own meaning. I had been like this before, back in the wild days of escape from school and home and certainty, in that restless wandering from thing to unknown thing, but there had been a closing-off after Billy was born, a loss of that freshness. That's why my painting had changed, first into the nostalgic dreamland of sleepers and sky and old farm-patterns turned mythic, and then into the sad, spare townscapes in which the figures were no more human than paper-clips or clothes-pegs.

Years went by. The children grew older and William was in and out of hospital with liver trouble. A doctor drew me aside one day and said the outlook was bad unless I could stop my husband from drinking. I asked him if he knew how, and he shrugged and admitted it was difficult. Sometimes I did some drawings, rapid inky things, water, stones, sun, a turned head, a figure that was half tree and half human. Martin got them framed for me and some of them sold. He looked at me and shook his head, and once he asked if he could lend me some money, then quickly added that I might like some little luxury – a couple of weeks abroad, perhaps. I refused, of course – but I was careful after that to put on the best clothes I could muster if I went to see him; it's very embarrassing to know that your friends are regarding you with concern. William did his best to be amiable if anyone came to visit us, but my mother came unexpectedly one day and found him in a rage, shouting incoherent abuse at the things and people that prevented life from being magnificent. "You try," he said when he saw her, "I'll give you that, you try. But you'll never understand magnificence." I took him into the bedroom and persuaded him to sleep for a while, and when I came out, my mother remarked that I'd got myself into a fine mess. Helen came occasionally, too, but her visits became less frequent as her sister, Frances, fell victim to arthritis and needed her help. I was glad she was spared the sight of William's sagging, red-rimmed eyes and the puffiness of the unburned side of his face.

One early morning, when the crack of daylight showing through the curtains was barely grey, I was woken by the phone ringing.

"Is that Mary? It's Mrs McBride – I doubt you'll remember me." The Argyll-accented voice was worried, and in that instant I knew what she had to say. I was already weeping as she explained that Mrs Dunbar had fallen yesterday in the yard, going out to a sick ewe, and Davey had carried her into the house but he couldn't wake her. "So he came across the fields to us, and we knew something must be wrong though we couldnae make sense of it, Davey being the way he is." They had gone back with him, Mrs McBride and her husband, and sent for the doctor, not Dr McNeish any more but the new young one, and he said she had taken a stroke. The ambulance came. "She died in the night, Mary, she never knew she'd left the farm. My husband says it's a good thing, she'd not have liked to be dependent."

I nodded, absurdly. I could see Mrs McBride so clearly, with her broad, anxious face and the grey hair braided round her head, I forgot she couldn't see me. Davey was with them, she said, but he kept asking for Mary. So they'd been into the house to look in Mrs Dunbar's address book for my number, they hoped I didn't mind.

William put his arms round me when I crept back to bed, having heard my side of the conversation. We lay together in kindness and grief, and my tears were almost as much for our own sad muddle as for the loss of the woman I had loved so much.

Later, I phoned Martin Fisher for the first time in many months. He asked no silly questions. I would want to go to the farm, he said, straight away. He'd be round to fetch me in half an hour. I wanted William to come, but he shook his head, not looking at me. Feeling a bit queasy, he said, not up to a long car journey. Poor William. He had his pride, too. He avoided looking in mirrors, and he certainly didn't want to meet other people's eyes.

It was surprisingly tranquil at the farm. Mrs Dunbar had taken on a foreman in the past year, a young man called Neil Currie, and although Davey's snub-nosed face was red with weeping, the work was being done, and I had no function except to comfort and, with Helen who arrived that afternoon, to plan the funeral for the following week. I stood for a moment at the back door and looked at the long slant of the hill which I saw so often in my dreams, and tears came again in a strange sense of release, as if at the end of a long hardship.

The week which followed was uneasy, as the time between death and burial always is. The spirits circle restlessly then, incomplete until this new one is added to their number – or maybe it is the person newly dead who watches the now separate body with its still-replicating cells and its motionless heart, the unseeing eyes and the slowly-growing hair and finger-nails, and cannot quite abandon it.

Alison and Joe, as I had finally learned to call him, came with me to the funeral, again in Martin's car, the same long green one which had driven into the yard all those years ago. Joe was nearly eighteen now, about to leave school, Alison four years younger. Again, William did not come. Nobody reproached him. "See you later," we said, as if he would be busy and occupied in our absence.

We did not go to the farm that day, only to the church, which was filled with the people who had been Mrs Dunbar's friends, formal and a little awkward in their dark clothes. It was Helen and I, with Davey between us, who stood at the door afterwards to receive the hand-shakes and condolences of those who filed out. I remember those hands now, and the warmth that came from their hard palms. Most of the women kissed me, and sometimes there was an arm round my shoulders. The comfort of it was very real.

The men carried the coffin out to the churchyard and the waiting grave. In the Scottish fashion, it was their task to attend to the burial, but no women were expected to be present. Davey understood, though he whimpered a little as he followed Mr McBride and the others. Helen and I, with the other women, climbed into the undertaker's two black cars, and were driven back to the McBrides' farm, to don aprons and make tea and set out the dishes of ham and chicken on the white-clothed table, together with a rabbit pie, scones and gingerbread, an apple flan, sliced and buttered tea-loaf, and shortbread of varying size and thickness. I knew these offerings had come from many different kitchens.

The men returned with a breath of the fresh air about them, and the steady carefulness of having seen a necessary task through to its end. They took up the small glasses of whisky that stood ready on a tray and drank respectfully. The women permitted themselves a little sweet sherry, but did not relax until every guest had been served with a plateful of food and pressed many times to take more.

I longed to be back among them, in this place where people valued each other. Wide distances of field and hill lay between one household and another, and yet each person was known. In a way, it was closer than the city. For exactly that reason, William would hate it. The warning startled me a little, coming as if to caution against too much happiness – and yet I was irrationally light-hearted, even on this day of loss and mourning. I kept having to stifle an odd excitement, and Mrs Dunbar seemed constantly at my side, her rough hand in mine, smiling as if in approval – of what? Of the well-set tables and the warm company, of my tall son and red-haired daughter whom everyone remarked on as being so much like me? There seemed to be something more.

A florid man came up and introduced himself as John Davis, Mrs Dunbar's solicitor. He had Helen at his side.

Could we, he asked, have a word in private? Mrs McBride showed us into the cluttered farm office, apologising because there was no fire lit, she hadn't been expecting to use this room today. And there, in the chilly afternoon light, we listened to the reading of Mrs Dunbar's will. She had left the farm to me and my family, on condition that Davey should continue to live there and be cared for.

Now I understood the smile. I protested, of course, and said that the bequest should have gone to Helen; she was Mrs Dunbar's daughter and Davey's half-sister, her claim was far stronger than mine. But Helen shook her head. They had discussed it a long time ago, she said, when I had first brought them together. Her mother had been worried about Davey – he could not manage on his own. And Helen had been honest. Farming was not for her, and the responsibility of looking after Davey was too heavy. She was sixteen years older than him, she pointed out. A different generation. The truth was, as we both knew, she could not love him.

The children were deliriously excited when I told them. Alison flung her arms round me. She had nagged endlessly about wanting to move to the country. Joe grinned and said, "Hey, my mother's an heiress!" It was the nearest he had ever been to the crock of gold.

I had kept the news until we were in the car, not wanting to get involved in all the explanations that would have resulted from a general announcement. Martin turned his head momentarily to smile at me as he drove. "That'll start you painting again!" he said. And I knew he was right.

But there was William. *Oh, my love*, I said to him, *what are we to do?* And then I reassured him, as I always would. *There's no need to worry. Nothing will happen unless you want it to. I promise.* As the car went along in the gathering dusk, I began to work, in enduring resignation, at the undoing of this magical bequest, this fairy-tale offer of my heart's desire, as the warning voice had told me I would have to. William could think himself anonymous in the city, but here, Mrs Dunbar's grandson would be watched and judged. It was impossible. Neil Currie, the young foreman, could run the farm; he planned to get married soon, to a fresh-faced girl called Susan. Perhaps she would care for Davey, if she and Neil lived in the house. It would be for Helen to decide.

I would not tell the children yet. They were in high spirits, laughing and pushing each other in the back of the car as if they were small again – let them enjoy their good news for a while. Martin, driving along Lomondside where the water reflected the clear evening sky, was planning how I could convert one of the outbuildings to a studio.

And then it happened.

William was with me, in a breath of small pink roses and the summer sweat of his young skin. His arms were round me and his smooth cheek against mine and his voice was close in my ear. *I'm sorry. Oh, my love, I'm so sorry.*

I put my hands over my face and wept. Martin looked at me in concern, and Joe said, "What is it, Mum?" Alison reached from the back seat to take my hand, but the tears would not stop. In their midst, one practical thought remained steady. When we got home, I must go into the flat alone.

At the corner of our street, I asked Martin to drop us off. "I can't ask you in," I said, "the place is too untidy." He looked puzzled – when had our flat ever been tidy? I came closer to the truth. "I don't know – how William will be."

Martin was always so kind. He said he absolutely understood, and as we got out, he put his hand on my arm for a moment and added, "Mary, dear, you will let me know, won't you, if there's anything I can do – at any time." Then he drove off to the villa he shared with his actor friend in Thornliebank.

When we reached the entry to the flat, I said we should treat ourselves to an Indian take-away, and gave Joe some money. Alison said she'd stay with me, and I had to tell her, "No, my darling. Just go. Please."

William was lying in a scarlet-soaked bed, his head back and his unseeing eyes open. A vein had burst in his throat, the doctor told me afterwards, due to a varicose condition not uncommon in alcoholics. He had drowned in his own blood.

*

Dark.
Sometimes it is warm dark. Close, hugging.
Outside is dark, too, very big. Things move, and a wind blows. There are spots of light up there, and a little curved thing, very pale. I put my hand up to touch it, and people laugh. Look, they say. Mari wants the moon.

*

I dreamed that I reached for the moon. There was such a richness of dreams in those free, empty days after William's death. The moon's tips are the last visible part of its circle, gently aching to close and be complete, and it seemed to me then that the same aching is inherent in being human "You see," William used to say in his drunkenness, "you see . . ." and his burned hand would grope for the thing that eluded him, the completeness that lay in the full moon and in the dark totality of the mind.

Martin was right, of course; once I was back on the farm, I began to paint again. The new perceptiveness was still with me, at an intensity which was almost painful, and it overflowed into the moon-dreams, blossoming in images of William, the grey-eyed Adam in the garden of innocence, sometimes with my young self as well, the sky above us blazing with stars and the searching moon. The sky became a rich field of ideas, and I painted it again and again, crowded with the newly dead who stared like children intrigued by a new toy at the small aeroplane that fell burning to earth.

It's not that I believe in life after death in the Christian, sitting-on-a-cloud sort of way – that lyrical, Blake-inspired view died with Miss O'Dell's sorrowful shake of her head. But how can there be nothing? The space between things is not nothing, it's filled with an active invisible soup of particles, constantly mating and dividing and reforming, and it seems illogical to think that we are different. It's just that we don't understand, that's all – and why should that matter?

On a practical level, things ran easily at that time. Joe had stayed on in the Glasow flat, having got himself a university place to read engineering. He let two of the rooms to friends, which paid the mortgage and made him a small income on top. He was very shrewd, my Billy. He came to the farm sometimes, and suggested how it could be made more profitable, but Neil Currie, though polite, took no notice.

Alison refused to have anything further to do with school. She had fallen in love with the farm at the first sight of it, and she said she would do all the housework and cooking so as to leave me free to paint. Davey adored her, and clapped his hands excitedly as she pegged out washing between the apple trees and her red hair blew in the wind.

Martin arranged an exhibition of my new work, which attracted quite a lot of notice. The more daring of municipal art-gallery curators bought paintings for their collections, and I was on a radio programme called 'New Talents'. And a young man from the *Glasgow Herald* asked if he could come to the farm and do an interview.

He was a new element in our pattern, Kenny, with his lean, smiling face and his Shetland-pony shock of dark hair. He was a man as transient and magical as a dragon-fly, and a wild electricity ran between him and Alison as soon as they saw each other. In the summer, he went down to London for an interview with the BBC, and took her with him, and when she came back, I knew she was pregnant.

Things were different now, she told me. Yes, she knew all about contraception and she could see that Kenny was not the kind of man to settle down, but this baby was not an accident. She wanted it. She put her arms round me and said again that things can be different now. I was afraid she was doing this for my sake, trying to make up for what she saw as a harsh past, not realising that these old sadnesses can bed down into a compost from which can grow all your understanding and joy.

Kenny got his BBC job and went off to London, then to Bristol. Alison stayed on at the farm and seemed content. She had no intention of following Kenny around, she said. He'd be back one day – or he wouldn't. At sixteen, she had a great quality of repose, very different from my own inclination to drift with the wind and feel safe when moving on. I found it hard to share her belief that things could be different. In spite of good people like Martin Fisher and Mrs Dunbar and dear, bumbling Davey, I still regarded other human beings with caution. I wanted to give Alison my grandmother's wedding-ring, which I had not worn since William put his own ring on my finger, but she gently refused it. There was no need to pretend, she said.

On a night when the first fine nail-paring of a moon hung in the sky, the baby was born in the little upstairs room where I used to sleep when I first came to the farm. The birth was cheerfully and lovingly supervised by a midwife called Mrs Green. There was much drinking of tea and easy chatting, and when the labour moved into full-time intensity, the easiness was still there, despite the authority of the well-scrubbed hands that held and pressed and guided, and of the voice with its firm, affectionate instruction. The child's hair seemed at first to be as dark as the night outside the small window, and I wondered if she was going to be of Kenny's kind rather than ours, but when it dried, the glints of redness showed, though she remained copper-beech rather than rowan.

Alison called her daughter Nimuë. It was, she said, the ancient name for the new moon.

*

Tree branches go by. Everything is moving. I kick my legs because I want to be on the ground, but my mother says, "You're too wee to walk yet. Keep still, we're going on."
Going on. It has a nice sound.
The sun is up there, caught in the branches, but it breaks free and comes with us. We are going on, going on.

*

So we went on at the farm, Alison and me, and Nimuë grew into a strong, active little girl who followed Davey about just as Billy used to. Kenny came occasionally, but he had got himself into overseas reporting, and never knew where he would be next. It was the perfect job for his restless energies.

Those gentle days lulled my watchfulness. It seemed as if all uncertainty centred round Kenny – but of course, he could not attract every scrap of it, any more than the fly-paper Neil Currie hung in the cowshed could lure every single fly to its golden stickiness. "All good things must end," my mother used to say when she came out to the evening lawn where the blackbirds sang, to put me to bed in the dark room.

One weekend in May, Kenny came for a visit. He and Alison went for a walk by themselves in the bluebell woods where the cuckoo sounded its mocking note, and Nimuë and I went into the garden to plant peas. I looked up from my trenching and saw her standing with the ball of string and the marker pegs bundled against her chest, but she was looking away, at something I could not see. After a few moments, her stillness passed. She turned her head and smiled, then came to me and put her hand on my rolled-up sleeve, and the smile became difficult. Kneeling there, I gathered her into my arms, and we grieved together for the time that was coming to an end.

There was hardly any need for Alison's halting, troubled explanation. The farm was lovely, she said, and she didn't want to leave me, but she had to think of the future. She ought to get some sort of qualification. And Nimuë should know her father better. It would be so much easier for Kenny to see them if they were in London. She was so sorry, she said as William had done, so sorry.

In one of those kitchen-table talks that go on late into the night, we reassured each other that the move would be a good one for us both. She, still only twenty, was too young to settle for routine domesticity, she would get bored and frustrated. We both knew she already suffered from this, but we were anxious to cause no hurt. She asked me to come with her, but that was too daring a charade, and the air between us tightened a little. I feared for what would happen to her in London – but we have no right to save other people from experiences that we think will be painful.

I must not be sanctimonious. The truth is, excitement was beginning to stir in me again. Things were moving on. I was getting to the end of what I could find to paint about, having used up my store of happenings. It was time to dip again into the unknown, let the pattern push me where it wanted to.

The excitement was irrational and impossible, I told myself, trying hard to subdue it. In the centre of the pattern was Davey, static and beloved, my anchor. I could not leave him.

This is what worries me, that again and again, any person who stood in the way of my heart's desire was obliterated. I loved Davey – of that I am certain – and yet it was with a sense of terrible inevitability that I watched him become huddled and finicky, pushing his food away like a fussy toddler. Very quickly it reached the point where I could only tempt him with the sweet things of childhood – junket, custard, the juice of stewed plums. I took him to young Dr Aitcheson, where he lay bravely on the leather couch that had been there in Dr McNeish's day, holding my hand and only whining a little as the clean white fingers pressed gently into his stomach. Davey was nearly fifty, I said in answer to the doctor's question, and he nodded absently, attending to what his hands were telling him. Then he gave Davey a last light pat and said we needed an X-ray and some tests. He'd fix a date with the hospital and let me know.

That night, Mrs Dunbar was sharply present beside me. I must not let Davey go into hospital, she said. It would frighten him. I needn't worry – she would take care of him.

But I did worry, of course, because it appalled me, as it still does, to think that the obstinate desire which I fought down so hard was sweeping Davey away, as it had swept William and Nana and my father, all of them pushed aside so that I could attend fully to the unfolding pattern which was so enchanting.

Perhaps Mrs Dunbar did indeed take care of Davey. The next day, he would not get out of his bed, but lay on his side with his eyes open, looking at the trees outside the window and sometimes sleeping. I phoned the hospital and said I would not be bringing him in for the tests. I remember that they made a fuss, but I took no notice. That night, I woke with his presence close about me, unalarmed, but smiling sheepishly as if a little embarrassed. I went into his room to find him lying as I had left him, his stubby fingers curled over his nose and mouth as if he was a baby. He was already almost cold.

Three weeks later, I leased the farm to Neil and Susan Currie, and went abroad.

*

Travellers, the country hantle call us, or tinkers, because of our trade in the tin-ware. I can see that they think us wild people, even those that are easy with us, needing what we offer and giving a fair exchange. There are others who see us as dangerous, and their eyes are wary as they frown through the crack of the door before closing it. They never think that they may be the odd ones, living their whole lives cramped in their houses, squatting each day over the same stinking hole, locking and barring themselves against the feared outer world. What are they so afraid of? Not of dying, surely, for there are no locks that can keep death from entering. Robbery, perhaps – but the protection from theft is to have nothing. Where no need for defence is felt, there is no fear. Sometimes, our young men take more than is needed to eat and stay alive, and my mother frowns at that. If they make the henwives afraid of us, she says, we will suffer for it. The house-dwellers make it their main work to collect this magpie-loot and protect it inside their locked houses.

The poor creatures – I pity them.

*

They were good, the travelling years. I had a little money from the sale of my last paintings, and occasionally sent Martin a frantic cable for some funds, but given any luck, my sketchbook acted as a source of small cash. Perhaps I ought to ask my current Bank Manager to supply me with cheque books that have no printing on them at all, just plain white paper, so that I can make of them what I can, once they are, as you might say, drawn on. That's what I did, in effect, during that lovely decade.

I wasn't a proper traveller, not like the Bedouin who live as the desert allows them and stock up their leather ware and their heavy silver jewellery against the drought year when the goats die – I had an umbilical cord to Scotland where the rent of the farm quietly accumulated, but I wanted there to be some money available to Billy-Joe and to Alison and Nimuë, should they need it. Kenny's accessibility had proved to be a transitory affair, and within a couple of years he had met and married a wealthy American girl who worked for *Time* magazine. Her father was in the running for the office of Mayor of his town, and would tolerate no illicit liaisons among his children – or perhaps it was that Kenny liked the money. I still see him on television sometimes, his lean face a little creased now but amused as it always was, and his dark hair grey-streaked but just as shaggy. Shaggy was the word for Kenny, Alison said waspishly at the time. Shagged his way to success, didn't he.

She was not seriously embittered, perhaps because she had managed after some basic exam-taking to get into the School of Oriental and African Studies, and had there met Mihir Sen, a tall and elegant young lecturer in Sanskrit who made paper boxes and shadow puppets for Nimuë, and eventually took the pair of them off to Kashmir.

On the Trans-Siberian train from Moscow to Beijing, filling my tea-glass in its pierced metal holder from the samovar at the end of the corridor, I met a Scottish woman who was more than merely a fellow-national on the otherwise solidly Russian train. In our long conversations as the birch trees and pine trees went by, she told me of her difficulty in selling the house which her mother had bequeathed her. It was too far north, she said, and not even in the town, but up the hill beyond it.

"Ullapool," I said aloud.

She was startled, but not very. Funny how you know these things, we agreed, and looked out at the red sun going down behind the birch trees and the pine trees. We exchanged addresses – I gave her Martin Fisher's, not knowing where I'd be – and parted company in China. I wasn't ready to buy a house then, even though Helen still lived in Ullapool and it remained the end of a journey which I had never completed. Nine years later, on a Christmas Day in Muslim North Africa, I walked up the steps of the white-walled Post Office in El Jadida, and put through a call to the barely-legible number on a scrap of paper kept in the back of a notebook. In the mahogany booth with its number painted on the glass, I heard the woman say, "You must be psychic. The people who bought the house are off to join their son in Abu Dhabi, and they've just put it back on the market."

With Martin's slightly askance help, I became the owner of a house I had never seen, for all the money I owned in the world. I went on travelling, but elegiacally now, looking at the dust under my sandals and the tiled watery-cool entry to a mosque in a slow goodbye, working my way to Tangier and across into Spain and up through France until, in Toulouse, I was struck by sudden urgency and flew home.

In Glasgow, Martin gave me a letter. I didn't at first recognise the writing, so confused and sprawling were the words, following each other down the slanting lines to end in a crowd in the bottom corner. Then I knew it was from my mother. Donald had died, she told me, and people were saying she should sell the house. Donald had died. It was lung cancer, did she tell me? The garden was getting too much for her. A man came to help once a week, but what he charged was ridiculous. Donald had died. Had I ever met Donald? She didn't think so.

I went to see her. She was white-haired and frowning, and when her trembling hand let tea spill down her cardigan, she didn't notice. "Oh, Mary," she said, and began to cry. "Oh, Mary, I'm so glad you've come."

I took her to live with me in the house I'd never seen, and for the seven years until she died we endured each other's company with fortitude and a kind of love, even though there were times when I would close a door behind me and lean back against it as I used to all those years ago, leaning against a wall at school and waiting for this time to end. I was careful to feel no impatience; enough people had died. Perhaps a trace of Catholicism came back with my mother's presence, persuading me that this was a penance rightly undertaken, a payment for carelessness and for the lovely years of solitary wandering.

Sometimes Helen would drive up from the town to my hillside house that gazed across the sea. Although she was almost as old as my mother, she was still lean and active, playing bridge with the group of ex-colonials she had found in Ullapool, marking in the clues in *The Times* crossword, scanning the local paper with amused impatience. "Leave your mother to me, my dear," she would say. "Off you go out. Have a little time to yourself."

It was the greatest gift she could give me. I would walk up the hill behind the house and follow the path that led through the woods in the sheltered crack between the hills, beside the burn that tumbled into pool after brown pool. In a grassy clearing between the trees, there was a ring of half-buried stones where unseen people watched, and sometimes tears of sudden slackening blurred the leaf-dappled light into melting diamonds. The gulf of time hardly mattered in that place where nothing had changed over the centuries except the slow collapse of habitations. I began then to like the gentle decay of houses, the coming-in of ivy through windows, the scurry of birds in the gap-tiled roof. Nos habebit humus, the earth has us, we are safe in its hands. Maintenance, as they call it, is only for the anxious.

I gave up painting my pictures. The patient years of watching over my mother's dwindling set up a defence against too much awareness. I took a step away from the reality of that trapped boredom and became my own observer, dispassionately interested in the ways of passing the present time by seeing it as part of the past – and temporal affairs are not the business of visual art. I turned to words, and managed to publish a volume or two of stories. I still find one occasionally in a second-hand shop or the dustier and less efficient libraries.

My mother was not good at dying. Like Donald, she developed cancer, though hers was of the stomach. It spread with merciful rapidity, but from its onset, she was in a panic of fury and fear. "Let go," I said to her at last, when each breath had become a torment, and put my hand on her heart. Her body gave a quiver of submission and accepted what I offered, but her eyes stared angrily into mine until the last arching of the back was over and the clouded pupils gazed at nothing. It was a strangely young spirit which stood beside me in that moment, at a little distance, hugging itself. I was afraid of you, it said. And I wept then, because I thought I was the one who had been afraid.

The doors and windows of the house stand open now, and the birds fly in. My black cat takes no notice – birds are a tiresome insubstantial food compared with the fat mice and voles that live on the hill. The garden is kept shortish by a goat, who leaves the buttercups standing in all their glory and comes in sometimes for a bread-crust or banana skin. These two can manage on their own if I go away, and I have no dogs now, though the old friends who sleep under the turf were kind and loving. I didn't start travelling again until the last of them was gone.

Sometimes my moving about is for its own sake, to unknown places, but sometimes to Kashmir, to see Mihir and Alison and their three slender, dark-eyed children, almost grown up now. Alison teaches in the university and writes poetry which I find hard to understand, though it is respectfully reviewed, but her frequent letters are still a joy, simple and funny and intensely alive. Nimuë is a journalist, based in Brussels, which is a handy place for a quick visit either way. We see each other often, and her smiling face looks up at me from the *Guardian*, Nimi McGuire, Eye-witness.

Martin moved to Nice when he gave up the gallery, and lives there with Robin in a white villa with red and mauve blossom tumbling over the walls and a couple of palm trees leaning towards the verandah. A cross, protective housekeeper serves her two old gentlemen with flageolets and mounds of tiny pink fried fish, and is rude to them while insisting all the same that they mustn't go out in the sun without their linen jackets and their comfortable, slightly unravelling Panama hats.

For me, the central question remains unsolved. Have I been guilty of changing the course of fate for my own purposes? Even now, in small ways, it is easy to have what I want. The weather is endlessly obliging, and I remember the old assertion that witches never get wet. I have not been wet for years. *Well, the rain will just have to stop for a bit*, I think, putting on my coat – and it does. People are no problem, either. A stirring interest in someone known long ago is enough to ensure that we meet on a bus or in some distant town or foreign country. Coincidence goes on working. And I must admit with a slight blush that the National Lottery is a most useful invention. I never do the serious gamble with its choice of six numbers, being afraid that I would win a stupidly big amount of money and ruin everything, but I do keep an inner eye open for that lift of confidence that prompts me to scrape the grey stuff off one of those little cards in the Post Office, revealing ten or twenty pounds when I most need it.

Things are very easy. People think I am eccentric, but I am careful to do them no harm, and they come here for a share of the easiness, pushing their way through the rainwet heads of columbine and poppy, bringing a pot of lemon curd or a good coat cast off by a fashion-conscious relative as a kind of payment for what they do not know they receive. Some stay away, of course. These are those who avert their gaze if they meet me on the road, though I feel them turn to stare afterwards. The fox-hound people are still amongst us.

*

My father comes back from the town. There is to be a hanging tomorrow, he says. And a burning. The gibbet has been built in the square, and the faggots are ready. Traders have been coming from miles around. It will be a good day for the selling.

"Duncan, no," my mother says. "Stay away." She is not looking at me, but she catches my hand and pulls me to her as if an evil threatens, and the younger ones come up, sensing her fear. "What is it?" they ask.

My father is frowning. "Surely, Agnes, that old story is forgotten?"

All of us crowd close to my mother like chicks when the hawk is in the sky. She shakes her head, and I do not understand her words. "Witchcraft," she says, "can never be forgotten."

*

I woke at dawn today, and the birds were singing. My sleep had been restless, the words I'd written in the afternoon still circling in a ceaseless half-work which had pushed into my dreams.

As I rolled on my back and became aware of the cool grey light and the singers in the garden, I heard for the first time the order which underlay their random-seeming chorus. A cantor thrush set out the line, and the other thrushes took up the same tune at the same pitch, except that each one began at whatever moment seemed right. This was a music which nobody had written, and there was no counting or giving of orders. It was the same for the finches and robins and blackbirds – each one was free to decide when to sing, and yet each contributed the notes of its kind, a part of the pattern.

So simple.

Breath went out of me like a laugh or a sigh, and a tear of relief came from the outer corner of each eye. I felt them trickle back into my hair and the accommodating pillow.

So simple.

The pattern includes our free will. If I am indeed of a strange kind, singing a witching tune, that kind still belongs in the order of all things. The finding of bizarre fulfilments and the struggle to avoid wickedness are an allowed part of my being; each decision is voluntary, but each one drops into the pattern, there to fit perfectly. I saw, too, that the working of coincidence is a natural thing, part of an old understanding which we have lost as we lean ever more heavily on the crutches of our clever modern machinery. Witchcraft, Mari tells me, can never be forgotten. We are – or can be – magic of all magic, just as water is of all water. Only unblock the connections, and it will run as it should, and join us to the lovely whole, that entity which we call by the many names of God.

The bird-song quietened, and I slept again.

When I woke for the second time, the simplicity was still there. When I had washed and dressed, I took the white stone from where it stood on the window-sill between a twist of driftwood and a seagull's feather, and went out. I walked up the path beside the burn until I came to the last and deepest of the pools, below the waterfall, and there I let the stone that was like a little full moon slip through my fingers into the brown water. It was not an end – just a small completing.

ALLISON & BUSBY FICTION

Simon Beckett
  Fine Lines
  Animals

Philip Callow
  The Magnolia
  The Painter's Confessions

Catherine Heath
  Lady on the Burning Deck
  Behaving Badly

Chester Himes
  Cast the First Stone
  Collected Stories
  The End of a Primitive
  Pink Toes
  Run Man Run

Tom Holland
  Attis

R. C. Hutchinson
  Johanna at Daybreak
  Recollection of a Journey

Dan Jacobson
  The Evidence of Love

Francis King
  Act of Darkness
  The One and Only
  The Widow

Colin MacInnes
  Absolute Beginners
  City of Spades
  Mr Love and Justice
  The Colin MacInnes Omnibus

Indira Mahindra
  The End Play

Susanna Mitchell
  The Colour of His Hair

Bill Naughton
  Alfie

Matthew Parkhill
  And I Loved Them Madly

Ishmael Reed
  Japanese by Spring
  Reckless Eyeballing
  The Terrible Threes
  The Terrible Twos
  The Free-Lance Pallbearers
  Yellow Back Radio Broke-Down

Françoise Sagan
  Engagements of the Heart
  Evasion
  Incidental Music
  The Leash
  The Unmade Bed

Budd Schulberg
  The Disenchanted
  The Harder They Fall
  Love, Action, Laughter and Other
    Sad Stories
  On the Waterfront
  What Makes Sammy Run?

Debbie Taylor
  The Children Who Sleep
    by the River

B. Traven
  Government
  The Carreta
  Trozas

Etienne Van Heerden
  Ancestral Voices
  Mad Dog and Other Stories

Tom Wakefield
  War Paint